THE FALL OF ROME

BY BETH CIOTTA

Jewel Imprint: Sapphire
Medallion Press, Inc.
Printed in the USA

DEDICATION:

For my sister, Barb. Thank you for all that you do.
Thank you for being *you*.

Published 2008 by Medallion Press, Inc.

The MEDALLION PRESS LOGO
is a registered tradmark of Medallion Press, Inc.

Printed in the United States of America
Typeset in Adobe Garamond Pro

ISBN# 9781933836041

10 9 8 7 6 5 4 3 2 1
First Edition

ACKNOWLEDGMENTS:

My heartfelt appreciation to—

Everyone at Medallion Press for giving my westerns a home and helping me to make them shine.

Booksellers and librarians for your enthusiastic support with a special shout-out to the fabulous and imaginative souls at the Brigantine Library.

All of the readers who embrace my tales and warm my heart with their kind and joyful feedback.

My friends and family, my critique partners, my agent and editor—you know who you are and why I adore you!

My husband, Steve. Writing about true love is easy when you're living it.

CHAPTER 1

Territory of Arizona, 1878
Gila Gulch

"AN OUTLAW'S WORST NIGHTMARE—Boston Garrett—R.I.P." The jailhouse cot creaked under the weight of a restless man trying to make light of his predicament. "Nah. Too cocky. What about, CHAMPION OF JUSTICE. SCREW CROOKED POLITICIANS AND THE LIES THEY RODE IN ON—Boston Garrett—R.I.P."

DISGRACED WELLS FARGO DETECTIVE— Rome Garrett—S.O.L.—stared up at the crumbling ceiling of the Gila Gulch jailhouse, thinking this was as bad as it gets. Listening to a sibling create his own epitaph. Yes, sir. After a month of drinking and carousing, he'd hit rock bottom. *Shit outta luck.* "You're not going to swing."

"We killed a man."

"I killed a man."

"We're both in the hoosegow."

"Me for pluggin' Wild-Man Dan. You for threatening

1

a law officer."

Boston swung his legs over the creaking cot and relaxed against the adobe wall. "This Marshal Burke's a weasel."

"No argument there."

"No call for arrest. You shot in self-defense."

But Rome wasn't altogether innocent. He massaged his pounding temples, contemplating the summer indiscretion that led to this evening's disaster. Admittedly, bedding a state senator's wife hadn't been his most shining moment, but did it deserve his being fired as a detective for Wells, Fargo & Company? Did it deserve the gut-dropping plummet from dime-novel hero to disreputable rake?

Guilty of adultery in the public's eye when all he'd been was a fool. A sucker for any woman who claimed she needed saving. He could deny it to the world, but not to himself or the rest of the Garrett brood. The fairer sex was his Achilles' heel. One had even managed to break his heart. But that had been a long time ago and he didn't think about her anymore.

Except on their anniversaries.

The first day they met. The first night they made love. The first time she lost track of the hour and the first time he took her for granted. Some sort of curse, the way he remembered the dates and details. Though today held no special significance, his recent game of distraction was her game of profession.

Poker.

If he closed his eyes he could see Katrina Simmons sitting at the tables, dressed in a colorful bustled gown with a scandalously low neckline. Waist-length chestnut curls twisted into a sassy updo. Pert nose. Full lips. Soulful brown eyes fixed on the cards just dealt. Expression serene as she contemplated her bet.

Eyes wide open, he got a big dose of little brother.

Out of boredom Boston had recently cut his dark hair short and shaved off his moustache. Made him look younger, but no less dangerous. The youngest Garrett had always had a rough and tough edge. "Regrets?" he asked.

"Plenty," Rome said, focusing back on the present. "But shooting Wild-Man's not one of them."

They'd walked into the Tarantula Saloon just as the locally feared rowdy backhanded a wrung-out dove. Her cut lip made Rome see red. He and his brother had only been in the boomtown two days—passing through on their tour of debauchery—but they'd heard a boodle of stories and complaints about a trigger-happy cowboy with a mean streak. Rome had intervened, knowing Wild-Man would strike back. Given his reputation, he wasn't surprised when he pulled his iron instead of throwing a punch. Probably thought he'd make a name for himself, gunning down one of the famous Garrett brothers. Except he'd underestimated Rome's lightning speed. Even if Wild-Man was a sure shot, a slow draw was a quick way to join the angels.

"Two hours ago we did what we've done for years," Boston said. "Faced down a low-down ruffian. Only this time we landed in a two-bit jail instead of a ten-cent novel. This time, instead of looking up to us, people looked away."

The observation chafed. Like he needed a reminder of how far they'd fallen. He wished Boston would shut the hell up, but instead of biting his head off, he stated logic. "Figure they wanted to distance themselves should Newt Gaffey come riding in retaliation." According to gossip, Gaffey was a big bug rancher and Wild-Man was his hired gun. "You heard the murmurs. *Gaffey ain't gonna like this.*"

"Seeing Gaffey supposedly pays Marshal Burke to look the other way, we're dead as a can of corned beef sitting in his jail." Boston rattled off another wry epitaph.

Rome didn't see the humor.

"Corrupt officials," Boston said with disgust. "Dangerous as standing bare-assed in a nest of rattlers."

Rome knew he was stewing on how Senator Smith had greased palms to exact revenge. The vengeful bastard had twisted the facts to ensure he and his wife came out of the scandal unscathed while Rome got skewered. He supposed he should count himself lucky that the senator hadn't paid someone to shoot off his offending member. Still and all, the powerful man had hurt Rome plenty without employing violence. One way or another, all of the Garretts were

4

paying for his sins.

Most notably, Boston.

When Wells Fargo cut Rome loose, his brother gave the company an earful, forfeiting his own job. *Principle of the thing*, he'd said.

Integrity, Rome thought, suffering another twinge of regret. For a month running, he'd been mourning the loss of his high-profile job and stellar reputation. Shouldering a wagonload of guilt because he'd taken his little brother down with him. He'd wallowed in whiskey and cards, hoping to numb anger and regret. Now a man was dead, and Rome sat on the wrong side of the bars for the first time in his life. He'd made a bad situation worse.

Mucker, he could hear Kat taunt. Gambler talk for someone who throws away his hand. Except he'd thrown away his purpose.

Wild-Man wasn't the only miscreant in these parts. The territory was littered with bandits, rustlers, and cold-blooded killers. But instead of wrangling outlaws, he was locked in the hoosegow.

Guilt intensified, bearing down on his shoulders and soul. If he was destined to dance with the angels, he'd swing alone. Necktie party for one. Boston would not be a part of it, and he would do the only thing he knew to separate his loyal brother from his side. He could at least do something right.

He sat up and set his brother square in the confines of the stifling moonlit cell. "*We* won't be shaking hands with Saint Peter, because *we* did not kill Wild-Man Dan. Sure as the sunrise, *we* did not have an affair with a married woman. I specifically recollect being alone in bed with the lovely, but treacherous Mrs. Smith. *We* didn't piss off her husband. *We* weren't scandalized in the newspapers. There is no *we* in the recent series of tainted misadventures, Boston." He took a deep breath and delivered the final blow. "Do me a favor and butt the hell out. Get your own goddamned life."

His brother's unspoken anger hit him like an invisible bullet, smacking the air from his lungs. They'd fought plenty in the past, but neither had ever been intentionally cruel. Rome rolled back his shoulders. "Just saying—"

"You've said enough."

"Marshal Burke wants a word with you, Garrett." Kerosene lantern in one hand, key in the other, the coyote-faced deputy unlocked the door and motioned to Boston.

Rome slouched against the wall. His brother didn't spare him a second look as he jerked on his Stetson and exited the cell. He was pissed alright.

Good. Better pissed than dead.

The men disappeared into the front office, a bit of a room, sparsely furnished and overburdened with documents and dust. Rome listened but all he heard was muffled garble. No shouting. No shooting. A good sign. Maybe.

A minute later, Boston returned, clasping the buckle of his holster. "Burke says I'm free to go, so long as I leave town."

The marshal hovered nearby, thumbs tucked in his sagging waistband. He glared at his prisoner while tapping stubby fingertips against his revolver. Coyote-Face struck a similar pose.

Rome rolled his eyes skyward then back to his brother. "You going?"

"I am."

He dragged his fingers through his hair, struggling with a response. Alienating someone he cared about wasn't new, but it was the first time he'd driven a wedge between himself and one of his four siblings. Even though he was doing it for the right reason, it felt wrong. The urge to make peace was strong.

Out of habit, he dipped his hand in his pocket and palmed his lucky coin. Which made him think of gambling. And poker. And Kat.

When the stakes are high, hold strong, steady. It had almost been six years. When the hell was he going to forget that heartbreaker's voice? *Focus*, she said.

He rolled the half-eagle coin over his knuckles, pondering his bad luck of late, hoping Boston would see the wisdom in this heated split when he cooled. "Where you off to?"

"To get my own goddamned life."

CHAPTER 2

Santa Cruz Valley

The Star Saloon was one of six buildings in Casa Bend, a small, lazy town smack in the middle of nowhere. South of Tucson. East of the Santa Cruz River and northwest of the Santa Rita Mountains. Rich bottomlands, rolling hills, and grassy range. Perfect for grazing cattle and horses. Perfect for escaping civilization.

Mostly it felt like heaven to Kat—freedom. As sole proprietress of the Star, she didn't care that her clientele was sparse. Didn't mind that they were scruffy cowboys, transient soldiers, and occasional drifters. As long as they didn't cause her any grief. Low profile was more important than high finance. She'd learned to do without. She'd settled into a new life even though that life was far from perfect. Pity her contentment, such as it was, teetered on ruin.

Change was in the air. She could smell it, feel it. Not wanting to dwell, she cast aside the anxious feeling that had

8

dogged her all night and manipulated a shiny new quarter with flourish. "Heads or tails?"

Johnson Pratt, a mountain of a man who doubled as barkeep and peacekeeper in Casa Bend's one and only saloon, smirked at his boss. "Like it matters. You always win, Jane."

Jane. Not her given name, but one of choice. One of a survivor. *Jane Murdock*—proprietress of the Star Saloon. She'd been living the lie so long, she'd started to believe it. Until recently. A string of articles from the *Arizona Weekly Citizen* had shattered the illusion. She itched to retire to her adobe, to snatch the newspapers—morbid keepsakes—from her secret drawer, but she resisted. The articles triggered a crushing sense of impending doom. Wallowing wasn't her style.

Hip cocked against the crude bar, she rolled the silver coin over her knuckles and grinned at her sole friend and confidant. She'd told herself to trust no one, but she trusted Johnson Pratt. Gut feeling. Good feeling. "You're exaggerating, Johnny. I'm certain you've won a toss of the coin a time or two."

He snorted. "Not with you."

She nabbed his meaty paw and slapped the quarter in his palm. "Toss and call."

He did. "Tails." And won. "I'll be damned."

She quirked a cheerless smile. "Had a feeling tonight

was your lucky night." Mostly because it felt like her luck had plumb run out. She'd been dodging her past for six years. Living under various assumed names, she'd been successful until now. Now everything, or rather everyone, was closing in. According to the newspaper, Rome Garrett was causing a stir up in Maricopa County and Bulls-Eye Brady was suspected of robbing a train and killing a female passenger west of Yuma.

The fallen hero and the heartless outlaw.

Both men were miles away, days away from Casa Bend, yet it felt like they were breathing down her neck. Tonight, especially, she'd felt threatened. Like someone was watching her, judging her, plotting revenge.

She shook off the ugly notion, but the truth of it was, she'd earned both men's ire. Six years had passed, yet when that brief and turbulent period flickered in her mind, it felt like yesterday. Smitten with Rome and intrigued by Brady, she'd recklessly encouraged both suitors' attention. Back then, Rome had yet to hit legendary status, and Brady was still Jed Brady, not Bulls-Eye Brady. Shifty, yes. Notorious, no. Although the signs of his bad streak *had* been present. If only she hadn't been blinded by his poisonous words and tempting promises. She'd been younger then. Normally a better judge of character, but she'd been off balance, shaken by the death of her cardsharp daddy, her friend and protector. She'd been vulnerable. Just that once.

It had cost her dearly.

She'd ruined what she had with Rome and despised what she had with Brady. Escaping the controlling man's clutches hadn't been easy, but when she did, she ran fast and far. Needing to lie low, she relied more on her wits and less on her beauty. When life had dealt her a wild card, she'd held it close to her heart, even though she'd had to give it away. She did what she had to do to carve out a life as an independent woman, a young sharper turned saloon proprietress. She focused on doing the right thing, no matter how hard.

"If you're gonna beat the devil around the stump, I'll do it," said Johnson. "I'd like to hit the mattress before sunrise."

She snapped back to reality. Jane Murdock's reality. Midnight. Closing time. All had vacated the saloon but one. She'd lost the coin toss and, as such, was obligated to send their last patron on his way. Skeet Appleby. One of the Star's few regulars. Presently, a table served as the booze-blind geezer's pillow. He'd been deaf to their verbal ousting, so one of them needed to physically rouse the man. She and Johnson had once bet on when the old miner had last bathed. They'd both been off by more than three months. "I'll do it." Tucking renegade curls into her loose bun, she rounded the bar and braced herself for the stench. "You won the toss fair and square."

The barkeep grinned. "That I did. Maybe I'll horn in on a card game tomorrow. Got me a pocket full of . . . Ah, blazes."

"What?"

"I plumb forgot to give you this." He repocketed a wad of cash and passed her a folded letter. "Came with the mail when the stage passed through. We got busy and . . . dang. Sorry, Jane."

She waved off his apology, heart skipping when she noted the originating town. She broke the wax seal and read. Her knees gave way. Fortunately, there was a chair in the vicinity of her backside.

"Bad medicine?" Johnson asked.

"Unexpected," she croaked. *Change.*

"I'll tend to Skeet," he said, and hurried off.

Stunned, she reread the letter. A meticulously written missive from Sister Maria of San Fernando, a Mexican convent devoted to educating and caring for young girls. The sister's English was impeccable.

I regret to inform you that we are no longer able to care for your sister's daughter. Frankie is disruptive and unhappy. We do not have the energy or time to track her down when she continually runs away. She's determined to live with family, Miss Murdock, and due to the unfortunate circumstances, that would be you. We'll expect you by month's end.

Except Frankie wouldn't be safe with her.

Not as long as Bulls-Eye Brady breathed free air.

Her heart bucked harder than a wild horse. Thoughts—past, present, and future—collided. Unfulfilled dreams. Missed opportunities. Bad judgment. Every action had brought her to this moment. Lucky in cards, unlucky in life.

"You were wrong, Daddy," she whispered. "You can't cheat fate."

She snapped back to reality. Kat Simmons's reality. Her shoulders sagged with the weight of her snap decision, but she quickly straightened, conviction singing through her blood. Even though she didn't know spit about rearing a kid, even though she'd hoped the girl would benefit from a better influence, it was time to embrace the hand dealt. Time to stop hiding. Time to take the bull, or rather Bulls-Eye, by the horns. She'd do anything to keep the notorious and deadly outlaw away from her only surviving blood.

That included hunting down the killer.

Body vibrating with anxiety and purpose, Kat pushed to her feet and stalked past Johnson, the missive clenched in her hand.

Arms full of drunken Skeet, he yelled after her as she breached the swinging doors and moved into the night. "Where ya headin'?"

"To set things right."

It was her.

He didn't ask outright. Didn't want to scare her off. He'd spent a good hour nursing a beer at a corner table, slouch hat tugged low to conceal the upper portion of his face. He'd been stone silent, minding his own business, a nameless, faceless drifter. After an initial once-over, the barkeep didn't pay him much mind. She paid him even less. He'd watched her plenty, though.

At an opportune moment, he slipped away and mounted up. Too dark to navigate the terrain safely, he camped on the fringes of town.

It was her.

She'd worked hard to conceal her true identity. Changed her name. Altered her appearance, her demeanor. She'd bamboozled him at first—fresh faced and dressed down—but he knew that voice, that smile. Only now she was stingy with her good humor, reserving that playful grin for a well-heeled protector—six-shooter at his side, shotgun nearby. A big cuss with arms the size of a barrel cactus. Testing the barkeep's patience by fishing for confirmation seemed foolhardy. Besides, there was no need. It was her. He'd bet his life on it.

Bedded down and staring up at the stars, he contemplated

the truth of it. His life *was* at risk. If he was wrong, Bulls-Eye would do worse than shooting off the tip of his finger like he'd done last time he'd messed up. If he was right . . . he'd win back his place in the Ace-in-the-Hole gang. Bulls-Eye was slick and ruthless, but he had one weakness—and Elroy had found her.

His cousin had ventured into Arizona Territory twice before, and Elroy remembered well the chosen hideout. A cautious and superstitious cuss, chances were he'd taken refuge in that same spot. At the crack of dawn Elroy would ride hard for the Rincons.

Yes, sir. After a year of misfortune, the future looked bright. "Hot damn," he muttered to the moon. "I'm turnin' back time."

CHAPTER 3

Gila Gulch

Boston's parting words gave Rome food for thought. He feasted through the night and the better part of the morning, chewing on the rise and fall of the man he'd fought hard to become.

Tracking outlaws and bringing them to justice, one way or another, was his calling. The passion bone deep and ages old. The skills that set him apart from his older brothers. Skills that made him feel worthy in their eyes and good about himself. As role models, they were damned intimidating.

London, the eldest, had adopted the role of caretaker when their parents had died less than a year apart. He'd forfeited his own dreams, for family. Ran the inherited Gilded Garrett Opera House and ran it well, for family. He provided, he lectured, he guided. Never mind these days the siblings were grown and self-reliant. The man was a patriarch to be reckoned with.

Athens was the mediator. The calm and wise one. The one who'd reasoned with an irate father, saving a then eighteen-year-old Rome from a shotgun wedding. The one who'd kept the brothers sane when their little sister, Paris, had run away to pursue a music career. The diplomat, the lawyer, the state legislator who, after losing his wife, retired from the political whirlwind to devote more time to his children. Athens—the saint.

When the Lord passed out selfless qualities, Rome had been loitering near the end of the line flirting with an angel. London had a tight rein on his emotions, his temper, and his sexual urges. Rome did not. When it came to dispensing justice, Athens preferred brains to brawn, words to guns. Rome did not.

He was hotheaded and fearless, a tad reckless and a lot fond of women, whiskey, and cards. He craved attention, adulation, and fame. He was more his theatrical parents' offspring than any of his siblings, except for Paris. Paris, however, had conquered her aversion to matrimony. Rome had not.

He worshiped women. But he didn't aim on hitching himself to one . . . ever. Hard to promise his heart to a lady when a she-devil had blown it to hell. Just thinking on Kat and their last few days—the lies; the betrayals; the angry, hurtful words—churned his innards.

He sat up on the cot and stuffed down the ugly emotions.

When tender ones welled, he stuffed those, too. "Dammit." Now his chest pained him as bad as his head. Too much whiskey. Too much recollecting. Soul searching was downright painful.

The front door slammed open and closed. People stirred. He heard multiple voices, though he couldn't make out the words. Must be Gaffey and a couple of his boys come to avenge Wild-Man Dan. Would Marshal Burke allow them to drag him off and hang him vigilante style? Or would he insist on a trial? Seeing most officials these days were crooked enough to sleep on a corkscrew, innocent or not, Gaffey could still get his way via a public necktie party. One thing was certain, Rome wouldn't leave this world without a fight.

The afternoon sun blazed through the lone, barred window, shedding light on his surroundings and lending clarity to his predicament. Arrested for killing a desperado. Locked up for aiding a defenseless woman. Alienated from Boston, the only brother who actually looked up to him. *Damn.* He hadn't thought he could sink lower than having his sexual indiscretions publicized.

He'd thought wrong.

"*Mucker.*"

The voices in the other room rivaled the one in his head.

He massaged his throbbing temples and made a pact with Him. If he got out of this alive, he'd purge himself of his bad habits.

Philandering.

Whiskey.

Thinking of Kat.

The connecting door slammed open.

His head snapped up. "Hell."

♥ ♥ ♥

London Garrett's grey mood blackened when he saw the subject of Boston's tirade locked up, just as he'd said, looking ragged as a gambler on a losing streak. A far cry from the dapper, cock-assured Rome the family accepted and loved. His fair hair was long and unkempt. His eyes were bloodshot and his jaw shadowed with a week's growth of stubble. His handsome features had been considerably compromised by lack of sleep and overindulgence.

He'd known Rome's pride had taken a powerful hit, his reputation and career shredded, but he'd assumed he'd bounce back after letting off steam. Apparently he didn't know his brother as well as he thought he did. London tucked away his concern, handling the situation as he and Athens had agreed. "You look like shit."

The tarnished dime-novel hero rubbed his hands over his face, transforming his haggard expression into one of shining amusement. "That's a helluva salutation."

19

"Apologies." London removed his hat and slapped it against his thigh, stirring up a cloud of trail dust. "Morning . . . you selfish son of a bitch."

"You could kill a man with that sarcasm of yours," Rome said with a wry grin. "Deadly as ever." He neared the iron bars, his normally fashionable attire wrinkled, his breath reeking of liquor. The smile slipped. "Guess Boston rode over to Phoenix."

"Good guess."

"Tell you what I'm in for?"

"He did."

"Tell you I chased him off?"

"Told me you're a horse's ass."

"Guess you didn't correct him."

London hitched back his duster, braced his hand on his hip. "Here's the deal."

"You mean the lecture."

"Marshal Burke wants you gone. He knows who you are. Knows you've got brothers in Phoenix—one with political connections. Knows you've got ties with Josh and Seth."

Rome grunted and London knew it was due to his volatile relationship with the latter two. Joshua Grant was their brother-in-law. Josh's friend, Seth Wright, married their sister's best friend, Emily—a woman the brothers considered family—which made Seth as good as kin. Both formidable and respected lawmen. Both Territory locals. Both at odds with Rome's quick temper and questionable peacekeeping tactics. Regardless, they'd stand up for him . . . or catch hell from their wives. A body, especially a bootlicker like Burke, wouldn't want to be on the bad side of two Arizona Rangers turned frontier peace officers. He'd told Boston to fetch the county sheriff—Seth—to escort Rome away from Gila Gulch and a bad sort named Newt Gaffey.

"Burke knows you shot that dove-beater in self-defense," London continued. "He doesn't want trouble should anyone try to prove different."

"So why am I still standing on the wrong side of these bars?"

"'Cause I've got a stipulation."

"Christ almighty, London." He pushed away and smacked the wall. "I'm not a damned kid anymore."

"Then stop acting like one." London tamped down his temper, something that proved unusually difficult these days. Athens was the diplomat. This was his plan. But instead of negotiating the deal, he'd sent his older brother to play the bad egg while he rode off with Boston to play hero. One way or another London was always looking after a sibling instead of seeing to his own life. Not that he generally minded. Just lately.

"You got a raw deal in the Smith case," he went on.

"But it could've been worse."

"The cuckolded blowhard could've shot off the family jewels." Rome grunted. "You've mentioned a time or four."

"Life's what you make it, and you're making a mess. Wouldn't care if you weren't family. Wouldn't care if our sister—"

"Is Paris alright?"

"Depends on your definition of the word. She's worried sick over your descent into idle carousing. Given her delicate condition, that's unsettling, wouldn't you say?"

To his credit, Rome averted his gaze. "Didn't mean to upset her."

"Guess you didn't mean to upset your niece and nephew either."

He came as close as the bars would allow. "What's wrong with Zoe and Zach?"

Rome had a soft spot for those kids, kids and women in general. London didn't shy from using the knowledge to his advantage. "The other children in town are teasing them about your publicized drunken brawls. Zach earned another black eye defending your honor. Zoe's refusing to attend church. Can't imagine how they're going to react when they get wind of this mess."

"I didn't want to venture too far from the region. Wanted to be near when Paris gave birth." He massaged the back of his neck. "I'm in a bad place, dammit. And I'm not talking about this cell."

"Stow it." London hardened himself to the shame in Rome's eyes. His brother was a good soul, but a troubled one. Too arrogant. Too stubborn and impulsive. He needed direction because he was sure as hell lost. "Gossip travels. Like I have to tell you."

"Would you just give me the damned stipulation so I can get out of this stink hole?"

London rocked back on his boot heels, preparing to deliver the humbling blow. "Think of it as redemption."

Rome narrowed his eyes. "What do I have to do?"

"Reunite with Katrina Simmons."

CHAPTER 4

Time crawled as Rome processed London's *stipulation*. His breathing slowed. His pulse ceased. A thousand images of Kat in action—at the tables, on horseback, in his arms, in another man's bed—exploded in his mind. Vivid, bitter-sweet shards that cut deep. His entire body ached. "What the hell for?"

"For the good of mankind."

"You're joshing me."

London arched a brow.

"Well, hell." Curiosity demanded details. "Define *reunite*."

"To resume your relationship. At the tables and be-hind closed doors. Strictly for show. Just long enough to lure a snake out of the grass."

Adrenaline jolted his seized vitals. "Deal."

"Simple as that?"

"Like I'm going to turn my back on mankind," Rome drawled, tongue in cheek. Not to mention the opportunity to exorcise Kat from his being. He'd reached a turning point in his life, and he couldn't move forward in any direction until he'd dealt with the past. Man to she-devil.

But concerns still tumbled through his whiskey-addled mind. "Last I heard, Kat married a city slicker and settled back east."

"You heard wrong."

"About the marrying or settling part?"

"Both."

"Huh." He gripped the bars, steadying himself as the news rooted. He hated that she could shake his world after all this time. "How do you fit into this? Personal vendetta?"

"In a way."

"Not like you to be so cryptic. It's irritating."

"My heart bleeds."

Rome fought to wrangle his stampeding emotions. Facing the man he looked up to from the wrong side of justice was near as vexing as learning Kat was still free and this side of the Mississippi. "Why Kat? You used to complain she was a troublemaker back when she gambled at the Gilded Garrett."

"She was."

"What, then? You want her to breathe life into that

new saloon of yours?" London had sold a thriving opera house and moved from San Francisco to Phoenix in order to be closer to their sister as well as Athens and his two kids. The saloon he'd purchased—Last Chance—was small and rustic and boring as a church social compared to the Gilded Garrett. Before the man could answer his first question, Rome asked another. "Who's the snake?"

London tossed a meaningful glance toward the outer office. "What I've got to say needs saying in private."

The implied secrecy pumped Rome's adrenaline. Questions burned, but he doused them while London called for the assistant marshal to unlock the cell. Once they entered main office, however, one question slipped free. "What are you doing here?"

He hadn't expected to find Seth Wright conversing with Burke. London hadn't mentioned the pain-in-the-ass lawman coming along, and Rome wasn't pleased. Though they acted on the same side of the law, they'd knocked heads more than once. He expected a spark of disapproval when he met the lawman's gaze, and that's exactly what he got.

"You're in my custody now." Seth barely spared him a glance before touching the brim of his hat, bidding the marshal farewell. He scooped up Rome's holster and made tracks. "Let's go."

"You telling me I'm still under arrest," Rome grit out as

they hit the boardwalk.

"Protective custody." Seth looped the holster over the horn of his saddle, then untied his bay from the hitching post and mounted.

Saddled and waiting, Rome's horse pawed at the dirt, anxious to get going. Rome commiserated. He mounted the spirited mustang, London swung on his sorrel, and the three men rode for the outskirts of Gila Gulch.

"How's Emily?" Rome asked while keeping his eyes peeled for a vengeful rancher.

"She's visiting with your sister for the next couple of weeks," Seth said.

"Then she's on top of the world," Rome said. "Can't believe I'm saying this, but I pity Josh." Paris and Emily were a heap of trouble, doubly so when together.

"Figure it will toughen him up for when the baby comes along," Seth said with a wicked grin. "Any offspring of Paris's is bound to be an ornery cuss."

London grunted, but they all knew Seth spoke the gospel.

Done with pleasantries, Rome fell silent, though his mind jawed plenty. He tugged down his hat, shielding his eyes from the sun as he scanned the desert landscape. A variety of prickly cacti and random mesquite, but not a man—present company excluded—in sight. "What exactly are you protecting me *from*? I don't see hide nor hair of

Gaffey and his lynch mob."

"That's because we stopped by his ranch on our way to town," London said. "Had a talk."

"Real polite," Seth added. "Over Arbuckles."

"I can fight my own battles," Rome said.

"Save your energy, Golden Boy. You're going to need it." He tossed Rome his holster and gun, implying he had worries other than the big bug rancher.

He reined Stargazer to a standstill and buckled his hardware around his waist.

London and Seth reined in on either side.

He glanced at his brother. "This thing that needs saying, I'm guessing Seth already knows."

"He does."

"Then let's hear it." He indicated the wide open desert. "Don't get more private than this."

London kneed his muscled sorrel closer, as if the cacti had ears. "Athens is heading a low-profile crime-fighting agency funded by the government."

"Come again?"

"Shocking, but true," Seth said.

Rome focused on London. "You're telling me our tolerant, diplomatic, nonviolent saint-of-a brother is in charge of an elite government agency?"

"The Peacemakers Alliance."

"PMA's mandate is to investigate hard-to-solve cases. To tame the West," Seth put in. "Personally assigned by President Hayes, Athens is the brains behind the outfit. The coordinator and strategist."

"Granted, he's as smart as they come," Rome said, swatting a fly from Stargazer's ear. "But that's book sense, not trail sense. Athens knows diddly about tracking and apprehending outlaws."

"That's why he's surrounded himself with the best of the best," London said. "Trusted advisors, a personal assistant, and a team of field agents. Former Rangers and lawmen with a flair for espionage. Men who don't think twice about bending the rules to dispense justice."

"Playing loose with the law, huh?" Rome slid a glance at Seth. "Not your style."

"It was for a spell. Fed up with the judicial system, I signed on. Then I met Emily." He smiled, the same stupid grin Josh wore when he talked about Paris. "Realized I can make a difference while sticking to my own moral guns. That means maintaining order on the local level, within the written law."

Knowing Seth detested murderers and thieves same as him, Rome raised a brow. "But you're still backing PMA."

The man nodded. "Serving as an advisor. Josh, too."

"And you?" Rome asked London.

"The Last Chance is a front for PMA headquarters."

"So Athens brought you into this, too."

"My reputation as an upstanding businessman puts me in the unique position of obtaining valuable information and making arrangements on the sly."

"You're working undercover?"

"As the need arises," London said.

"If that don't beat all." Rome sleeved sweat from his brow. What else had happened while he'd been getting his ass kicked due to the Smith affair? "How long has PMA been up and running?"

"Nearly two months," Seth said.

"Yet this is the first I'm hearing about it."

"It's a semi-covert operation," London said.

"I can't be trusted with sensitive information?"

"Don't be an ass."

"Comes natural," Seth teased.

"Go to hell," Rome said, his mood worsening as he absorbed the revelation.

"Athens recognizes you and Boston as top-notch detectives," London said. "But when he organized the team, you were high profile. First the dime novels. Then the scandal."

"Noted. And now we're undesirable due to our current reputations for drinking, brawling, and gambling."

"Actually," Seth said, resting his forearm on the pommel,

"the lower you sink, the more valuable you become."

"In this case, anyway," London clarified. "Athens enlisted Boston and rode south to lay the groundwork. He wants *you* to tempt the devil out of hell."

"Using Miss Simmons as bait," Seth added.

Rome's mind doubled back, then raced ahead. "You want us to lure a snake out of the grass by pretending to be a couple." His gut twisted with deep-rooted jealousy. *The betrayal.* "Considering our short, but colorful history, only one man would care."

CHAPTER 5

The Rincon Mountains

Bulls-Eye Brady paused mid-shuffle. Irritated, he glanced from the deck of cards to the newest member of the gang. "Sit down, Cody. You're getting on my nerves pacing like that."

"Can't help it," he said, spurs jangling. "Feel like a caged animal."

Brady's hand fell to his six-shooter. "Want me to put you out of your misery?"

The man stilled at the sound of a hammer cocking. He dropped into a vacant chair, a good distance from where Amos and Mule, two of the gang's original members, sat playing five-card draw with their boss.

Expressionless, the gambler-turned-outlaw holstered his piece. If he was going to kill Cody, he would've done it directly after the Southern Pacific debacle. He'd had good cause. But the gang was comprised of seven. There had to be seven. Still, that didn't mean he couldn't or wouldn't inflict some pain, and Cody knew it.

Brady shuffled and dealt, ignoring the ache in his wounded shoulder, enjoying the boost to his wounded pride. John P. Cody was a gunslinger, mean enough to reserve a seat in hell. Knowing he could manipulate the rowdy soothed his smarting ego. No one crossed him without suffering the consequences.

Not even a woman.

The recent train heist had been his first qualified disaster. He studied his cards—most notably the pair of queens, which caused him to fixate on two dark-haired bitches. One had dared to slap him. He'd struck back, a natural response. There'd been a river of blood and an unexpected uprising from a male passenger. Pulling a concealed weapon, the fresh-faced kid got off one shot before Brady cut him down. Stupid bastard was dead now, same as the feisty whore. Didn't trouble his conscience none, but it did rile his temper. Killing a man was one thing. But a woman?

The law would pursue him twice as hard.

He blamed the other gal, the skinny one who'd refused to give over her damned necklace. What nettled more was the fact that Cody had hustled him out of the chaos before he'd had a chance to snatch the locket from her birdlike neck. Wasn't the necklace that rankled as much as her defiance and the fact she'd complicated his life.

It agitated an ancient gripe, festered as they escaped the ragtag posse and took refuge in the mountains. So much so, he'd sent Boyd and Itchy back to Yuma, the train's final destination. If she thought she'd escaped him, she was dead wrong. Unlike the rest of his boys, Boyd and Itchy were weasel smart. They'd circulate in Yuma with relative ease, ask the right questions. Either they'd return as instructed with that necklace or news of the woman's whereabouts. He knew the gang expected to ride for Mexico, but he wasn't going anywhere until he got even. Unlike the charismatic cardsharp who'd once roped and hog-tied his heart, this wisp of a woman would bend to his will.

"A week," Cody complained. "We've been here a damned *week*."

Mule took his time contemplating his hand. "What's yer hurry?"

"If we would've kept ridin', we'd be across the border by now, drinkin' tequila and sparking senoritas. Instead, I'm starin' at your ugly puss, drinkin' tonsil varnish." He snapped his fingers at Amos.

The seasoned outlaw tossed him the corked bottle of whiskey, then signaled Brady for three cards. "For a cooped-up cuss, his jaw's gettin' exercised plenty."

"Reminds me of someone else," Mule said. "Least Elroy wasn't bossy."

Brady had to agree. His cousin had more wind than a horse with colic, but he'd followed instruction without complaint. If he hadn't crossed the gang by inadvertently flapping his gums to the wrong people, he'd be sitting here instead of Cody, and Brady would have that necklace in pocket. Back on the train, Elroy would've given him free rein instead of taking charge, no matter the risk.

The four men rose, guns in hand, at the sound of two short and one long bird caw. A warning from their lookout—the cantankerous hermit who owned this secluded shack. Brady had bought his hospitality and silence before. It helped that the crotchety coot held a grudge against the law. His signal was clear. Visitors. Three seconds later, Snapper burst in, filling the decrepit cabin with nervous energy and a dose of afternoon sun.

"Posse?" Brady asked.

"Boyd and Itchy," he countered. "But they ain't alone."

He peered past Snapper through the open door, saw his men riding up, noted the trail-weary cowboy lagging behind, his horse lathered and winded. The man raised a hand in greeting, his index finger a knuckle shorter than the rest. "I'll be damned."

"If that don't beat all," said Amos.

Mule spit. "What's he doin' here?"

Bulls-Eye wondered the same. He sidestepped Snapper and moved outside, intent on knowing what had caused his cousin to defy him. Elroy was a lot of things. Stupid wasn't one of them.

Boyd and Itchy dismounted first.

"We rode up on him as he was ridin' through the hidden pass. Couldn't talk him into vamoosing," Boyd said. "Woulda plugged him, but he's your kin and . . ."

"What?"

"You'll wanna hear what he has to say, boss," said Itchy.

Curiosity piqued, Brady noted his cousin, who, so far, had had the good sense to sit quiet. "What about you?" he asked of the men he'd sent off to Yuma. "What's the news?"

"Name's Tori Adams," Boyd said. "She's an entertainer. A lawman's escorting her to Phoenix."

"Specifically, and you ain't gonna believe this," Itchy said, "to London Garrett. Guess she's gonna perform in that new saloon of his."

Brady clenched and unclenched his fists. The gang knew about his beef with the Garretts. Hell, they all had a beef. Rome and Boston had tracked them more than once on behalf of Wells Fargo. But Brady's grudge ran deeper. Years ago, London Garrett had barred him from his family's highfalutin opera house. The slight still rankled. But it was Rome whom he hated with a vengeance. He'd celebrated for three days and nights when he'd read Wells Fargo had fired the famous brothers. Had noted with interest the gossip regarding their current antics and whereabouts. Good to keep track of your enemies. Now it seemed a new enemy, Miss Tori Adams, was in cahoots with the old.

Brady stabbed a fresh cheroot between his teeth. "Have me a mind to ride north."

"You can't be serious," said Cody from behind.

"You don't want to go to Phoenix, Jed." This from his cousin who finally slid from his saddle and approached real careful-like. "You want to ride south, to Casa Bend."

"Never heard of it."

"Not surprised," said Elroy. "Barely a one-horse town."

Brady fired up his tobacco and studied the man through a cloud of blue smoke. Elroy had always been on the wiry side, but the man had lost so much weight, if he turned sideways, he'd disappear. His clothes were ratty; his boots wore thin. He was pert near unrecognizable. Killing him might've been kinder than kicking him out of the gang. Surely ill luck had plagued his cousin a good long while. "I'll bite. What's in Casa Bend?"

Elroy had always been good for a tall tale and a laugh, but just now he was dead-dog serious. "Kat Simmons."

The name burned through Brady's body, igniting dormant frustration and desire. He didn't flinch, but his men gave him space. All except Cody. He didn't know about Brady's obsession with Kat. This past year, he hadn't mentioned her name because he'd given her up for dead. It was that or go *loco*. Rumors that she'd married another man . . . Just thinking about it spurred murderous thoughts. "If you're wrong, Elroy—"

"I'm not. It's her."

He turned to his men. "Get ready to ride. I want that necklace, but the skinny bitch will have to wait until I visit Kat."

Cody bristled. "Who the hell is *Kat*?"

"Bulls-Eye's woman," Boyd said.

"From what I've witnessed," the gunslinger said, "a wink and a smile lands you any lady you want, Brady. What's so special about this one?"

She's the only one who got under my skin. "That's my business."

Cody gritted his teeth and glared at their boss. "So instead of making for the border, we're going to risk our necks so you can make time with some skirt and then swipe a stupid necklace?"

Snapper whistled low.

Brady snuffed his smoke. "Counting on you to lead the way, Elroy."

"You're invitin' him to ride with the gang?" Cody griped.

"I am." He glanced at his kin. "If he's learned his lesson."

Elroy nodded. "I have." Then he buttoned his lips.

Unlike Cody. "But he's a damned liability, slow on the draw, quick on the talk. Besides, you said it yourself, Bulls-Eye. The gang's comprised of seven. Lucky seven. Don't be an idiot."

Mule and Amos peeled away.

Brady relaxed his bandaged shoulder and smiled. "You're right, Cody. If Elroy comes along, we'll be one too many. Admittedly superstitious, I'm the last one to tempt bad fortune." He pulled his iron quicker than hell could scorch a feather.

"Bull's-eye," whispered Mule as Cody took a slug to the heart and crumpled to the dirt.

Brady winked at Elroy, the man who'd offered up his most earnest desire. "Seven it is."

CHAPTER 6

Santa Cruz Valley

On the rare occasions Casa Bend felt like a prison, Kat saddled her horse and rode like the devil was on her heels. Which he was. Unless he'd given up. She prayed he'd given up, but given current developments she couldn't count on it.

Believing Frankie was safe at the convent for another few weeks, she'd telegraphed a law official in Yuma stating she could bait Brady out of hiding. The first time she'd divulged her real name in more than five years. He'd wired back, saying she'd be visited by a couple of top-notch bounty hunters posthaste. That meant any day now.

Today, she'd been too anxious to tend bar, so she closed the Star and saddled Blaze. Kat gripped the reins, leaned low, her head ear-to-neck with her horse, and kneed the spirited creature faster. She raced along the Santa Cruz River, the circumstances that had led her to this moment crawling though her mind. Regret, shame, and anger pumped through her body like a runaway locomotive.

She was so busy berating herself for her past mistakes, she lost track of the present. She didn't hear or see the two oncoming riders until they were nearly upon her. Fearful Brady had materialized from her thoughts, she pulled up too hard and fast. Spooked, Blaze reared. Unfocused, Kat went head over back end. She landed in the grass with a bone-jarring thud. By the time she caught her breath, the men had dismounted.

They closed in, their faces shadowed by their Stetsons, their bodies silhouetted against the brilliant blue sky. Judging from the attire and aura, they weren't cowboys or sheepherders. Rangers, maybe. Or Federal marshals. Even though she couldn't read their expressions, she was keenly aware of their powerful confidence.

The taller one offered her a hand up. "You alright, ma'am?"

He didn't sound threatening, but all the same she refused his help. "Backside's bruised along with my pride. Other than that," she said, pushing to her feet, "right as rain." Mortified, was more like it. She brushed off her britches and smoothed damp curls from her flushed face. A gifted horsewoman, she hadn't been thrown in a coon's age. Frazzled nerves had made her sloppy. She shifted to make sure Blaze had settled and in doing so, locked gazes with the tall man's friend. *Dear God.*

"Hell's fire." He swept off his hat. "Kat?"

No way, no how was she going to bluff her way out of this one. "Morning, Boston." *Boston Garrett.* She couldn't believe it. With the exception of numerous dime-novel sketches, she hadn't seen him in years. Coincidence?

Breathless, she scanned the area for Rome as the two were typically attached at the hip. She'd invested an awful lot of energy trying to remember how she'd betrayed him and trying to forget how he'd forsaken her. She could handle the days. It was the nights, the dreams of what had been, what was, what could never be, that tortured her soul. Even though Rome had broken her heart, she'd clung to the best parts of him. If she were ever to get on with her life in the romantic sense, she needed to let go of fairy-tale expectations. The newspaper article touting his scandalous fall from grace had damn near done the trick. Maybe seeing him in person would cinch the deal. Only the man was conspicuously absent.

Dizzy with relief and disappointment, she palmed her forehead.

The taller man steadied her.

"I'm fine." Because she had long ago mastered her poker face, he believed her.

He removed his hat, revealing a head of barbered blond

hair. He was handsome in a quiet way, gentler in manner than Boston. "You're Katrina Simmons?"

He looked so incredulous, she almost laughed. "Unfortunately."

"Athens Garrett," he said, remembering his manners. He offered his hand again, this time in greeting.

This time she took it, mostly to convince herself that these two were real and not figments of her crawl down memory lane. They were real all right. "The politician of the family," she noted, fighting to keep calm. The only Garrett brother she'd never met, and now here they were in the middle of nowhere—face to face. *Fate*, her mind whispered as dread iced down her spine.

"Former politician," he said while surveying the area. Wasn't a whole lot to see beyond the blue sky and wide open spaces, but he surely took his time. "You riding alone, Miss Simmons?"

"Obviously."

"Convenient."

"How so?"

"We were riding for Casa Bend in regards to your telegram." He fingered the brim of his hat, studied her with kind green eyes. "Given the sensitive nature of the subject, the more privacy, the better."

Thrown for a loop, she dabbed the back of her hand to her moist brow. "Are you saying you're the bounty hunters

43

I was told to expect?"

"Yes and no."

"Meaning?"

"The bounty hunter portion's a cover."

She stood riveted as he explained that he was the director of a new government agency. Her throat constricted when he stated the agency's overall mission. If they intended to tame the West by tricking and trapping elusive outlaws, then surely a man as menacing as Bulls-Eye Brady was at the top of their list. Were the Peacemakers her and Frankie's salvation? Were her days of running and hiding numbered?

"I assume you heard about Brady's latest train robbery," Athens said.

She curled her fingernails into her palms. "Read about it in the *Arizona Weekly Citizen*." Unlike the article on Rome, she'd had no desire to read the awful report more than once. This time a woman had died. A woman who'd stood up to Brady. She'd mourned Victoria Barrow's death. She'd also spent sleepless nights worrying that the incident had happened near Yuma. She'd worried that Brady was headed deeper into the Territory, closer to Casa Bend. Were the Peacemakers on Brady's tail?

"I heard he rode for Kansas," she said. Barroom gossip. Wishful thinking.

Athens shook his head. "We think he's holed up in

the region."

She crossed her arms over her roiling stomach, breathed deep. Various scents teased her nostrils. The smell of horses ridden hard. The smell of the swollen river. The smell of confidence—the Garretts. The smell of fear—hers. They filtered through her system, reminding her this bizarre moment was real. "I haven't been with Brady for several years."

"We know you headed east, then essentially dropped out of sight," Athens said.

"Brady and I didn't part on good terms."

"So you thought it best to stay clear of the bastard," Boston said. "Smart."

"If I were smart, I wouldn't have gotten involved with him in the first place," Kat said. She refused to show the extent of her shame and fear. Strong and steady. "I've tried hard to put the past behind me, but it won't let me be."

"I sympathize," Athens said.

She wagered he had his own demons, given the flash of pain in his green gaze. A gentle soul, her instincts told her, with a guilty conscience.

"So you've decided to go to war," he said.

She shifted and struck a confident stance. "I've decided to take a stand against a despicable menace."

Boston smiled. "Smart *and* brave."

"Not brave," Kat countered. "Selfish."

45

"How so?"

She pondered what to share. "I have a niece. Five years old. My responsibility. Brady's obsessed with me, and I defied him. No telling what he'd do if . . ." she trailed off, not wanting to speak the unthinkable.

"Having a five-year-old daughter myself," Athens said, "I understand. What we have in mind—"

"I'll do it."

"You haven't heard the plan."

"Being a politician, excuse me, government agent, I'm sure it's clever. Men like you don't play to lose. I'm in."

Boston studied her down-to-earth appearance. "You'll have to slick up."

Time was, she'd take offense. Instead, she took Boston's comment as a compliment. She'd worked hard to downplay her so-called beauty. Given her appreciation for frippery, initially the transformation had been a trial. These days she didn't give her plain attire and lack of face paint a second thought, although her new persona had never felt completely natural. Blending with honest, hard-working folk had kept her safe, but it wouldn't aid PMA in their quest to snag Brady. "In other words, you want Kat Simmons, not Jane Murdock."

"We want a woman qualified to compete in a poker tournament. A woman who'll garner attention and spark talk."

"A woman who'll make the newspapers. Between

word of mouth and the press, Brady will know where to find me faster than chain lightning with a link snapped." She smiled. "Like I said, you're clever."

Athens angled his head. "As you said, you haven't been with Brady in years, and he has strong reason to stay in hiding. We want to ensure he'll come around by resurrecting an old rivalry."

That could only mean one thing. "You're going to pair me up with Rome." Amazing, she said his name without flushing. Amazing, she actually looked forward to the ruse. If she played her cards right, she'd condemn Brady to hell for eternity and banish Rome from her heart for good.

"That a problem?" Boston asked.

A nonchalant shrug belied her inner anxiety. "Whatever it takes."

"You'll be protected," Athens said.

"What about my niece?"

"Whatever it takes."

CHAPTER 7

Phoenix

The day crawled into night, and the night stretched on forever. The Last Chance was locked down, and London was locked away in his office, restless as hell. He sat at his desk, tapping a pencil on his accounts ledger. Hard to concentrate on numbers while contemplating problems of another nature. Hard not to obsess.

London loved his family. Unconditionally. But sometimes they taxed his patience. Take Athens. He had no business putting himself in harm's way. To London's knowledge, he'd never fired a gun, yet he was determined to personally bring down one of the West's most notorious outlaws, Bulls-Eye Brady.

As director of PMA, Athens, alias: *Fox*, had a list of targeted desperadoes. Bulls-Eye Brady was one of many. Until he killed a woman. Then he became public and personal enemy number one. Athens's first wife, Jocelyn, had been gunned down in a train robbery, and though Victoria Barrow hadn't died from a bullet, she'd sure as hell died by Brady's hand.

London figured his brother was dealing with demons even bigger than Brady. "Regret's a helluva thing," he muttered. Even though he understood Athens's motivation, he begrudged his active role in the case. Proficient with guns and fists, London should've been the one riding with Boston. The one scheming with Rome and Seth. Instead, he was holding down the fort, so to speak, business as usual in his boring-as-hell life. "What is it, Parker?"

Parker, Athens's personal assistant, had an annoying talent of creeping up on a person. Silent as a ghost, only London was used to sneaky people. Entertainers snuck into rehearsal late. Dishonest patrons snuck out on bills. Rival opera house owners snuck in to check out the competition. Unscrupulous gamblers cheated the house, fate, anybody and everybody. A lifetime in theater, a peddler of liquor and chance, he'd seen and heard it all. So, much to Parker's disappointment, he always sensed his presence before he made it known.

"A telegram, sir."

"From?"

"Fox."

London rolled his eyes at the unnecessary intrigue. Past closing time and holed up in his office, they were very much alone.

CAT IN THE BAG. ON OUR WAY TO RENDEZVOUS WITH A DOG. SEND A PEACEMAKER TO PARTNER WITH B AT SAN FERNANDO. –FOX

Athens left Boston behind? The practiced gun? The experienced tracker? What the hell? The rendezvous point with Rome and Seth was a good day's ride. Where the hell was San Fernando? And what did Boston need a partner for?

"Fox will protect Miss Simmons," Parker said.

To the best of his ability. Absolutely. But who would protect Athens? "Dammit."

"Sir?"

Of the handpicked Peacemakers, all but one was currently on assignment. "Contact Manning and—"

"On it, sir."

Parker was out the door before London could finish his sentence. Not that it mattered. The man had a knack for knowing his thoughts. Another annoying talent.

He looked back to the telegram, trying to read into it. So Kat had agreed to team up with Rome to catch Brady. Unlike Athens, he hadn't heard about the trio's history secondhand. He'd been in the thick of it. He'd seen Kat and Rome fall in love. He'd witnessed Brady's obsession with Kat, her obsession with games, and Rome's obsession with work. The situation took an ugly twist. He still couldn't accept what Rome had been too willing to believe. Then again, he'd never been infatuated with a woman to that extent. Though his brother claimed to be over Kat Simmons, the look in his eyes at the mention of her name indicated otherwise.

He envisioned the reunion of *Cat* and *Dog*. If anyone could keep the fur from flying, it was Athens. A gifted diplomat, he'd manipulate a truce—at least until they trapped a snake. If reason failed, Seth would keep Rome in line. Maybe.

He resented not being there. Resented being on the sidelines, though Athens had supposedly left him in control. Of what? All of the Peacemakers were in the field. Any paperwork was handled by Parker. Athens's woman, Kaila Dillingham, had moved into his home to care for Zach and Zoe and, though she seemed a bit uptight, he pegged that due to her fiancé's current mission as opposed to his kids' erratic behavior.

Emily was in Chance with Paris and Josh. Not that he wanted the headache, but if his sister and her friend were here, at least there'd be a crisis or catastrophe to handle. Individually, those two women courted trouble without even trying. Together, mayhem circled like vultures. He almost felt sorry for his brother-in-law.

That left him with the Last Chance. One of sixteen saloons in Phoenix. Broken down and lacking female entertainment of the musical or social kind. Undesirable location. Not exactly a gold mine and he worked hard to keep it that way. The last thing he wanted was another Gilded Garrett. He'd sacrificed success and stability for an adventure. So far this venture was a bust.

He locked away the telegram. Needing to escape his own depressing company, he stood and shoved his arms into a black frock coat, buttoned his paisley vest, and finger combed his dark hair. Wasn't his style to frequent a pleasure palace, but a lustful toss in the hay with an imaginative dove might provide a dose of fleeting excitement. At this point he'd take what he could get. "What I need," he grumbled as he strode outdoors into the night, "is a distraction."

♥ ♥ ♥

She bolted upright, wrapped in a rough blanket, drenched in sweat.

"Just a nightmare, miss. I'm here. You're safe."

She blinked in the dark, focused on a short, pudgy silhouette. John Fedderman, former town marshal of Yuma. A campfire crackled and burned, backlighting the kindly retired peace officer who'd insisted on escorting her from Yuma to Phoenix. He'd said he had business in Phoenix anyway. She suspected that was a lie, but she'd been nervous about traveling on the Overland stage. What if the coach was attacked by road thieves? According to the newspapers, it happened frequently in this rough and wild region. She'd already lived through one robbery.

Sort of.

"You all right now?" he asked softly.

Not trusting herself to speak, she nodded, then lay back in her makeshift bed. She'd resisted his entreaties to spend the nights in any of the station houses or missions they'd passed along the way. She wasn't ready to be around people. They'd ask questions she didn't want to answer. Mindful of her delicate state, Mr. Fedderman had acquiesced. They camped in the open desert. Each night he made a place on the ground, near the fire. Each night she curled up in the back of the buckboard alongside a trunk of clothes, her clothes now, she reminded herself. Her only worldly possessions.

Chest tight, she watched Mr. Fedderman walk away, watched him settle onto his bedroll, a goodly, but not so far as to be unable to defend her, distance away. She told herself she was safe with him. She told herself she'd be safe with London Garrett. She willed her pounding heart steady and mentally recited her new reality. The sooner she accepted it, the less delicate she'd be.

Victoria Barrow is dead.

To the father who never loved her.

To the fiancé she'd never met.

Dead, buried, and soon forgotten.

Thanks to a kind and brave woman who'd gifted a wounded soul with a new identity.

"Tori Adams." She mouthed the name to the starry heaven. A name that would be with her forever . . . one way or another.

"*How funny,*" the woman had said as the Southern Pacific rolled out of San Diego, "*my name's Victoria, too. But everyone calls me Tori.*"

Though they couldn't be more opposite in personality and background, they'd connected like sisters. After day two of the tedious train ride, they knew each other intimately.

Tori envied Victoria's betrothal.

Victoria envied Tori's freedom.

They'd joked about swapping places. Then that outlaw and his gang had boarded the train and the joke became reality.

She'd blocked most of the horrific moment from her mind, stress-induced amnesia the doctor in Yuma had told the various law officers who'd questioned her. Truth was, she didn't want to remember. However, Tori's final moment was clear as a sparkling diamond. "*Remember everything we talked about,*" she'd whispered as Victoria had tried to stem the bleeding. "*You can do it . . . Tori.*" She pressed her reticule into Victoria's trembling hands, spoke her last words with a smile. "You're free."

Victoria, no *Tori*, squeezed back tears. To refuse this gift would be an unforgivable insult. She concentrated on everything they'd talked about. Beneath the blanket, she clutched the reticule to her heart, protecting the enclosed identification and the letter from one London Garrett. "I'm free."

CHAPTER 8

Rincon Mountains

"You nervous?"

"I don't get nervous."

"You look as twitchy as a prostitute in church."

Lazing on an upholstered armchair and using a padded footstool as a makeshift table, Rome frowned across the high-ceilinged parlor at Seth. "I'm not nervous. I'm concentrating."

He continued to manipulate the deck of cards—riffle, cut, faro shuffle, a strip, and another riffle. If he was going compete with cardsharps then he needed to practice his technique. He played poker for pleasure. He wasn't a professional like Kat. She knew all the tricks—flashy moves, subtle moves. Reading body language and manipulating minds. Her knowledge of the craft had fascinated him, and he'd dogged her until she'd shared random tricks of the trade. In return, he'd taught her to ride. Turned out she was a better horsewoman than he was a gambler. Then again, back then he believed the sun rose and set with Katrina Simmons.

At the sound of rustling paper, he glanced over at Seth. "Any mention of Brady?"

The lawman peered over the wire rims of his reading glasses. "You read this newspaper front to back. Twice. You see any mention?"

"Just wanted to be sure I didn't miss anything." He'd already missed plenty. Fed up with bad press, he'd steered clear of newspapers and dime novels for more than a week. He hadn't read about Brady's latest, deadly heist. Hadn't heard about the woman murdered until London had filled him in. He'd felt like a damned idiot. He'd also acquired new reason and drive to crush the man he already loathed. Purging Kat from his heart was no longer his primary motivation for reuniting with the she-devil. But it would sure as hell be a bonus.

Seth abandoned the newspaper and sidled up to a pine table draped with a cloth. He nabbed a crystal decanter and poured himself a brandy. "Want a drink? Might help you relax."

Rome noted his cocky grin. "Enjoying yourself?"

"Seeing you squirm? You bet."

"Peddler robbed you when he sold you those spectacles, Wright. I'm sitting as calm as a toad in the sun."

"Uh-huh." Seth raised his glass in a mock toast.

"Cartwright stocks his house with premium liquor. He told us to make ourselves at home. Could be a long night. Athens and Miss Simmons are already overdue."

"Get used to it. Kat's always late." One of the things about her that drove him crazy, and not in a good way. Memories flashed—good and bad. He rolled back tight shoulders, shuffled, and cut. Seth was right. He was tense, not that he'd admit it. He eyed the decanter, craving a drink like air, but that pact he'd made with God five days ago was too fresh in his brain. What had he been thinking, bargaining away his bad habits?

Seth settled in a plush chair, sipped brandy.

"Have to give it to you," Rome said, gesturing to the comfortably furnished room. "As a rendezvous point, this spread is first water." Located east of Tucson in the lush foothills of the Rincon Mountains, the two-story Spanish-style residence was isolated but offered similar comforts to his childhood home. More rustic than the Napa Valley estate, but a mansion compared to the boomtown inns he'd been sleeping in since the Smith fiasco. "How do you know the owner?"

"Matt Cartwright's an old friend. Josh and I rode with him when we were Arizona Rangers. Turns out he's independently wealthy. Doesn't flaunt his money, but likes to live in style."

"I can see that." In addition to favoring luxurious furnishings, the man employed a housekeeper and caretaker.

Maderia, a plump, brown-skinned woman and her skinny-as-a-rail husband, Paco, had greeted them yesterday, seen to their needs, but otherwise made themselves scarce.

"Last month Matt met a nice young lady. This month they're celebrating their nuptials. So. How'd you meet Kat?"

Rome's lip twitched. "Smooth."

"I have my moments."

Conversation had been sparse on the journey from Gila Gulch to the Rincons. It's not like he and Seth were friends by any stretch of the imagination. Though Seth had made it clear he was curious about Kat, Rome had evaded his questions. Now that she was due, make that overdue, it seemed pointless to skirt issues that would no doubt resurface during this mission. Still and all, discussing details exceeded his comfort level.

He set aside the deck of cards, eased back, and propped his feet on the stool. "How much did London tell you?"

"Not much." Seth nursed his brandy while waiting for Rome to relay his story. When he didn't, Seth prodded. "I know your relationship ended badly. Bulls-Eye Brady was to blame."

He pulled a cheroot from his vest pocket, struck a match. "London would tell it that way."

"Meaning you blame Miss Simmons."

"Meaning I blame Kat and Brady equally."

"Huh."

Rome blew out a plume of smoke, grateful he hadn't mentioned tobacco in his pact. "If you've got something to say, say it."

Seth took off his reading specs and squeezed the bridge of his nose. "Just think it's interesting that you're holding a grudge after all this time. Especially given your own loose morals."

He referred, of course, to the Smith affair. "Passing judgment?"

"Making an observation." He set aside his spectacles and moved to the window.

Rome sat and stewed. He didn't want to see the logic in that.

"She's here."

A nerve jumped in his cheek. Rome stood, puffed the cheroot, and eyed that brandy. He'd had five days to prepare. It may as well have been five minutes. Last time he'd seen Kat, he'd spewed ugly, hurtful words. His last exchange with Boston hadn't been as explosive, but the fallout had been the same. He knew an apology and a joke would mend bridges with his brother. He didn't know what he wanted to do about Kat, aside from purging her from his being.

Trouble was, there'd never been closure. He might've cooled off, might have forgiven her, if she'd bothered to ask forgiveness, which she didn't.

"I know in my heart, I didn't do anything wrong."

That's when he'd broken. Engulfed in a red haze of fury and hurt, he'd called her god-awful names and damned her to hell. Instead of fighting back, she'd shut down. He'd stormed out of the hotel room and later that day, she'd blown out of his life. With Brady.

Not long after he heard rumors that she deserted that bastard, too. Rome clenched and unclenched his fists, wondering how many men she'd seduced and grown bored with over the last few years.

Seth moved to the front door.

Rome stood his ground. He stuffed down tumultuous emotions. Did she ever think of him? The first time they kissed? The first time they played poker? The first time they rode double?

He slipped a hand in his pocket, fingered his treasured coin. He wasn't superstitious precisely, but he was—to his detriment—sentimental.

For chrissakes, Garrett, you've faced down countless outlaws. You can sure as hell weather one deceitful woman.

Wary, but curious, he joined Seth on the shaded porch. A Texas buggy, sturdy and reliable, bumped and rolled over rough terrain, pulled by two harnessed horses. Athens was at the reins. Kat sat beside him. Even though he couldn't see her face clearly yet, he recognized her flamboyant style.

A free-spirited woman who'd grown up in theatrical and gambling circles, Kat drank and cussed like a man, but she dressed like a well-to-do lady with an adventurous streak. She'd never been one to hide her bountiful curves and cleavage and, like the actresses she admired, she utilized face paint to accentuate her stunning features. She was, in his estimation, unique.

"Beautiful," Seth said with a note of awe.

"Aren't you married?" Rome snapped, feeling protective of Emily and possessive of Kat.

"I was talking about the sunset."

He crushed his cheroot beneath his boot, glanced at the desert sky, a wash of orange, purple, and red. He looked back to Kat, thinking he'd rather drink his fill of her.

The buggy rolled to a stop. Paco appeared out of nowhere and took the horses in hand. He jabbed a bony finger at the baggage, indicating he'd handle that, too. Athens handled Kat. He rounded the buggy and handed her down. Then he waited patiently while she shook wrinkles and trail dust from her blue satin skirt and adjusted her frilled bonnet. Always fussing with her appearance. Mostly the reason she always ran late.

Rome noted the riderless horse tethered to the back of the buggy. Athens's horse. "Where's Boston?"

Seth shrugged. "Don't know."

Rome couldn't venture because his brain was fixed on

the women sashaying her way to the porch. He noted her tall, graceful form, more slender than her former voluptuous self. Her cleavage wasn't as pronounced as in the past. Then again, the neckline of her bodice wasn't as low. Her complexion was still flawless, but no longer alabaster. Sun-kissed, he thought, noting the freckles beneath the powder. She still favored cosmetics, but with a subtler hand. Instead of crimson red, she'd painted her lips dusty rose. Kohl liner enhanced her doe-brown eyes. Eyes that had yet to meet his own.

"Stunning," said Seth.

"Can't believe you're obsessed with a damned sunset."

"I was talking about Miss Simmons."

Rome shifted. "I'm going to kick your ass before this assignment's over."

The grin widened. "You can try."

Athens whispered something in Kat's ear, squeezed her elbow. She smiled and Rome felt a stab of longing. He remembered with aching clarity the last time she'd smiled at him.

"Sorry for the delay," Athens said as they climbed the steps.

"Worth the wait," Seth said.

"You must be Seth Wright," she said with an easy smile. "Heard you're a charmer."

"Heard you were beautiful. That's an understatement."

"Definite charmer."

"So says my wife."

"Lucky woman," said Kat.

"I'm the lucky one," Seth said.

Rome folded his arms, feigning boredom. Was she ignoring him to perturb him? Playing coy to disguise her nerves? Two could play at that game. One thing he knew for certain, Kat loved games.

"Katrina Simmons," she said, offering Seth a gloved hand. "Everyone calls me Kat."

"Always lands on her feet," said Rome.

At last she looked his way . . . and nearly knocked him on his ass. "Been a long time, Rome."

Her pointed gaze grated and enflamed at the same time. He hadn't counted on being this seduced by her presence. After all the hurt. All the years. He fought to disguise any flicker of attraction as she took stock of him. He tried picturing himself through her eyes. Last she'd seen him, he'd been cocky, reckless, and temperamental. Come to think of it, he hadn't changed all that much. Except his hair was longer and his patience shorter.

"I'd say it's good to see you," she said, "but I'd be playing loose with the truth."

"God knows you never lie, sweetheart."

She didn't flinch, but he caught a flash of something. Just a spark. Anger. Hurt. He couldn't be sure. He was never sure with Kat.

"Shame about your losing face with Wells Fargo and

the populace," she said.

He couldn't tell by tone or expression if she was being sympathetic or sarcastic. Given he'd just insulted her, he banked on the latter.

Athens frowned. "Let's take this inside."

Seconds later they all faced off in the parlor. Rome eyed the brandy. Kat eyed him. Athens eyed the both of them and Seth looked amused. *Hell's fire*, Rome thought.

"This is why I wanted to meet in private, prior to setting this trap. Let's get this out and over with," Athens said. "Deal with it squarely."

"Fairly, you mean," said Seth.

"Bulls-Eye Brady doesn't play fair," Athens said. "Life isn't fair. Forget fair."

"Where's Boston?" Rome asked, maybe too forcefully, but hell, their even-keeled brother had turned cynical. All was not right with the world.

"Protecting Miss Simmons interests."

He waited for Athens to elaborate. When he didn't, he looked to Kat.

After a tense moment, she spoke. "I have a niece. If this scheme goes bad, I want to make sure she's protected should Brady retaliate."

"It won't go bad," Rome said. Partly out of arrogance. Partly to ease the trace of worry etched in her brow. Then he remembered. "Thought you were an only child."

"I had a half sister. Never mentioned her, as we were estranged."

"Had?"

"She passed on and now I'm responsible for Frankie."

"Sorry for your loss," he said. "What about the girl's pa?"

"Also gone."

"Fate can be cruel," Athens said.

And warped, Rome thought. He couldn't imagine Kat in a maternal role. She'd never been comfortable around children. Besides, she was a professional gambler. Someone who moved from town to town, bawdy to bawdy. What kind of a life was that for a kid?

The same life Kat had.

She folded her arms, set her jaw. "Go ahead and say it."

"Just trying to wrap my mind around the notion."

"Don't bother. I can see it's paining you."

"I think it's right noble of you, Miss Simmons," Seth cut in. "Taking in an orphaned girl."

"She's not an orphan," Kat countered. "She has me. I intend to protect her from the heartless miscreants in this world. Starting with Brady."

Rome eyed her hard, pondered the bitterness in her voice. "How long did it take you to recognize him for the devil he is?"

"Not long." She glared back, waited. "Aren't you

going to say *I told you so*?"

"Why state the obvious?"

"I've arranged for another Peacemaker to join Boston," Athens said in a tight voice. "Not that he needs backup, but better safe than sorry."

Rome had to ask. "He still pissed at me?"

"Can you blame him?"

"I'll take that as a yes."

"Would you like something to drink?" Seth asked Kat. "Cider? Coffee? Brandy?"

"A glass of cider would be refreshing," she said as she removed her stylish bonnet. "If it's not too much trouble."

"No trouble. While I'm in the kitchen, I'll let Maderia know we'll be ready for dinner after you've had a chance to freshen up. Long ride. You must be famished."

"Pleasant man," she commented when Seth was gone.

Rome grunted.

"The sooner we complete this mission, the better," Athens said. "So I'm going to be blunt."

More proof that the world was askew. A born diplomat and career politician, Athens pretty talked, double-talked, and talked in circles. Talking plain was not in his repertoire.

"I'm not privy to details, but I know you two were romantically involved. I know Brady came between you, and things went bad."

He turned to Kat. "I heard Brady's obsession with you didn't end when you called it quits."

Then to Rome. "And that above any rival, he resented you the most."

Rome braced hands on hips. "Not privy to details, huh?"

"What I'm hoping," Athens continued, "what I *need* is for you two to set aside your differences. I need you to put on a show. To tempt Brady out of hiding. I need to put an end to his senseless killing."

Rome paid particular attention to his wording. The raw edge in his tone. His rigid stance. An expert at reading people, Kat's thoughts no doubt mirrored his own. For Athens, this mission was personal.

"Be assured," she said, "I want Jed Brady behind bars as much as you do."

"I've got men interviewing victims of the gang's last robbery. If I can secure an eye witness willing to testify about the killings," he said, "Brady will swing."

Kat didn't flinch, intimating that punishment was fine by her. Rome had never known her to wish a man dead. He understood Athens's agenda. Her motivation was less clear. The lioness protecting her cub didn't wash. She'd always been self-absorbed.

"Like my brother, I'll be blunt," Rome said, gaze locked on hers. "How far are you willing to go?"

"To hell and back." She feigned a sugar-sweet smile. "Figuratively speaking."

He grinned. Couldn't help it. Physically, she'd changed, but she was still an enchanting spitfire. The only woman who'd ever kept him on his toes and off balance. She'd just insulted him, but the only thing she'd stirred was his interest.

"So it's settled," Athens said. "You're united in your commitment to trap Bulls-Eye Brady.

"Whatever it takes," Kat said. She offered a hand in agreement to Rome, her gaze never wavering from his.

Intrigued, he clasped her gloved palm. "Whatever it takes."

"It's going to take more than a handshake to make Brady believe you're lovers," Seth stated bluntly as he reentered the room.

"I believe your friend is suggesting we kiss and make up," Kat said.

"He's not my friend," Rome said. He'd yet to let go of her hand. She'd yet to pull free. One or the other or both had closed the distance. They stood toe to toe. Honeysuckle teased his nostrils. Rosy lips tempted him to feast.

"Do you hate me that much?" she whispered, when he didn't succumb.

"I've felt a lot of things where you're concerned," he said honestly, "but never hate."

"Wish I could say the same."

The admission shouldn't have surprised him, especially since they were speaking frankly, but it did. *He* was the injured party for chrissakes.

"We're in trouble," Seth said.

"For the good of mankind," Athens prodded.

Rome leaned in, wanting to prove she'd mistaken disillusionment and regret for hate. Needing to prove some part of her still burned for him. "For justice."

"For show." Kat pressed her mouth to his, and though her lips lingered longer than considered decent, the kiss was chaste. She eased back and cocked a brow at the two voyeurs. "I trust that will suffice for now. Rest easy, gentlemen. When it matters—"

Rome nabbed her wrists and hauled her against his body. It mattered now. He crushed his mouth to hers, demanding yet tender—the way she liked it. He cradled her head, tongued the seam of her mouth. His blood heated in anticipation. Kissing Kat nearly always sent him over the edge. She opened to him. He feasted.

But there was no satisfaction.

Instead of melting in his arms, she iced over. Not visibly. Internally. Outwardly, she appeared an eager participant. But there was no passion in her response. No sincere fire.

He broke off, pissed that, despite the betrayal, she still stoked his lust. Marveling at his inability to stir her blood in kind. To rekindle an old flame. He'd been her first, dammit. There had to be some lingering affection.

"Good God," said Athens, notably uncomfortable.

Seth whistled low. "When you two put on a show . . ."

Only *he* hadn't been acting. Kat on the other hand . . .

Riled by the defiance sparking in her eyes, Rome lowered his gaze. That's when he saw it. Her tell. The beet-red flush staining her slender neck. *Desire.*

She'd been acting all right, just not in the way he'd thought. He'd bet his Stetson her knees were wobbly under that fancy gown. If he gripped her wrists *now*, he'd detect a racing pulse. He held the high card, but still she bluffed.

"This will be easier than I thought," she said with a cocky grin.

He squelched his own smug smile. *My thoughts exactly.*

Athens cleared his throat, nudged Seth. "Show Miss Simmons to her room?"

"My pleasure."

Rome felt better than he'd felt in weeks as he watched her go. She'd be back and the game would be on. This was definitely a win-win situation. By bagging Brady, he'd regain good favor in the public's eye. By bagging Kat, he'd regain full possession of his heart. All he had to do was romance the sassy vixen and recapture what they'd had before.

Only this time, he'd be the heartbreaker.

CHAPTER 9

Ear pressed to the secured door of her assigned bedroom, Kat remained calm until she was certain Seth Wright had descended the stairs. She counted to ten, then pushed off the door and flung herself on the bed. She screamed her frustration into a pillow. How could she be so shallow? So susceptible? The man was arrogant and unforgiving. Yet it had taken every ounce of her willpower not to melt in Rome Garrett's arms.

All had been well until he'd initiated that second, deeper kiss. Up until that moment she'd been convinced that what she'd mistaken as undying love for Rome was six feet under.

She'd pondered their reunion on the lengthy journey, her stomach knotted and queasy. Would he strike her dizzy with his good looks and charm much the same as the first night they met? Would her heart ache to regain the passion and joy they'd initially experienced? Would she burn with shame, knowing she'd done him wrong, but not remembering the how or way of it? Or, the worst fear of all, would she relive the humiliation and hurt when he'd refused to give her the benefit of the doubt after discovering her in Brady's bed? She'd anticipated any and all of those scenarios, calculated how she'd deal with each one.

She hadn't anticipated the overwhelming, all-consuming anger.

No guilt. No regret. No sadness or affection. Just white-hot anger. Standing on that veranda, it had taken massive restraint not to slap his face when they locked gazes. All of the things she wished she'd said in response to his hurtful name calling that awful night begged, no, *ached*, to be shouted. Instead, she'd swallowed the tirade. Now was not the time. She needed Rome to catch Brady. She knew him well enough to know he wouldn't think twice about trading barbs, but if she told him what she really thought of him, it was possible he'd tell her to go to hell, just before slamming out the door and hitting the trail.

He'd done it before.

So she'd lassoed her rage, donned her poker face. She'd played nice. Sort of. She'd even told him about Frankie. A split-second decision based on their tense reunion. She'd asked Athens not to divulge specifics about her current life—the location of her home, that she owned a saloon, that she had a niece—but Rome adored kids. She figured if he knew a little girl was in danger, he'd go the extra mile to catch Brady. She knew he already had fierce motivation to squash the notorious outlaw, but he also held a grudge against her. She needed to stack the deck in her favor. She'd do whatever she had to do. That included kissing the man who'd crushed her heart.

She pressed her fingers to her tingling lips, still warm from his hot mouth. She willed her heart to settle. Assured herself that the attraction was purely physical. Some damned chemical reaction. She was only human, and he was exactly as she remembered him, only intensified. More handsome. More cocky. More charismatic.

Difference was, she no longer craved his adoration and good favor. She was no longer drawn to his larger-than-life edge. Their affair had ignited at a vulnerable time in her life. She'd needed a hero. Someone to admire. Someone who made her feel safe and cherished. Someone who made the future less daunting. She'd pinned her hopes and affections on Rome, and when he'd fallen off his pedestal, she'd panicked. She'd looked to another champion. For a moment in time she'd forgotten everything her daddy had told her about reading and playing people. She'd been impulsive and foolish and suffered the consequences of her poor judgment.

That moment in time was history.

She pushed upright, confident she'd recovered her composure. Seeing Rome in person, withstanding a kiss that would have brought the young, needy, and reckless Kat to her knees, was a victory. Yes, he still sparked an almighty hunger, but she'd pretended numbness, held the upper hand. She'd done it. She'd won! She was no longer a slave to girlish infatuation.

In hindsight, she realized the majority of their relationship had been based on the pleasures of the flesh. It hadn't been enough. She was mature enough now to know it would have never been enough.

After six long, painful years, she could finally chalk Rome Garrett up to her favorite mistake. She could let go of fairy-tale expectations. As long as she kept their physical interaction to a minimum, as long as she retained control of her sexual urges, her heart was safe. All that was left was to banish Brady from her life and the lives of his future victims. Her determination tripled. The sooner they trapped the man, the sooner she could embrace Frankie and a new life. The sooner she could shed the somber persona of Jane Murdock and the baggage of Kat Simmons.

She curled her fingers into her palms, her pulse skipping with anxious hope. "I'm almost free."

♥ ♥ ♥

Kat sat down to dinner with a hopeful heart, a nervous stomach, and three handsome men. In her younger days she'd been wined and dined plenty. Her social-bug daddy had trained her in the art of conversation while teaching her the finer techniques of gambling. As a result, she felt comfortable socializing with two or twenty people. Men or women. Given her daddy's profession, which eventually became her own, she had generally found herself surrounded by gentlemen—the term in some circumstances applied loosely.

As far as social gatherings went, tonight was not unlike any of a hundred nights she'd experienced in her twenty-four years. Trouble was, she'd spent every night of the past two years taking dinner dressed down. It had been a long time since she'd gussied up in feminine finery. She felt out of sorts. Not Kat Simmons—cardsharp. Not Jane Murdock—saloon owner. Someone undefined.

Athens had requested they leave off talk of Brady until Maderia had retired to the caretaker's adobe with her husband. Presently, the woman shuffled back and forth between the kitchen and dining area, intent on serving her guests an array of dishes. Spicy scents from the ethnic food and the amber lighting from assorted candelabra created a pleasing atmosphere. Athens and Seth accepted glasses of wine while

Kat opted for coffee. She was surprised when Rome followed her lead. She easily recollected his fondness for liquor.

After acknowledging the delicious fare and toasting their absent host's nuptials, Seth waded into personal waters. "So, Miss Simmons. When did you first meet Golden Boy over there?"

She imagined the nickname vexed Rome and couldn't help smiling. "Six years ago."

"Five years and ten months," Rome corrected.

"Not that you're counting," Athens said.

"Got a mind for dates, is all."

His tone was matter-of-fact, but that he'd recalled their acquaintance so accurately troubled Kat.

"Where'd you meet?" Seth asked, pushing her past the uncomfortable moment.

"The Gilded Garrett. In addition to featuring premium theatrical performances, I heard some of San Francisco's finest card players frequented the Gilded."

"So you met Rome at the tables?" Seth asked between bites.

"Under the table," Rome said.

"I dropped a coin and it rolled under a faro table," Kat clarified. "Thinking back, I'm sure I looked the fool scrambling to retrieve it while dressed in layers of fine satin."

"Must have been a coin of great value," Athens said, forking shredded pork and peppers.

"Only if you're superstitious." Kat drank coffee to dissolve the sudden lump in her throat. "My father gave it to me for luck."

Seth glanced at Rome, then back to her. "Let me guess. Rome was at that table, and when you crawled under, he was already there, coin in hand."

"Always coming to a lady's aid," Athens said.

"A habit I'm trying to break," Rome said, finishing off his steaming rice and beans. "Tends to end in misery. Mine."

Kat waited for a spiteful glare, but instead he smiled into his coffee. Laughing at his own misfortune? A glimpse of his old sense of humor? One of the things that had attracted her to him in the first place. She quickly turned her attention to her food.

"Did he give it back?" Seth asked.

Kat blinked.

"The coin that rolled under the table," Athens clarified.

"I did," Rome answered.

"But a few weeks and several games of chance later, I gifted it to him. He needed it more than I did." It had been an impetuous act, one she later regretted because she knew the coin meant more to her than him. Unlike her, he'd never produced the coin for luck, just stowed it somewhere. God knew where it was now. "Not that he's superstitious."

"Interesting," Athens said, trading a knowing look

with Seth.

Puzzled by the exchange, she added, "At least he didn't used to be."

"Speaking of luck," Rome said, seizing her attention. "How've you been faring at the tables lately?"

"Luck has nothing to do with how I fare at the tables," she said by way of avoidance. "Skill is on my side."

"Your confidence is reassuring," Athens said.

Only she wasn't confident. She hadn't participated in an actual game since purchasing the Star Saloon. Preferring not to talk about her present life, she steered the conversation back to the Garretts. "Speaking of skill, how's London? Still dazzling the city and turning an impressive profit at the Gilded?"

"London recently relocated to Phoenix," Athens answered.

"I'm surprised he trusted someone else to run the opera house in his absence. I recall him being a controlling man."

"You recall correctly," said Seth. "Bossy. Domineering."

"Sounds like you don't like the senior Garrett, Sheriff Wright."

"Like him fine. And, please, call me Seth."

"I expect *Seth's* right fond of London seeing he hurried along his marriage to Emily," Rome said. "I still can't believe that sweet kid fell for this arrogant SOB."

Kat scrunched her brow. "We're not talking about your sister's friend, are we? Not Emily McBride. The preacher's daughter?"

"That's my girl," Seth said. "She's with Paris now. Helping her to prepare for the arrival of her first child."

"Paris is expecting? But she's so young." She remembered Rome talking about his baby sister, a girl with spunk and a talent for music. Of course, they were all older now. Still, Kat's recollection of Paris was rooted in the stories Rome had relayed, those of a mischievous, eccentric kid.

"To our dismay," Athens said, "she's grown and married."

"To a good friend of mine," Seth said. "Josh Grant."

"Small world," Kat said. She looked to Rome. "Didn't Emily fancy—"

"She did and she doesn't. My loss," Rome said.

Seth toasted him with his glass. "Good answer, Golden Boy."

Sensing a tethered animosity between those two, Kat stepped away from further talk of Emily. "So Paris is married. Given her musical aspirations, I take it Mr. Grant is artistic?"

"Hardly," Seth said. "Although he did inherit an opera house. Primarily, Josh is a lawman. These days he sheriffs a mining town in the foothills of the Superstition Mountains."

"Not far from Phoenix," Kat said.

"That's right."

"So the Garretts have transplanted from California to Arizona." Same as her. What were the chances?

"First Paris," Rome said, "then Athens and his kids. The rest of us followed. Nothing more important than family."

Kat's stomach tightened. She felt the same way, in her own way. A way Rome wouldn't understand. Not that she needed his approval. She eyed the decanter of wine. She hadn't had a taste of liquor in years. But she remembered how it altered her mood. How it made her giddy and brazen and numbed negative emotions. She also feared it had contributed to her faulty memory that fateful night. She sipped coffee instead.

"Your niece," Rome said out of the blue. "How old?"

"Frankie's five," Kat answered without making eye contact.

"Bet she's a cutie."

Now she glanced over. "Why would you bet that?"

He shrugged, smiled. "All kids are cute. Even when they're terrors. Especially little girls."

The observation warmed her heart. It also proved unsettling. Yes, she'd counted on his fondness of kids to advance her goal. She hadn't counted on him being amiable. Where was the hostile man who'd greeted her at the door?

"*My* niece," he pointed to Athens, "his daughter, Zoe, is also five."

Kat arched a brow. "A terror?"

"A handful," Athens said. "Although not as cantankerous

as my son, Zach, who's nine. Luckily, Kaila doesn't mind. In fact, she seems to enjoy the challenge."

"Kaila?"

"Kaila Dillingham," Seth said. "The beautiful and sophisticated Englishwoman he proposed marriage to."

Kat had read about Athens's first wife's tragic death in the newspapers. Killed in the midst of a train robbery.

Just like Victoria Barrow.

So that was it. She'd sensed earlier that Athens had a personal stake in thwarting Brady. Did he think Brady was responsible for his wife's death? She'd heard Rome and Boston had tracked and dealt with her murderers. Maybe Miss Barrow's death had simply opened old wounds. She prayed he'd find peace and happiness with the Englishwoman. She smiled across the table at the lawyer turned lawman. "When's the wedding?"

"Soon."

Rome grunted. "He's been saying that for a month."

Athens wiped his mouth with a napkin. "I'll tell Maderia that we'll clean up after ourselves. The sooner she's out of earshot, the sooner we can get down to business."

Hot damn. Kat knew Athens's plan for trapping Brady was pretty straightforward, but the sooner he dispensed the details, the sooner she could retire to her room. She didn't trust Rome's lightning-quick transformation. She resented the way it quieted her anger. The physical attraction was bad enough. She didn't want to like him. Not even a little. *Dangerous*, her gut warned.

"Good luck," Seth said to Athens. "Matt said Maderia has a problem with men in her kitchen."

Kat pushed away from the table while nabbing two empty plates and a serving bowl. "I'll do it."

The men stood when she did.

Rome eyed her with curiosity. "You're going to wash dishes?"

She smirked at his incredulous look. "Believe it or not, it's another one of my skills."

"Since when?"

Since trading one profession for another. "Let's just say I'm a woman of many talents."

"Thought I knew them all," Rome said quietly as she walked by, careful to keep her distance.

Her pulse quickened at his flirtatious tone, but he didn't render her weak in the knees. Not even when he flashed one of his devilish lopsided grins. No, sir. She didn't trust this transformation one bit. Instead, she took enormous pride in knocking him down a peg. "You thought wrong."

CHAPTER 10

Santa Cruz Valley

They struck in the middle of the night.

They didn't find her at the saloon. Didn't find her in the adobe out back. But they did find a daguerreotype of her pa. Proof enough for Bulls-Eye that Elroy hadn't been mistaken. Up to that point Elroy had kept his fingers curled into fists, worried his cousin was going to rid him of a few more digits.

Instead, Bulls-Eye took his frustration out on the bar-keep they'd found sleepin' in the back room of the Star Saloon. "Ever see a man try to walk without his toes?" he'd asked after Amos and Itchy tied the buffaloed cuss into a chair and pulled off his socks.

Elroy couldn't decide if Pratt was brave or stupid. He was sure as shit tough. He didn't scream when Bulls-Eye shot off his big toe, or even the next two after. Didn't give up no information either.

Bulls-Eye was getting more huffed by the minute, Elroy more squeamish. The front door slammed open, and Snapper stepped in draggin' a clammy-faced poke by the scruff of his neck. A tin star hung from his sweat-stained shirt. "This," Snapper said, "is what I guess passes as the law in this one-horse town. I'm guessing he serves more tax notices than justice. Came runnin' down the middle of the street still strappin' on his hardware. Lost hold of the buckle when Boyd sent a bullet whizzin' past his ear." Snapper wrinkled his nose. "Pissed his pants, too."

Elroy was happy for a reason to look away from the barkeep's bloody stump.

Bulls-Eye strode over to the piss-pants sheriff. "I'm looking for the owner of this place."

"Jane Murdock?" the man croaked.

"If you say so."

The sheriff's Adam's apple bobbed when he looked over and saw Bulls-Eye's handiwork. "Rode out two days ago with a couple of men."

The barkeep finally spoke. "Shut your trap, Gus."

"Fond of your fingers and toes?" Bulls-Eye asked the wide-eyed sheriff.

The boy nodded.

"Then I'd ignore Stumpy over there and flap your gums. Those men got names?"

"Not that I caught, but one of them looked familiar. I'd swear he was one of—"

"Dammit, Gus," Pratt bellowed. "Shut the hell—"

Bulls-Eye whirled and shot and, lickety split, Johnson Pratt was pushin' up daisies. Leastwise, Elroy thought, he wouldn't lose anymore toes.

Bulls-Eye worked his bandaged shoulder, turned back to the twitchy sheriff. "You were saying?"

"He looked like one of the Garrett Brothers," he droned, eyes riveted on Pratt's bloody corpse. "You know. One of those detectives from the dime novels."

The room got real quiet, and Elroy braced himself for an ugly moment. Bulls-Eye hated the Garretts, especially the one who'd seduced Kat first.

"Fucking Rome Garrett," Bulls-Eye said in an eerily calm voice.

No doubt about it, Elroy thought. *This is bad.*

"Overheard something about Tucson," Gus spewed through chattering teeth. "A poker tournament. That's all I know, mister. Swear."

Chewing over the information, Bulls-Eye tapped his revolver against his thigh. "I believe you, Gus. Take a seat."

The man wilted into a chair, and Elroy ventured out loud, "You don't think they're back together, do you, Jed? I mean, I didn't see hide nor hair of Rome the night I was here.

Didn't hear no mention of him neither. From what I saw, Kat only had smiles for Pratt over there and . . ." He trailed off, his own stupid rambling echoing in his ears.

"Thank you for the detailed report, Elroy," Bulls-Eye rasped, plugging Pratt with a second bullet even though he was already dead.

"Here it is!" Amos smacked a page of the newspaper he'd found on one of the tables. "Week from today. High-stakes poker tournament hosted by Foster's Gambling Emporium."

"If that's the case," Itchy pointed out, "Tucson will be a hotbed of activity. One of them professional gamblers might recognize you from the old days, boss."

"Heard they got a *real* sheriff in that city," Snapper said, throwing a smirk Gus's way. "There's a fort nearby, too. Not that I'm tellin' ya anything you don't know, Bulls-Eye."

"I hear you." He nabbed a bottle of whiskey and poured a double. "Give me a minute."

While he sipped and thought on the matter, Mule burst through the back door. "Kept searchin' her place like ya said, boss. Found a hidden drawer in the back of her wardrobe. Some dime novels featuring the Garrett Brothers in there, couple of newspapers—one running an article about our latest heist—and a bundle of letters from a Sister Maria." He thrust out a folded missive. "This is the most recent."

Cheroot clamped between his teeth, Bulls-Eye nabbed

the letter and read. "Niece, huh?"

Elroy and the rest of the gang stood silent while their leader devoured three more letters. He looked as cool as a skunk in the moonlight, but Elroy knew better. He could see his cousin's wheels turnin'. Could feel the intensity of his brewing rage.

"You can relax, boys," he said. "I won't be goin' after Kat. She'll come to me." He threw back the last of his drink, bundled the letters, and headed for the door.

Snapper jerked a thumb. "What about Piss-Pants?"

Bulls-Eye paused about six feet away. "You a betting man, Gus?"

He swallowed. "No, sir."

"Bet you I can shoot that fly off the crown of your hat."

Before the man could counter, smoke curled from the nozzle of Brady's gun.

Blood spurted from the hole in between Gus's eyes.

"Oops." Bulls-Eye tossed a quarter at the dead man's feet as he walked out into the night.

Elroy followed, thinking his cousin had turned a whole lot meaner this past year.

CHAPTER *11*

Rincon Mountains

Seth had waxed poetic about the sunset, but Rome was more taken with the sunrise. Maybe it's because he'd seen so few. The few he had witnessed had been through bleary eyes. Whenever possible, he slept in. The only time he rose early was when necessitated by a case. He wasn't the most hospitable person in the morning, or so he'd been told. Cranky from too little sleep and too much whiskey. Not to say he woke with a hangover every day, but he confessed to tying on a bear most nights.

He hadn't touched a drop since his pact with Him. Each day that passed, especially the nights, proved more of a challenge, but he'd be damned if he'd succumb. He'd never lost a battle of will in his life. Until he was certain he could partake in moderation without it becoming a nightly routine, he wouldn't partake at all. As for the other habits he'd promised to purge—philandering and thinking of Kat—he figured he was on track in a roundabout manner.

Hopefully, the Almighty would cut him some slack, seeing he'd given up one of them cold.

This morning his head was acutely clear, and all manner of thoughts buzzed between his ears. Wide awake predawn, he'd risen and dressed. Restless and not wanting to wake the house, he'd gone out for a walk. The air was dry and cool, the deep blue sky a dramatic backdrop for massive clouds of red and orange, their edges tinged in explosive gold. He'd stared up at the colorful phenomenon a good ten minutes before setting off down a rocky path flanked by saguaros, prickly pears, mesquite, and cottonwood trees. The quiet would be deafening if not for the crunch of his boots over rough terrain and his riotous thoughts.

He kept thinking on the night before. Dinner with Kat. One thought dogged him throughout: *She's changed.* Namely, she was more subtle. In appearance. In manner. In the past, she'd had a way of demanding attention, but last night she'd shunned the spotlight, preferring to talk about the Garrett clan. He wanted to know about her mysterious half sister. How did she die? How did her husband die? When? Had Kat taken Frankie under her wing days ago? Months ago? Years? Where was her niece now? How had Kat looked after her while gambling at the tables? Did she resent the responsibility? When he'd asked about the girl, she hadn't taken the opportunity to brag, so he assumed she wasn't a doting guardian. Then again she was eager to entrap a murdering outlaw in order to protect the kid. That was a powerful indication of affection.

His mind swarmed with additional questions. Why would Brady target the kid? Why did Kat break off with the man? Last night she'd refused wine. In the old days, she'd been as much of a drinker as he. She'd also been a night owl, staying up all hours and sleeping late. Self-indulgent, like him. Impetuous, like him. Cocky and flirtatious, exactly like him. They'd been the perfect match.

Until a no-account sidewinder had slithered into their lives.

Rome perched on a boulder and lit a cheroot. He savored the smoke and the knowledge that, if all went according to plan, he'd catch the rat that had continually eluded not only him, but also the Pinkertons and a passel of local lawmen for years. Snagging Bulls-Eye Brady, a man who'd robbed countless stages and trains and who killed without conscience, would be a personal and professional pleasure. It wasn't wholly because the rat had seduced Kat—though that figured in heavily—but more that he and Boston had failed to apprehend Brady the two times Wells Fargo had assigned them the task. Rarely had they failed to get their man. Rarely had Rome been so motivated to set things right.

Whatever it takes.

If nothing else, he and Kat shared a common motto

and goal.

"Dammit!"

Rome looked from the desert vista to a copse of trees. He knew that voice, though it surprised him she was up and out so early. He pushed off the boulder, peered around the sprawling branches of a mesquite, and saw a conservatively dressed Kat bending over to free her skirt from the pointy spines of a barrel cactus. Her shiny curls bounced around her head like a chestnut halo. Thick locks that once reached her waist now flirted with her shoulder blades. He wondered when and why she'd cut her hair. If she'd meant to heighten her seductive aura, she'd succeeded. Once a she-devil. Now an *angelic* she-devil. Christ.

He crushed out the smoldering cheroot and moved in.

Startled by his presence, she jerked and winced. "Dammit, Rome!"

"Prick yourself?"

"Thanks to you." She squeezed her forefinger and frowned. "I thought you begged off coming to a lady's aid."

"Some habits are harder to break than others." He gestured to her wound. "Let me see." When she didn't comply, he took charge. As soon as their hands connected, he felt a surge of lust. He imagined suckling her finger, kissing away the hurt. He imagined flicking his tongue over her palm, her wrist. He envisioned an array of erotic images, all of which he'd performed in the past, but instead, produced a bandana from his pocket and wrapped it around the wound. It was then that he noticed her skin wasn't as soft as it used to be. He smoothed his thumb over a rough patch. She hadn't earned those calluses dealing cards.

She jerked back her hand as if privy to his thoughts.

He sensed a query wouldn't be welcome so, for now, he let it go. Pensive, he stooped to free her skirt from the spiny cactus.

"I could've done that."

"You're welcome." He straightened and met a pair of contrite brown eyes.

"I just . . . I wasn't expecting to run into anyone," she said in a less hostile tone. "You of all people. Unless you've been up all night."

"Slept fine. Woke early. You?"

"Same. Thought I'd take a walk. Mull over last night's talk in preparation for the impending charade." She lifted a brow. "You?"

"Same." More or less.

"You're staring."

"I know." He was hypnotized by her face much as he was by the sunrise. Rarely had he seen Kat without face paint. This morning her face was scrubbed fresh. She was twenty-four now, yet she looked younger than when he'd first met her at eighteen. How the hell was that possible?

On second thought, it wasn't about youth, but innocence. She looked wholesome, *vulnerable.* He was particularly smitten with the freckles scattered across her nose and cheeks. Smitten and curious. "You used to be meticulous about shielding your skin from the sun."

"If you're wondering how I'm going to attract Brady looking like this, you can stop fretting. When it matters, I'll slick up and dress to the nines."

He stuffed down a surge of jealousy, hoping to strike up an illuminating discussion. "I wasn't criticizing your appearance, Kat."

"No?"

"No. Just wondering what would tempt a night owl like you into spending time in the sun, unprotected no less. As I recall, you owned numerous bonnets and parasols."

"I was obsessed with maintaining a pale complexion. A sign of sophistication and gentility, as you know."

"And now?"

"I'm no longer obsessed."

"Guess that extends to high fashion." He gestured to her brown cotton skirt and calico shirt. "Don't recollect you ever wearing anything that wasn't frilly and just shy of scandalous."

She quirked a brow. "Little early for superfluous finery."

"Wouldn't have stopped you before. Time was you wouldn't step out of your room until meticulously dressed and coiffed."

"That's because the illusion was vital."

"What illusion?"

"If you knew me at all, you'd know the answer to that question."

"You're joshing."

"Mercy, but I'm exhausted from this scintillating conversation." She passed him his sullied bandana. "Thank you for your medical attention, Rome. I'll leave you to your walk and continue with mine."

What the hell? He'd kept his tone pleasant throughout, yet she was pricklier than any one of the surrounding cacti. *Don't let her get under your skin, Garrett.*

He fell in beside her and matched her stride. "I know you're not married, but is there a man in your life?"

"There are lots of men in my life. In case you haven't noticed, women are greatly outnumbered in this region."

"Just pondering your circumstances. Single woman, raising a little girl on her own."

"An unreliable woman, you mean."

"That's not what I said."

"Frankie and I manage just fine, thank you."

"So she's been with you for a spell?"

She stopped in her tracks, crossed her arms, and set her chin. "Why are you so all-fired intent on knowing my business?"

"Friendly interest," he said kindly, holding tight to his temper. Her cool tone and closed-off posture chafed.

"We're not friends."

"We used to be."

"We were never friends, Rome. We were lovers."

Well, damn. Though stated calmly, that sure as hell sounded like an insult. "There was more to our relationship than the physical, Kat. I recall—"

"No offense, but your recollecting is getting tiresome."

Don't let her rile you. "You mean to say you don't think about those days? Ever? How it was between us before it went wrong?"

A flash of anxiety contradicted her nonchalant shrug. "I refuse to live in the past. I have enough to worry about in the present."

"Like Brady?" Maybe her prickly mood was rooted in fear. He matched her stance and dug in. "Why do you see that man as a personal threat, Kat?"

She looked away. "If I tell you, will you leave this be?"

"Depends on your answer."

She met his gaze, all emotions in check. "He wanted to make our relationship permanent. I didn't. I fled. He followed. I don't know if he's obsessed with me or the fact that he can't have me. Doesn't matter. I crossed him and, just like you, he won't forget."

The low blow, intended or not, obliterated his calm. "You're comparing me to *Brady*?"

She blew out a disgusted breath. "Your ego is mountainous. I just bared my heart, and all you can think about is yourself."

Incredulous, he moved toe to toe. "You call that baring your heart, sweetheart? Between last night and this morning you haven't revealed spit about where you've been and what you've been doing these past years."

She stepped back. "It's called survival."

"What the devil does that mean?"

"It means I did what I had to do. It means lying low, making changes. It means putting someone else's welfare above my own happiness."

"You speaking of Frankie?"

Another step back. More distance.

Rome dragged his hand through his hair, his patience spent. "You think Brady would use Frankie to get to you, to get even with you."

She narrowed her soulful brown eyes. "What do you think?"

He thought she should've listened to him and steered clear of the bastard when he'd first warned her off. "I think you're playing me."

She fisted her hands. "*What?*"

"You're not showing all your cards, Kat. I don't trust this."

"You mean you don't trust me."

"Can't say you didn't give me reason to doubt you in the past." Except she didn't live in the past. Lucky her.

They faced off in stony silence. Sunbeams sliced through the vibrant clouds. The warm air sizzled with frustration. His. Hers. In the past their arguments had exploded into passionate tumbles, landing them in bed. Fight. Make love. Fight. Make love. Damn, if he wasn't hoping for a row.

"I'm not ready for this conversation," she said.

"What conversation?"

"Our first conversation . . . alone . . . since that night."

He hadn't thought about it that way, but she was right. Out of all of the questions burning to be answered, one seared his heart. *Why did you sleep with Brady?* He yearned for the explanation she'd denied him in the first place. An excuse, a confession, an apology . . . Anything except that flippant statement that had made him see red.

"I know in my heart I didn't do anything wrong."

As if their six-month relationship had meant no more to her than a one-night stand.

He slid his hands in his pockets, settled into the moment. It occurred to him that their previous relationship had existed primarily after dusk. Conversing at dawn, sober and alert, was a new and interesting twist.

"Why do you hate me?" he asked. Not his top question,

but a source of agitation.

"I don't hate you."

"Yesterday you said—"

"I despised you for a spell, but it passed."

"Because of the things I said that night? Surely you understand—"

"That you were hurt? Angry? I understand the emotions, Rome. What pains me is the reaction. The lack of sensitivity."

"*What?*"

"Let's get something straight," she said.

"I'm all ears." Except his heart was pounding so hard it threatened to drown out whatever she planned to say.

"I'm not here to resurrect an ancient fight."

No fire in her voice or gaze. No sarcasm. No welling tears. If he'd thought she'd kept him on his toes before, he was floating now—the earth plumb yanked out from under him.

"I don't want or need your forgiveness. I don't care what you think of me. Despite my past, I'm a good person who's striving to be a better person. Part of that entails ridding the world of a murdering scoundrel. As long as Brady is on the loose, lives are at stake. Tonight, when we hit that first saloon and launch our mission, you will see the Kat Simmons you so strongly recollect. I will be everything I was and more. Just do me a favor and try to keep up."

With that she turned and headed back to the house.

Not exactly a she-devil, but neither was she a shrinking violet. Who *was* that woman?

For the first time since London presented this mission, Rome second-guessed his commitment. Hell, yes, he wanted to annihilate Brady. But he'd also aimed to purge Kat from his heart and thoughts. He'd aimed to seek revenge. Two days in her company and she had him more twisted than ever. She had him wondering about her beef with Brady, her relationship with Frankie. *His similarities to Brady*, for chrissakes. She had him questioning the past, doubting his conclusions. *"You owe her the benefit of the doubt,"* London had once said. Did he? Had pride and whiskey clouded his judgment?

Now, instead of focused, he felt confused. Instead of righteous, he felt petty.

"Horse's ass," Boston taunted from afar.

He thought about Kat's challenge. He wasn't worried about keeping up, but he'd prefer to stay a step ahead. In order for that to happen, he needed to know his opponent inside out.

"If you knew me at all, you'd know the answer to that question."

His detective instincts kicked in. To get to the heart of the mystery, he needed to get to the heart of Kat. He watched her retreating form—the bouncing halo of curls, her purposeful stride—and marveled at his eagerness.

CHAPTER 12

Phoenix

"What is it, Parker?"

"How did you know it was me, sir?"

"Anyone else would have knocked." London cracked open his lids just as the man wrenched open the curtains. Sunlight pierced his eyeballs. He grimaced at the rude awakening, then noted Parker's fallen expression. "What's wrong?" He swung out of bed stark naked and stalked to the antique bureau transported from his apartments in San Francisco. A half-dozen scenarios flashed through his mind in the half second it took Parker to answer.

Josh telegrammed. Baby's coming.

Athens telegrammed. Fur flying.

Kaila panicking. Zach injured in a fistfight. Zoe ran away.

The saloon's on fire.

"I'm distressed by the fact that you always hear my approach, sir."

London froze, hunched over, one leg stuffed into a pair of trousers. "What?"

"I take great pride in my ability to come and go unnoticed. I have researched and practiced and strive for a ghostlike existence."

"Why?" Perturbed yet intrigued, London finished tugging on his pants.

"I had hoped your brother would eventually recognize the value of said skill."

"Why?"

"Is it not obvious?"

London straightened and glared across the room at the man who'd awakened him from a restful sleep. A third night with an adventurous dove had rendered him sated and exhausted. "No. It is not obvious, Parker. Enlighten me, fast, or go away."

Athens's personal assistant straightened his already-impeccable posture, gave the lapels of his wrinkle-free jacket a crisp snap. "I wish to be utilized in the field."

Welcome to the club, London thought. "Your organizational skills are top-notch, Parker. You're invaluable in a behind-the-scenes capacity. Just as a qualified and efficient stage manager is integral to a flawless stage performance, *you* are integral to a smooth-running PMA."

"Kind of you to say, sir." Parker pushed his wire-rimmed

glasses up his long, straight nose. "I am, however, determined to play a more active part. Unfortunately, it seems I am not as advanced in my espionage skills as I'd previously determined. I have yet to catch you unaware."

London suppressed an eye roll. He commiserated, after all. He, too, wished to be utilized in a more active capacity. Providing a front for PMA headquarters wasn't a challenge. Nor was watching over Kaila and his niece and nephew, who seemed to be getting on fine. Just now, he'd prefer standing in any one of his brothers' boots as opposed to his own. "Tell you what. First time you successfully sneak up on me, I'll have a word with Athens on your behalf."

Parker smiled. "Truly?"

"Absolutely." Hell would freeze over first, but no harm in giving the man hope. He liked Parker, even though he was an annoying bastard. "We done here? Since I'm up, think I'll head over to Becker's Bath and Hair Dressing Emporium, indulge in a leisurely soak."

"Miss Effie Go-All-Night is famous for riding a man sore," Parker said matter-of-factly.

The crude observation didn't surprise London as much as the mention of the dove's name. He hadn't told Parker about his trip to the pleasure palace, certainly hadn't shared the pretty and imaginative dove's professional name. "How did you . . ." He held up a hand. "Never mind."

Parker strode to the armoire, chose a shirt, and passed it to London. "No time for a bath, sir. You have business."

"No, I don't. It's Sunday." His day off. A day typically devoted to family.

"She said it couldn't wait until Monday."

"Who?"

"Miss Tori Adams."

The name rang a distant bell.

"You hired her, sir."

He hadn't hired anyone aside from two barkeeps and Mrs. Chen, an Oriental woman who cooked and cleaned.

"She's a pianist," Parker added. "If that helps."

It did. He remembered now. A vibrant pianist recommended by a friend. At the time she'd been booked in Dodge City. London had hired her for a two-month engagement at the Gilded Garrett. Negotiations had been handled via wire months ago. The actual engagement set for this past month. The new owner of the opera house, renamed the Gilded Lily, had promised to honor previous contracts. Perplexed as to what *business* he therefore had with Miss Adams, London buttoned his shirt. "Where's the telegram?"

"What telegram?"

"The one that can't wait until Monday for a response."

"Miss Adams didn't wire you, sir. She's here."

"In Phoenix?"

"I was walking over to give you an update on the Peacemaker you instructed me to send to San Fernando."

London knew now that San Fernando was a Mexican convent north of Tubac. What he didn't know was why Boston was babysitting nuns. "Manning in place?"

"I don't know. I asked him to wire us when he arrived. Nothing yet. I'm concerned, sir."

"Don't borrow trouble, Parker."

"Could be as simple as not having immediate access to a telegraph office," the man mused.

"Exactly."

"I'm sure he'll check in soon."

London smiled. "About Miss Adams . . ."

"Ah, yes." Parker cleared his throat. "As I neared the Last Chance, I noticed an old man and young woman preparing to knock. I introduced myself, as did they. A retired lawman, John Fedderman, and Miss Tori Adams."

"They're waiting downstairs?" he asked while tucking in his shirttails. Surprising he hadn't heard any voices or activity, given he lived directly above the saloon. He'd renovated the second floor into spacious and comfortable living quarters. Until he decided where he wanted to build a home, it would suffice.

"Mr. Fedderman wished to speak with you in private, so I escorted Miss Adams to the Café Poppy and introduced her to Mrs. Dillingham, who in turn invited her to have tea and scones."

London fought to make sense of Parker's words. On Sundays, Kaila didn't open her bakery until early afternoon and only for a few hours. "What time is it?"

"Noon."

No wonder his head was fuzzy. It had been years since he'd slept this late. "Fine. So Miss Adams is with Kaila and Fedderman is downstairs. Why didn't you tell me right off?"

"I confess to being sidetracked by your infuriating awareness, sir."

London smiled at that, finger combed his hair while sparing a glance in the mirror. No time to shave, but minimal ablutions and bladder relief were a must. "Tell Fedderman I'll be down momentarily. In the meantime, do me a favor and—"

"There's pot of coffee brewing on the stove," Parker said as he whisked out of the room.

But of course there was.

Five minutes later, London was shaking hands with his mysterious visitor. "Sorry to keep you waiting, Mr. Fedderman."

"Be pleased if you'd call me John. Sorry I woke you."

London scraped a hand over his stubbled jaw. "Long night."

"Had a string of those myself this week."

Indeed, the white-bearded codger looked like he'd been dragged backward through the bushes. London motioned him to sit. They had the entire saloon to themselves, except for Parker, who neared with a pot of coffee and two mugs. After pouring, the hopeful *ghost* drifted back into the kitchen.

"I'll get right to it," Fedderman said as London sharpened his wits with a gulp of strong Arbuckles. "I'm sure you read about the train robbery that recently occurred west of Yuma."

London didn't flinch, but his brain cells sparked to life. "Held up by Bulls-Eye Brady and the Ace-in-the-Hole Gang. Three passengers died as a result."

"The woman who's with me, Tori Adams, she was on that train. Seated alongside the woman who died."

"You don't say?" He relaxed against his chair, sipped more coffee. Fedderman couldn't know he was with PMA. Chances were, he didn't even know PMA existed. Few did. Yet he'd delivered an eyewitness—the very thing Athens needed to nail shut the coffin on Brady—to their headquarters' door. A woman London had hired for the Gilded, sight unseen, several months back. Serendipitous?

"She's a bitty thing, on the delicate side. Didn't take well to what she witnessed."

"Few would."

"Thing is, she's blocked it from her mind."

"Doesn't want to talk about it."

"Can't talk about it 'cause she can't remember."

London angled his head.

"Doc called it stress-induced amnesia."

"She lost her memory?"

"Not all of it. Just the parts pertaining to the robbery. Much to the disappointment of the local law, Wells Fargo, a team of Pinkertons, and a couple of smooth-talking bounty hunters."

Undercover Peacemakers. Athens had sent two men to interview the surviving passengers. Even a promise of a reward had failed to entice anyone to bear witness against Bulls-Eye Brady.

"Weren't too many passengers in the car where Miss Barrow met her Maker. Those who were refused to testify that it was Bulls-Eye Brady who struck the lady down, but they did provide law officials with a rundown."

"You privy to that information?" London asked.

"I am." Fedderman slurped coffee, then continued. "When they ordered everyone to hand over their valuables, Miss Adams refused to give over her necklace. Brady asked her if it was worth dyin' for. When he made a grab for it, the other woman, Miss Barrow, interceded. Folks reported the woman gave him an earful and smacked the outlaw in the face to boot." Fedderman tapped a finger to his forehead. "Kind of off the mental reservation, if you catch my drift."

He did. But he didn't agree. The way London saw it, Miss Victoria Barrow had a barrel full of courage. Was it smart to assault a man as dangerous as Brady? No. But he couldn't fault her for standing up for another human being. A damned admirable quality.

"Anyways, Brady buffaloed her so hard she crumpled and hit her head again. Was that second blow that did her in." Fedderman sighed. "Poor thing took her last breath as the gang made their getaway. Died, it's reported, in Miss Adams's arms."

"Hell of a thing," London said, imagining both women's misery.

Fedderman nodded. "I first saw Miss Adams when the train rolled into Yuma and a porter helped her disembark. Covered in blood, dazed. A haunted, anguished look in her eyes. Couldn't get the pitiful sight out of my head. I dropped by Doc's, checked in on her, and introduced myself. That's when I learned she was headed here, to you. Seeing I know your family in a roundabout way, I felt obliged to see her safely to your doorstep."

"I'm not familiar with your name, John."

"No reason to be. It's your brothers, Rome and Boston, I interacted with. Was a time I maintained the law alongside Joshua Grant. Back when we were policing Yuma."

London snapped his fingers. "You're the one who answered their bulletins regarding our sister." Over a year ago, Paris had run away from home to pursue her musical dreams. She'd ended up safe and sound with Josh, but the brothers had shared a few angst-filled weeks not knowing if she was dead or alive. "You tipped them off to Paris's whereabouts."

"Was happy to do it. My daughter ran off a couple years back. Haven't heard from her since. Helluva thing, not knowing."

"Yes, it is." London ached for the man. "So you've made it your mission to look out for young women in distress?"

Fedderman smiled over the rim of his mug. "Guess I have."

"Noble."

"Selfish. Makes me feel better. Gives me hope that maybe someone's looking out for my girl."

London raised his mug in a toast. "Here's hoping." He'd have to have a conversation with Athens about tracking the man's daughter as soon as they closed this case on Brady.

Fedderman set aside his mug and leaned forward. "Miss Adams told me you hired her to play the piano. Being a professional performer, I reckon she's outgoing when she's herself. Sure is a pretty thing. Just now though, she's skittish. I'm hoping you're a patient man, Garrett. Hoping you won't send her packing before she has a chance to come around."

He was still confused about why Tori Adams was under the impression that she'd been hired to perform at the Last Chance, but he didn't 'fess up. Way he saw it, she was a gift. The distraction he'd prayed for. The challenge. He didn't care if she played the piano or not. What he wanted were the memories she'd blocked. He wanted an eyewitness who'd testify against Brady once PMA had him in hand.

London reached over and clasped the old man's shoulder. "Rest easy, John. She'll be safe with me."

"Mumbled that same thing in her sleep a couple of times. Guess you two have met before."

"No. Just a mutual acquaintance who must've portrayed me as a respectable man."

The old man raised a brow. "Are you?"

London thought about his scruffy appearance, the fact that he'd slept until noon. He thought about Effie Go-All-Night.

Parker appeared with the coffeepot. "The man's a veritable saint," he said to Fedderman, topping off their mugs and setting the pot on a folded towel.

London smiled. "Why don't you go and get—"

"I'll return with Miss Adams posthaste." He was already halfway to the door.

"And while you're at it—"

"I'll bring back a couple of scones." Parker disappeared onto the boardwalk.

"How in tarnation does he know your thoughts?" Fedderman asked.

London smiled over the brim of his steaming cup. "An annoying skill."

CHAPTER *13*

The Café Poppy was an enigma. A quaint, upscale bakery in a sprawling low-down town. Delicious aromas overwhelmed the uncomfortably warm room. Every manner of man and woman stood in line waiting to place orders. A few others congregated at small tables, sampling confections and engaging in hushed gossip. They all stole glances at Victoria as Mrs. Kaila Dillingham served her a second cup of tea.

"A lovely girl such as yourself, new in town no less," she said in an endearing accent, "is bound to attract attention." She smiled kindly, as if knowing Victoria's discomfort. "Pay them no mind."

The exchange was cordial but brief. They'd been having sporadic conversations ever since Mr. Parker had ushered her in and seated her next to the window. Kaila, as she preferred to be addressed, excused herself once again to attend business. Victoria strived to blend into the pretty calico curtains. She was accustomed to being invisible, her father had insisted upon it, but her new wardrobe screamed, *"Look at me!"*

The wardrobe of a professional entertainer.

The townsfolk whispered behind their hands, no doubt wondering who she was and what she was doing in Phoenix. Their curiosity was natural, but unnerving. Victoria ignored them and focused on the Englishwoman who graciously oversaw her bustling bakery. Kaila Dillingham was regal. No other word for it. Except perhaps elegant. Beautiful and confident, too. A successful businesswoman. She was also betrothed to London Garrett's younger brother. *Athens*, the woman had said, affection and worry sparking in her eyes at the mention of her beloved's name. *Away on business*, she'd said.

Victoria wondered about his profession. She wondered about a lot of things. Like what lured someone as cultured as Kaila Dillingham to this raw territory and why a woman who reeked of money and good breeding would need to work. She wondered about the two young children, Zach and Zoe, who only created more chaos and work for the woman as they poorly cleared vacated tables and loudly traded barbs. Kaila had the patience of a saint.

She burned to question the Englishwoman about her exciting life, just as she'd questioned Tori Adams. Only she didn't want to reciprocate by answering questions about her own life, as she was no longer Victoria Barrow. Besides, that life—the only child of a coldhearted jewel merchant in San Diego—had been dismal, and the future—betrothed to an elderly cow baron in a remote region of Texas—had promised no better. Blessedly, Kaila's attention had been torn between her many customers and her two little helpers, leaving scant time to converse with the woman Mr. Parker had left in her care.

Now that same man strolled back in. "Two scones to take with, please," he said to Kaila, then addressed Vic— *Tori*. "Mr. Garrett will see you now, Miss Adams."

Merciful heavens.

For the first time since *the switch*, she'd truly be called upon to lie at length. Tori, the *real* Tori, would call it acting. Victoria wasn't certain she could pull it off, but she had to try. No matter her trepidation, she would not squander this opportunity to reinvent her life.

"Miss?"

"I'm ready." She stood and resisted the urge to fuss with her inherited gown. An emerald satin day dress with a cinched bodice and revealing neckline—the most conservative gown in the trunk, yet more flamboyant than any dress ever owned by Victoria. Her father would pronounce her appearance scandalous. *Trollop*, he'd say. She didn't care. He'd called her worse. A burden, for one. An annoyance. A mistake. Oh, yes, he'd called her much worse.

"*Three* scones," Kaila said, thrusting a bag into Mr. Parker's hands. "Miss Adams didn't have time to finish her refreshments."

Victoria blushed. She prayed she hadn't insulted Kaila. She'd had plenty of time, but lacked the appetite. Just now it was all she could do to keep down the tea.

"I had hoped to engage in pleasant conversation, Tori," she said. "I must apologize for being so scattered. I . . . oh, Zoe, sweetie, no!"

The woman raced off just as the little girl flung a gooey pastry in her brother's face. "You take that back!" Zoe screamed. "Sparkles is real!"

Vic—*Tori*—didn't know who Sparkles was, but she welcomed the distraction. All eyes turned to the pastry melee as Mr. Parker guided her onto the boards. *I'm Tori. I'm Tori*, she chanted on the stroll from bakery to saloon. She endured the curious looks from passersby, pulled deeper into herself. She recollected every detail uttered by the woman who'd sacrificed her life just because Victoria had refused to part with her mother's locket. Her stomach churned. She became one with a woman she admired. *I'm Tori. I'm Tori*.

They breached the doors of the Last Chance Saloon—how fitting—and words failed her. *Tori* had led her to believe she'd be safe with London Garrett. A nice man, she'd said, respectable. A proper and boring gentlemen.

He looked anything but. He looked dashing and rakish. *Dangerous.* Though slightly disheveled, his clothing was tailored and fashionable. Devilish black hair curled above his collar, and dark stubble shadowed a strong jaw. Tall and broad-shouldered, he seemed to take up the entire room. Her heart pounded as she absorbed the knee-buckling sight of London Garrett.

Mr. Parker made the introductions. Mr. Fedderman stood nearby, a supportive figure to be certain. But Victoria couldn't move. Her stomach bumped to her throat, and her brain clouded, negating coherent speech.

Her protector's eyes sparked with curiosity and intelligence. *How would she ever fool this man?* He moved in and grasped her hand. "Pleased to make your acquaintance, Miss Adams."

His warm palm and cool fingers did strange things to her senses. Her skin goose pimpled even as her body burned. Her cheeks flushed as she willed herself to speak. The enormity of the deception rendered her ill, but she refused to allow the real Tori's death to be in vain. She refused to return to her own stifling life. She wanted more. *You deserve more*, she could hear Tori say. Summoning a backbone, she opened her mouth in greeting . . . and promptly retched on London Garrett's expensive boots.

CHAPTER *14*

Tucson

Normally, Kat had an ironclad nervous system, but as the buggy bounced over rocks and ruts, she thought she might be sick. She'd been raised by a famed practitioner of the art, a man equally proficient at faro and poker and wise to crooked games such as thimblerig and three-card monte. She'd accompanied him from riverboat to mining camp to boomtown. Developing a thick skin and sharp wits was integral to survival. And by God, Kat was a survivor. Still, so much was at stake. So much depended on adopting her younger, wilder, and more reckless persona and playing the role so convincingly that word would spread like brushfire, drawing Brady to Kat.

She dreaded the moment with every fiber of her being.

She shivered. Even though she was dressed in layers of frippery. Even though it was hot enough to wither a fence post.

No turning back now.

Rome and Seth had ridden ahead in order to set the ruse in motion. Even now they were probably at the tables. Kat and Athens would roll into town within the half hour. Kat had labored over her appearance just as she would have back in her cardsharp days. Athens had transformed himself into a book peddler with a gambling addiction. According to their concocted story, they'd met in Texas at a craps table and become fast friends. Upon learning they were both bound for San Francisco, they united as traveling companions—strictly platonic.

Already established as a woman of questionable virtue, few would be surprised by Kat's association with an unmarried man, especially a dandy. After checking into separate rooms at the Cosmopolitan Hotel, they'd visit the El Dorado Saloon where she'd coincidentally bump into her former lover, the famed Rome Garrett.

Another dreaded moment.

The journey from the Rincon Mountains to Tucson had transpired without incident and in the blink of an eye. Or so it seemed to Kat, who'd spent most of the buggy ride reflecting and obsessing. On Frankie. *On Rome.*

Understandable she felt rattled by their rise-and-shine exchange. She'd been suppressing her emotions for so long, she couldn't help but feel like a stick of dynamite with a short fuse.

Rome had lit the wick.

Though he no longer rendered her witless with a mere smile, no denying the sensual thrill when he'd tended her pricked finger. The touch of his hands had ignited a dozen erotic memories. Skin on skin. Mouth on breast, stomach, thigh . . . Intimacy and passion the likes of which she'd never felt before or since. Her first lover, her only lover, as far as she was concerned. For that reason alone, he held a special place in her heart.

He also taxed her patience.

Why did he have to be so nosy? She'd made it plain she didn't want to talk about her private life, but still he pried. His comment on her appearance had made her self-conscious. His questions about Frankie rubbed raw. His *friendly* interest was about as refreshing as being burned at the stake. Hell, yes, she had an ace up her sleeve. She hated that he noticed. She used to excel at deception. Or maybe Rome was just better at detecting. Six years ago he hadn't seen through her ruse. Six years ago he'd fallen for the woman she pretended to be.

The illusion.

If you knew me at all, you'd know the answer to that question.

The shock in his eyes, the confusion in his tone, had hurt. *Friends.*

Like hell.

Thankfully, she'd had several hours to recover.

Presently, the sun dipped on the horizon. The city of Tucson, a metropolis compared to Casa Bend, loomed up ahead. A sprawling succession of adobe buildings set amid sparse grass and plentiful cacti. When in need of premium supplies for the saloon, Kat sent Johnson into Tucson with a shopping list. On occasion, she'd accompanied him in order to handle personal purchases. Dressed down and quiet as a stone wall, she'd blown in and out of town without gaining interest, but not without noting the town's layout.

Populated by a colorful mix of Mexicans, Americans, and Chinese, the town boasted several mercantile firms, a Catholic girl's school—which made her think of Frankie— a public school and a public library, a brewery, and dozens of saloons and gambling halls—which also made her think of Frankie. In order to secure the girl's safety, Kat needed to spend the next week making a spectacle of herself at the gaming tables. Adopting her old ways didn't make her happy. She'd fought hard to abandon that lifestyle and mind-set, but it was necessary to her cause. *Whatever it takes.*

Breathing deep, she shifted her gaze to the Santa Catalina mountain range, rugged and beautiful with serrated summits etched against a brilliant blue sky. Despite her efforts to relax, she felt as rocky as the distant terrain.

"I say, Miss Simmons, are you feeling peaked?"

She glanced at her companion, still amazed by his transformation. No longer lawyer-turned-lawman, but a book peddler with a British accent and foppish taste in clothing. He held the rig's reins with a delicate touch, yet the horse obeyed his every whim. Apparently the broomtail sensed what she knew: despite his absurd attire, the driver was a capable, confident man. "A little anxious is all," she said. "Don't worry about me, *Sherman*."

"Just easing into character," Athens said, reverting to his own voice.

"You're a character alright." She quirked a lopsided grin. "Where'd you dig up that suit anyway?" The knee-length frock coat with a contrasting collar lay between them. He'd shed that miles ago due to the heat. But the matching waistcoat and trousers and fancy accessories still pegged him as highfalutin. "You didn't purchase those duds in this area, I can tell you that."

"I didn't purchase them at all. Kaila did."

The Englishwoman he intended to marry. *Soon.* "The top hat, too?"

He thumped the shiny brim. "Pretty, huh?"

"More ornamental than useful."

Athens pointed to her flower- and feather-laden bonnet. "You're one to talk."

They both smiled, and Kat marveled that she used to actually collect such nonsense. Rome had been right on that score. She'd owned a steamer trunk filled with frivolous bonnets, parasols, and gloves.

"Kaila thought I should have something appropriate to wear when I meet with President Hayes," Athens continued.

"You're meeting with the president?"

"Eventually."

Because Athens was so down-to-earth, it was easy to forget his elevated status. In good favor with the president of the United States, she imagined there were greater things in his future than duping outlaws. Were he inclined, she easily imagined him as governor of the Territory. Maybe even a U.S. senator.

Kat noted the gold watch chain dangling from his tailored waistcoat, the wide ascot tie fastened with a jeweled stickpin. "I suppose this getup would be considered distinguished over in London."

"It would."

"But not in Washington, D.C."

"Not unless I'm meeting the president at the opera house. Even then . . ."

"Not really your style."

"Not really."

She commiserated, still readjusting to the rib-crushing

effect of a corset. It had been years since she'd laced herself into misery for the sake of a miniscule waist. "I assume you found a tactful way to break the news," Kat said.

"Didn't have to. She knew the clothes didn't fit the man—so to speak—the moment I tried them on."

"Still, you kept the suit."

"How could I refuse her good intentions? English has a heart as deep and vast as the ocean."

She noted his pet name for Kaila Dillingham with a wistful smile. His affection for the woman was evident, and it plucked a melancholy cord within. She'd never been the recipient of true love. Just lust. She swallowed a lump of regret. *Your own fault, Kat.*

"I told her that I'd find a need for this suit someday," Athens said, as he navigated the horse and buggy through a rocky patch of road. "And I did. Not my style, but I'd say it works for Sherman Shakespeare, wouldn't you?"

She laughed at the absurd name. "Along with that fake moustache and beard."

"My face isn't famous like Rome's and Boston's," he said, "but it doesn't hurt to take precautions. Not to mention, the costume helps me to feel like I'm someone else."

She understood that concept well. "Although you didn't follow in your parents' theatrical footsteps, you certainly inherited their gift for acting."

"We all did. Especially Rome."

She frowned. "I don't follow." When she'd first met Rome, he'd been twenty-two with three years under his belt at Wells Fargo. "I don't recall any mention of him ever gracing the stage."

"You don't need a stage to act."

She was living proof of that. But Rome? She scrunched her brow. "Are you saying Rome's not who he appears to be?"

"I'm saying there's more to him than he lets on."

"How so?"

"If you knew him well," Athens admonished kindly, "you wouldn't need to ask."

Words failed her, but a hundred thoughts swirled. She'd blamed Rome for their shallow relationship when perhaps she was equally at fault. She'd never pried beneath his cock-assured surface because she'd been desperate for a protector. No weakness. No vulnerability.

Did she really know Rome Garrett at all?

"Speaking of acting," Athens said, intruding on her thoughts, "you should start easing into character yourself." He pointed out their proximity to Tucson. "Won't be long now."

"Like I said before," Kat mumbled, her mind still on Rome, "don't worry about me."

"So, who does?"

She blinked out of her reverie. "Excuse me?"

Athens, aka *Sherman,* glanced over, one bushy brow raised. "Who worries about you, Katrina Simmons?"

Rattled further, she fussed with the satin ribbon of her fancy bonnet. "No offense intended, but why should it matter to you?"

He smiled. "It matters because I like you."

She didn't detect sexual interest, just friendly interest. Remnants of her early morning discussion with Rome flared. Guilt pricked. What if his interest *had* been genuine? "You don't know me." The theme of the day.

"I'm an excellent judge of character."

The confidence in his tone coaxed a smile out of her. "That so?"

He nodded. "Famous for it."

"You're famous for a lot of things," Kat said as the buggy rocked from side to side. "Most notably your political achievements and diplomacy skills."

Now it was his turn to frown. "Concerned I won't be able to handle myself with a rotten egg like Brady?"

"No," she said kindly. "Just curious as to why you're inspired to try."

He focused back on their destination. "President Hayes put me in charge of taming the West. Currently, Bulls-Eye Brady is public enemy number one."

Part of the speech he'd delivered when they'd first met.

She pursed her lip. "Strictly business, huh."

"That's right."

"I don't buy it." Kat shifted in her seat and regarded the man beneath the costume. "I think it's personal."

His shoulders stiffened, and she smiled.

"I read people, too, Athens. It's what makes me good at playing cards. So. Want to discuss what's really driving you to nail Brady's worthless hide?"

"I do not. Want to talk about your true motivation?"

"Can't say I do."

Athens nodded. "If you ever change your mind . . ."

"Same goes here." They fell into companionable silence, and Kat contemplated the possibility that she'd just forged a positive bond with someone other than the generous and kind soul currently overseeing her saloon. Given her upbringing, given her history, Kat didn't trust easily. Especially men. But she sensed she could trust Athens Garrett. Still and all, she wasn't ready to confess her sins. For Frankie's sake, she'd take those to her grave.

A short time later, they rolled into Tucson.

With great effort and anxiety, Kat regressed several years, pretending to be the woman her daddy had raised her to be. An outrageous flirt. A free-spirited creature who used beauty and sensuality to distract and manipulate. *"They won't be concentrating on their cards, Kitten, if they're focused on you.*" She ignored the self-disgust gnawing at her gut, envisioned Frankie's smiling face. *Whatever it takes.* She primped, shaking trail dirt from the linen duster she'd donned to protect her stylish gown. She winked at the male passersby who openly gawked.

"I say, everyone should have someone who worries about them."

Kat cast Athens a sideways glance. He'd affected Sherman's accent, but he'd referenced a previous conversation. The man was relentless. No wonder he excelled at politics. "Johnson Pratt," she gave up in a whisper. "The barkeep at the Star. He's my friend. He worries."

Satisfied, her companion smiled as he sought out the Cosmopolitan Hotel. "Excellent. Including Rome, Boston, Seth, and me, that makes five."

CHAPTER *15*

Phoenix

"What do you mean, she can't stay here?"

"I confess to an accent, London, but it's not as if I'm speaking another bloody language. Were circumstances different, I'd happily take in Miss Adams until you arrange for suitable housing. But circumstances are currently dreadful."

They were certainly tense.

Kaila Dillingham hovered over the stove in Athens's kitchen, fussing with a castiron kettle. London loitered next to the pie safe, hat in hand. He hadn't known his brother's intended for long, but in that time he'd never seen her agitated. She'd seemed the perfect match for Athens—always calm and logical. Always diplomatic. Always accommodating.

Until now.

"Anything I can do?" he asked, temporarily distracted from his own personal crisis.

"Absolutely not." She whirled, fists clenched at her side.

Several red ringlets had escaped her chignon and now hung limp against her pale, sweaty face. Her normally friendly expression was hostile. Her bodice was stained with . . . something. The always impeccably dressed and coiffed Kaila Dillingham had come undone in more ways than one. "I would be most distressed if you attempted to fix this matter, London Garrett."

More distressed than she was now? He bit back that question and asked another. "What *matter*?"

"Earlier today, Zoe instigated a pastry fight."

His chest eased. "Is that all?"

"In the bakery," she snapped. "During peak business hours. I had to close early in order to deal with the mess."

"I'll send over Mrs. Chen to clean—"

"Not that mess. Zach and Zoe. I'm referring to the two out-of-control children whom I am presently watching over."

"I'll have a word with Zoe."

"It's not entirely her fault. Zach taunted her."

"Then I'll have a word with him."

"It's not entirely his fault, either." She turned back to the stove, lowered her voice. "He's anxious because his father is away."

Understanding dawned. Knowing Miss Tori Adams was currently medicated and under the watchful eye of Parker, London perched his hat on the pie safe and straddled a kitchen chair. "Zach's not the only one who's anxious."

"Of course, I'm concerned." Her hands trembled as she procured two teacups from the cupboard. "He's out there taunting a ruthless beast. Athens is a brilliant motivator. A brilliant strategist. But he doesn't possess an iota of practical experience when it comes to dealing with outlaws."

"Rome, Boston, and Seth have plenty of practical experience."

"Which is why he should have left the task of catching Bulls-Eye Brady to them."

London agreed, but didn't say so. His brother had his loyalty, although he questioned his judgment of late. He understood Athens not wanting to keep his future wife in the dark regarding his job as director with the Peacemakers Alliance. But why wouldn't he shield her from unnecessary worry? It would have been far kinder to be vague. *Going away on business. Be back in a few days.* A belated thought caused him to frown. "Athens didn't tell the kids about—"

"Of course not." She spooned dried leaves from a tin into the china cups, her movements jerky but efficient. "He just said he'd be away a few days on business. Apparently, he used to travel quite a bit when he served as state senator."

The traveling had intensified, London thought, directly after Jocelyn's death. His brother had dealt with the guilt and loss by burying himself in work. London remembered those days well. The entire family had pitched in to look after Zach and Zoe until Athens came around. Not to say he'd wholly put Jocelyn's death behind him.

"Whilst Zach and I had developed a comfortable relationship," Kaila continued, "he now worries that, with a stepmother around, his father won't think twice about traveling frequently once again."

"I'm pretty certain this is a one-time deal."

"I know exactly what it is," she said in a scratchy, hushed voice. "I know it's something he needs to do. I just want it over and done. I want Athens home safe."

Her voice broke, and London rose. He placed a comforting hand on her shoulder. "My brother lucked out when you walked into his life."

"Actually," she said, sniffing back tears, "I didn't walk. I fell."

"Out of a tree, into his arms." He smiled. "I heard." Encouraged that the dust devil moment had passed, he repeated an offer meant to further ease her distress. "Let me talk to Zach."

"No. Please. I need to do it." She looked over her shoulder and regarded him with a watery smile. "It's important to our future."

He'd been watching over his brothers and sister for a long time. That tendency naturally overflowed to extended family. It was hard to pull back, but he did. "Understood."

He stepped aside, crossed his arms. "About that tea you're making. I'm more of a coffee drinker."

"This isn't for you," she said kindly, pouring hot water into the cups. "It's for Zach and Zoe. Catnip tea. Known for its calming effects. I intend to stack the deck in my favor when we have our heart-to-heart."

"Where are they anyway?"

"After I cleaned them up, I made them an early dinner and then sent them to their room to ponder their disgraceful behavior."

"Surprised we haven't heard them going at it since they're bunking in the same room."

"Yes, well, they're not speaking at the moment."

"But you're going to remedy that."

She gave a curt nod. "I am. But shall I make you coffee first?"

"Thank you, but no." He moved to the pie safe and snagged his hat. "I should get back to Miss Adams."

"Miss Adams. Good gracious. I didn't mean to . . . I was . . . self-involved." Her cheeks turned pink. "She's welcome to stay at my house, of course. It's small, but comfortable, and, as I am sleeping here, quite vacant."

London shook his head. "I'm afraid that won't do. She's ill. Nothing serious, according to Doc Vargas, just exhaustion and a mild case of influenza."

She frowned. "All the more reason not to bring her here. Influenza is contagious, and children are exceptionally vulnerable. If—"

"You're right. I wasn't thinking." Not straight anyhow. Tori Adams had his brain working every which way. His heart raced every time he thought about the fragile woman who'd walked through his swinging doors. Visually, she was stunning, and it had little to do with the dipping neckline of her form-fitting gown. Frankly, the woman could stand to gain a few pounds. A passing thought as he'd fixated on her unique face. Almond-shaped eyes. Button nose. Lush lips. Sleek, brunette waves cascaded down her back, the front portion anchored back with ornamental combs, accentuating her quirky, yet striking, features. Unlike most women in the theater, she didn't favor face paint. Nor did she seem aware of her beauty. Hard to believe she was a veteran performer, which by virtue of profession meant she was somewhat worldly. Those pale green eyes said different. They said shy, wounded. Then again, she'd been traumatized by Bulls-Eye Brady.

"Maybe you could acquire a room at Mrs. O'Malley's boardinghouse," Kaila mused aloud. "If you pay extra, I'm sure Mrs. O'Malley would look in on her."

"She has nightmares. The man who brought her here said she wakes up screaming in the middle of the night." He mentally coldcocked Bulls-Eye Brady. "I doubt Mrs. O'Malley or her other boarders would appreciate the intrusion."

"How dreadful," she said, hand to heart. "Do you know what tortures her dreams so?"

He did, but in light of their very recent discussion, he wasn't all-fired eager to bring up the famed outlaw. "A recent tragedy," was all he said. Vague to be kind.

She furrowed her brow. "Mr. Parker said you hired Miss Adams to perform."

"I did and I didn't."

"I don't understand."

"Neither do I, but I intend to sort that out."

She tucked limp curls behind her ears, expression intense. "Clearly, you're responsible for this girl."

"Not so clear, but I agree."

"She's ill and troubled, and you have a guest room at the Last Chance, do you not?"

"She's there now. But I was thinking of her reputation—"

"I do not profess to understand the stereotypes and prejudices when pertaining to theatrical artists, but am I wrong to assume conventional rules do not typically apply?"

London raised a brow, intrigued by her tolerance. Although he didn't know her background, it was obvious she was well bred. He would have guessed her more conservative. "You're not wrong."

"She'll be prejudged by nature of her profession, yes?"

"Probably."

She glanced at the steeping tea, and he registered her sudden impatience with his presence. "Right," he said, then made a spontaneous request.

Two minutes later, he bid his future sister-in-law a hasty farewell and, clutching a spare tin filled with the makings for catnip tea, made his way back to the Last Chance. Tori Adams filled his head and heart. He realized now that seeking out Kaila had been a knee-jerk reaction. He realized fate had already determined a specific course. He not only understood John Fedderman's desire to protect the woman, but upon locking gazes with the troubled soul, he experienced the same bone-deep urge. His feelings, however, were far from pure and paternal. The delicate beauty had upchucked on his boots, and all he could think was, *I'm going to marry this girl.*

A longtime bachelor, he was dumbstruck, to say the least. Of course, he had spent the last year pining for an adventure, anything to shake up his boring-as-hell life. Taking a wife certainly applied.

"Maybe you should try courting her before dragging her to the altar, Garrett," he murmured to himself.

Right. As soon she recovered from the flu, and exhaustion, and, Christ, amnesia.

"You wanted a challenge," he said to himself as he pushed through the swinging doors. "You got it."

CHAPTER 16

San Fernando

The half moon illuminated the desert landscape in eerie lights and shadows. A coyote howled in the distance, a haunting cry that echoed Brady's own desolate mood. He fidgeted in his saddle, anxious and loaded to the muzzle with rage.

As soon as the convent came into view, he signaled his men to halt. "Make camp here. I'll venture closer and keep watch. Sister Maria's last letter reported the kid's in the habit of running off. If Frankie makes a break tonight, I'll snatch her. If not, I'll ride in at the crack of dawn, claiming Kat sent me to fetch the girl in her stead."

Amos reined closer. "You sure you want to go in alone, Bulls-Eye?"

"No need to terrorize a bunch of nuns and little girls." Brady wasn't a religious man, but he didn't figure he should tempt hell further when he could rely on manipulation to get what he wanted.

He wanted Frankie Hart.

He'd ridden night and day to get her and shot an Arizona Ranger along the way. A man he'd once escaped. All Brady and the boys had wanted was a meal. Same with Manning, he supposed. The badgeless lawman had looked up from his plate just as the gang strode into the remote cantina. Brady had had the advantage since he wasn't holding a pair of utensils, otherwise likely he'd be the one staring up at the sky and seeing nothing. Manning was a quick and sure draw. Or at least he used to be. Now he was dead.

After gorging on beans, pork, and tequila, the gang had covered their tracks and moved on. Brady had promised them, once they had Frankie, they'd hole up until Kat came calling. He knew they were uneasy since he'd littered the region with dead bodies. But since robbery wasn't involved, with luck, the law wouldn't associate the killings with Bulls-Eye Brady and the Ace-in-the-Hole gang. Not that there'd been much to steal from that fly-ridden cantina or the Star Saloon.

He still couldn't imagine a pampered, cultured creature like Kat living in an isolated pit like Casa Bend. Couldn't imagine she'd been happy pouring rotgut for rank cowboys. She'd gone to a lot of trouble to hide from him, so far as abandoning her profession and name. After reading the bundle of letters in his pocket and absorbing the image of Frankie he'd found tucked within, he was pretty sure he'd pegged the reason for her sacrifice.

Brady tucked his .45 into his waistband at the small of his back and passed Amos his holster for keeping. He traded his black duster and Stetson for his cousin's worn brown coat and slouch hat, hoping to look less menacing, then he spurred his horse onward to San Fernando.

If Kat thought she'd won this game, she was sorely wrong.

CHAPTER *17*

"You in or out, Casanova?"

Rome held his dog-eared playing cards close to his chest while gauging the bushy-browed, barrel-chested man seated to his left. Tall and broad as a sequoia. Loud as a foghorn in a funeral parlor. Giant Jim, they called him. Rome preferred Big Bastard.

A foul-smelling miner looking to increase his recent good fortune, Jim's mood turned black when his luck got to running muddy. Though the rest of Rome's opponents paid more mind to hygiene and manners, they were a far cry from the perfumed and sensual Kat Simmons.

The El Dorado Saloon was situated at the far end of Tucson, the designated starting place of their whirlwind poker spree. The place where Kat was supposed to sashay in on the arm of her traveling companion . . . over an hour ago. Rome didn't know whether to be worried or pissed.

Because she was notoriously late, and because he preferred to think of her dawdling in her room over a gown, rather than lying in the desert alongside his brother, bleeding to death—he went with pissed.

On any other night, the surrounding activity—the chatter, the laughter, the clinking of glasses, and the tinkling of the piano—would've blurred into seamless cacophony. On any other night, after wiling away several hours in a bawdy, Rome's senses would've been dulled by booze. Tonight, he was stone-cold sober. Tonight, he was acutely aware of every sound and movement. He didn't feel quite himself. He felt better.

Big Bastard drummed sausage-sized fingers on the tabletop. *Thumpety-thump. Thumpety-thump.*

Contemplating his bet, Rome resisted the urge to pull Kat's coin from his pocket. Seth had already ribbed him on the ride. *"Don't suppose that coin you're always fingering is the same one Kat gave you for luck? I mean, you wouldn't treasure a gift from a woman you despise, right?"*

Rome had responded with silence, chafing at the amusement in Seth's tone. The man was a damned pain in the ass.

Though not as irritating as Big Bastard. *Thumpety-thump. Thumpety-thump.* "Any day now, Lover Boy."

If he'd been drinking whiskey, he would've bloodied the man's big mouth by now.

When a barmaid had recognized Rome as one of the famous Garretts, the bastard had slammed Rome with the Smith scandal, citing him a fool for diddling the wife of a powerful politician, an even bigger fool for getting caught.

Hard to argue the truth, plus, somehow, bar-brawling without Boston around lacked appeal. They'd always fought their battles side by side. He wondered how his little brother was faring with Frankie. A terror, Kat had said. Rome's lip twitched. No doubt Boston had his hands full. At least he and Frankie were safe.

Though the other players silently waited for Rome to make his play, Giant Jim muttered under his breath, using double-barreled syllables seasoned with cuss words.

Fed up, Rome pushed his remaining chips into the pot, even though he held a weak pair. "All in." *A good bluff takes guts and consistency*, he could hear Kat say, her voice as smooth and intoxicating as aged brandy.

Where the hell was she?

Focus, she would say.

He didn't smile, didn't fidget. No tell. No tilt. True to his behavior for the past few hours, he drank coffee and mentally rolled his pocketed coin over his knuckles. He didn't need to throw a punch to hit the bastard where it hurt.

Seth, under the guise of Dwight Dupree, a professional gambler who moonlighted as a hired gun, studied his hand through oval, blue-tinted glasses. "Fold."

Charlie, a gap-toothed geezer with a long, red beard, sighed. "Too rich for my blood."

The fifth player, Silent Pete, dropped out with a shake of his bald head.

Giant Jim gnashed his teeth while gauging the situation. Thinking he held the winning hand, he'd contributed the bulk of his chips. Rome had rattled his confidence. He'd also raised the bet beyond the man's immediate means. To call, he'd have to rustle up some silver ore or hidden cash. "You're bluffin', Casanova."

Rome didn't answer, didn't react. He envisioned manipulating the coin—fluid motion, consistent pace—and sipped coffee.

Dupree lit a cheroot, calm as an early morning pond even though the stale, smoky air rippled with tension. If he sensed an altercation, he didn't let on. Still, Rome knew he was steeled for trouble.

Giant Jim studied Rome through squinty eyes, then slammed his greasy, dog-eared cards facedown. "Out."

Feeling cantankerous, Rome splayed his hand.

"Hell's bells," Charlie said in awe. "Pair a fives. You were right, Giant Jim. He was bluffin'. If I didn't know better, I'd think you was a professional gambler, Mr. Garrett."

Silent Pete nodded in agreement.

"Figure I'm good enough to compete in the upcoming poker tournament. Thanks to Jimmy-boy here," he winked at the man, "I'm only a hundred shy of the buy-in."

The burly loser bared rotten teeth and growled like a pissed-off bear.

Rome braced himself for a fight when Big Bastard pushed out of his chair. But instead of swinging his fist, he swung his body away and stalked across the saloon, muttering about *pulp heroes who believe their own press*.

Except I. M. Wilde, the dime novelist responsible for their legendary status, no longer chronicled the Garrett Brothers' adventures. Not that their adventures of late were worth penning. The triple-W vices of the frontier—whiskey-drinking, whoring, and wagering—weren't exactly heroic feats. Of course, they'd be celebrated in plenty of headlines when they brought down Bulls-Eye Brady and the Ace-in-the-Hole gang. Thing was, they needed Kat for that.

The bat wings swung in Giant Jim's wake. The man disappeared into the night just as Sherman Shakespeare, Book Peddler Extraordinaire, made his grand entrance—sans Kat. "I say, good chaps, someone point me to the bar. I am in dire need of a cocktail."

Rome collected his winnings and stood. "Need to stretch my legs. Deal me out of this hand, boys."

Dupree shuffled the deck, his voice accented with a

lazy Southern drawl. "Whatever you say, Huckleberry."
Translation: *Don't do anything stupid, Golden Boy.*

Rome passed several gaming tables—faro, monte, chuck-luck—on his way to the bar. He saw the curious looks, heard the hushed musings.

"Looked taller in those dime-novel renderings."

"Now he's hustlin' cards instead of wranglin' outlaws."

"Best keep our wives under lock and key."

"Heard he shot a man in cold blood up in Gila Gulch."

That last one took him by surprise. *Wasn't the way of it,* he wanted to say, but kept walking. He reached the ornate bar and caught sight of his reflection in the huge back-bar mirror. His rough-around-the-edges image belied his inner sharpness. Unshaven jaw, unruly hair. No tie, no jacket, just a loose-collared shirt and a black vest—unbuttoned. In keeping with his new fallen status, he'd dressed down. In some ways, he felt naked.

He'd always been meticulous about his looks, his wardrobe. Some called him arrogant. Some, shallow. Truth of it was, the façade bolstered his confidence. He'd needed a passel of grit to face down the heartless marauders he'd dealt with as a Wells Fargo detective.

The illusion.

He leaned against the bar as a notion took form. Could it be? Was Kat's previous preoccupation with her appearance a shield? If he'd stripped her bare all those years ago, seen her as he'd seen her this morning, what would he have found? An insecure girl? A frightened girl?

The illusion was vital.

To what?

Survival.

Backtracking, he could see the signs, the vulnerability. He'd been blind to them then because he'd been seduced by the illusion. Consumed with the pressures of work, he'd considered her the perfect distraction. Carefree and independent. A good time. He'd fallen in love with the *idea* of her.

Kat was right. He never really knew her.

And he'd accused *her* of being self-involved.

"I say, haven't we met?"

Jaw clenched, Rome eyed the dandy standing next to him. He had to admit he was impressed with his brother's dedication to this case. Instead of sitting behind the desk, spouting orders like most men in charge, he was in the trenches. Rome even detected a firearm under that outlandish frock coat. Definitely a side of Athens he'd never seen. "I'd remember," Rome said, eyeing the fancy getup.

"Sherman Shakespeare," he announced, sticking out his hand. "Book peddler."

"Rome Garrett." He grasped his brother's palm, no longer certain of his own label.

"Thirsty." On demand, the barkeep served up a glass

and a quart bottle. "Buy you a drink, Shakespeare?"

"Most generous of you, good chap." He stroked the long, wheat-colored whiskers of his newly acquired beard, deep in thought. "I say, I believe I'll have a brandy sour."

"Figures." Smirking, the barkeep turned to the shelf of liquor.

"Rome Garrett," Shakespeare mused loudly. He snapped his fingers. "The legendary Garrett Brothers. Of course! No wonder you look familiar. I've seen your face on dozens of dime novels." He glanced around. "Where's your sidekick, Boston?"

"Otherwise engaged."

"Pity. Dual autographs would have fetched a pretty penny."

Rome rolled his eyes as Shakespeare sipped his *cocktail*.

"It may surprise you to learn that we have a mutual friend, Mr. Garrett."

"You don't say." This scene wasn't going as planned, but coming from a theatrical family, Rome knew the value of improvisation.

"Miss Katrina Simmons."

"Kat Simmons?" he asked, feigning surprise.

"Best poker player this side of the Mississippi."

"That's a pretty tall compliment, mister." This from the ruffle-shirted cardsharp standing to Shakespeare's left.

"You talking about Charles F. Simmons's daughter?"

asked the barkeep.

"I am," said Shakespeare.

"I've heard of her. Long time ago. Thought she took to the riverboats."

"Indeed, she did, sir. But now she's bound for San Francisco. As am I."

"Charles F. Simmons," said the cardsharp. "Now *him* I've heard of. Broke several faro banks in New Orleans about ten years back. Heard he walked away with $50,000."

"$55,000," Rome corrected.

"Yes, well," Shakespeare said, "Miss Kat is her father's daughter."

"If that's so," said the cardsharp, "I'd like to see her in action."

"Likely you will, Mr. . . . ."

"Lewis. Tom Lewis."

"Sherman Shakespeare. Book peddler." He gripped the man's hand and pumped. "You a reader, Mr. Lewis?"

"Not unless it's the newspaper or a treatise on gambling."

"Ah. So I wouldn't be able to interest you in a first edition of Charles Dickens—"

"About Miss Simmons," Rome prodded. *Damn, Athens. Where is she?*

"Yes, yes. As I was saying, we were on our way to San Francisco when we heard about the upcoming poker tournament here in Tucson."

The barkeep nodded. "Next week at the other end of town. Foster's Gambling Emporium. Professional sporting men have been trickling in for days."

"I'm one of them," Lewis said. He fingered his watch fob. "Buy-in's steep."

"We'll possess the necessary funds in due time," Shakespeare said.

"We," Rome said, holding tight to his patience. Athens was feeding necessary information, hopefully inciting gossip, but where the hell was Kat? *Feed me a clue, dammit.* "You and Miss Simmons cozy?"

"Gracious, no. Traveling companions. Strictly platonic. We're staying at the Cosmopolitan."

"So am I."

"You don't say? You wouldn't be heading there now, would you?"

Here we go. Rome shifted. "As a matter of fact—"

"Splendid." He rapped Rome on the shoulder. "Perhaps you'd be so kind as to show Miss Kat about town. I'm sure she'd be thrilled to see an old friend such as yourself. I told her I'd be back within the hour, however, I see a game of monte—"

"My pleasure." He pushed off the bar, whiskey untouched.

A barmaid distracted Lewis, and Shakespeare leaned into Rome, voice hushed. "Maybe *you* can talk her out of her room."

CHAPTER *18*

Except for the usual stares he received as a dime-novel legend (now fallen), no one paid Rome any mind when he crossed the lobby of the Cosmopolitan Hotel. He was a guest, after all. He took the stairs two at a time. He knocked lightly on the door marked 10. Two doors down from his own room.

No answer.

He knocked again. "Miss Simmons?" he called, for appearance's sake. "Rome Garrett. Heard you were in town. Hoping you'll take a late supper with me."

No answer.

He leaned into the woodwork, spoke low but firm. "Kat, dammit, I know you're in there."

"Go away."

The voice was hushed and shaky and directly on the other side of the door, though closer to the floor. "Kat."

"Can't do it."

Can't do it? She'd been the one to contact Athens. She'd been the one who'd been on an all-fired crusade to protect Frankie from the—quote—*heartless miscreants in this world. Starting with Brady*—end damned quote.

He tried the door.

Locked.

Clearly, she wouldn't open it.

Clearly, he couldn't break it down.

Chest tight, he moved on to his own room and walked to the window. This side of the building faced away from the main street. Pedestrian traffic was minimal. It was pitch-black, and the ledge was just wide enough for him to edge along. If he fell, well, hell, he was only two stories up. A dime-novel legend, he thought with a self-deprecating grunt, wouldn't think twice.

Five seconds later, he eased through another window and into Kat's room. A kerosene lantern burned, so he saw her right off. Clad in only pantaloons and chemise, she sat on the floor with her back against the door, knees pulled up to her chest, head lowered, face hidden.

"Hard for me to keep up," he taunted gently so as not to scare her, "with you hiding out."

Instead of starting at the sound of his voice, she slowly raised her head, her dark curls in wild disarray. "How did you get in here?"

Reaction time sluggish. Voice slurred. Hell. "Never mind that." Hands on hips, he scanned the room. It looked like her steamer trunk had exploded. Gowns, petticoats, corsets, shoes—strewn everywhere. "What's going on?"

Hand limp, she gestured to the mess. "None of them are right."

Something told him this was more than an *I-don't-like-anything-I-have-to-wear* dilemma. He'd witnessed plenty of those in the past. "I'm sure you looked beautiful in any one of those dresses," he said, while moving forward.

"But I didn't look like *her*."

"Who?"

"The Kat everyone knows. The young cardsharp who wins the attention of every man in the room with a sly smile and saucy laugh. I abandoned her years ago. The name, the persona, the profession. I thought if I dressed the part, everything would come back."

He hunkered down in front of her, noted the face paint smeared from crying. Christ.

"I tried on every gown," she continued, glassy-eyed. "I looked in the mirror. But I couldn't see her."

"You're not making sense, sugar. What do you mean, you abandoned the profession?"

"Everything depends on my creating a stir playing

poker. Only I'm rusty." She pointed to a deck of cards littering the floor. "I tried a riffle and a flourish, and I bobbled. What if I can't bluff? What if I forget what beats what?"

What the hell was she talking about? He dragged a hand down his face, stated the obvious. "You've been drinking."

"I thought it would help. Part of my old routine. I used to take a couple of swigs before leaving my room. To loosen up."

He glanced at the bureau, noted the bottle of liquor. "You took more than a couple of swigs, Kat."

"Because it wasn't working." Her forehead lulled back to her knees. "It's still not working. It used to make me giddy."

"I remember."

"And brazen."

"Remember that, too."

She peeked up. "You recollect an awful lot."

His lip twitched. "Wearing on your nerves?"

"A little."

"Why?"

"I'd rather not say."

"Hmm." He rose and sought out a chamber set, soaked a cloth with water, and returned. "Look at me, sugar." When she did, he smiled and gently washed away her streaked face paint. "You used to hold your liquor a whole lot better."

"I haven't had a drink in a long time."

"How long?"

"Since that night."

"What night?"

She raised a brow.

Well, hell. He poked a tongue in his cheek as a boodle of thoughts stampeded through his mind. Best not to explore them now. Instead, he focused on her face, the face he'd seen this morning. Sun-kissed and sprinkled with freckles. Funny, he was having a hard time seeing the "Kat everyone knew" himself.

He eased down on the floor, positioning himself next to her with his back against the wall, legs stretched and crossed at the ankle. "The illusion."

She slid him a glance.

"That's what this is all about, right? Your daddy was a smart man, from all I've heard. Knew how to read people, manipulate people. That's what made him a top-notch practitioner."

She didn't correct him, so he kept rolling. "He was all you had, except for that half sister I never knew about. You said the two of you were estranged, so I guess her mother raised her. I'm thinking Charles F. Simmons taught you his secrets and technique so you'd have a way of earning a good living. I'm thinking, since rumor has it he was a doting father, he thought he was doing you a favor."

She wet her lips. "What else are you thinking?"

Mostly, about kissing her. She looked so vulnerable. So sweet. But she was also roostered and he was sober and that combination was a first. Instead, he eased his arm around her, pleased when she didn't object. "I'm thinking when you lost your daddy, you also lost your sense of security. I'm thinking you adopted a tough and wild persona that allowed you to survive in a male-dominated profession, but on the inside you were a scared young girl."

Her flushed cheeks burned brighter. "Early on, he told me I was pretty. Told me I could move mountains with a wiggle and a smile."

"You certainly moved me," he said, heart heavy. "Gotta admit, it dings my ego some, thinking it was all an act."

"I thought you liked me that way."

Guilt reared and kicked. "I did."

"I wanted you to like me. I wanted . . ."

He looked down at her bowed head. "What?"

"It's embarrassing."

"Tell me." Maybe he was a bastard for pushing, but he was afraid she'd clam up when she sobered. He honestly wanted, *needed* to know.

She looked at him, tears in her eyes. "You're right. I was scared. When Daddy died . . . Don't get me wrong. I loved cards. Loved the excitement. The challenge. But I was afraid of being alone. I wanted a companion. Someone to laugh with, to live with." She stumbled over her words, but her feelings rang loud and clear. "I wanted a champion. A protector. I thought you were that man, Rome. I thought . . ." Her voice cracked and she swiped away a tear. "I fell in love with you that first night, under the faro table."

His heart pounded against his ribs.

"At least the man I sensed you were. I don't think I ever really knew you. I think I put you on a pedestal and then . . ."

"I fell off." He thought about the ugly names he'd called her when he'd walked in on her and Brady. Yes, he'd been hurt and angry, but he'd also been drunk. He'd seen everything— Kat naked in bed, Brady sitting in a chair, shirtless and pulling on his boots—through a rotgut haze of fury. He'd coldcocked the man and blasted the woman. He'd stormed in and out in a rage. An emotionally charged, whiskey-addled scene frozen in his brain for six damned years.

"Every time I got used to you being around, you took off on a case for Wells Fargo. I know it was your job and I know it was important, but then *I* didn't feel important. We'd only been sparking for six months, yet I already felt like old news. I started thinking, why would you want to stay on permanent with me? You liked kids, and I wasn't good with them. You'd want a wife and a family, and I was a cardsharp. Some part of me panicked. Some insecure, wretched part of me latched on to Brady's interest. He was charming at first and," she lowered her gaze, "I was a fool."

"You were young." Rome smoothed her curls from her face, winced at her tortured expression. "And I was an ass." He banged the back of his head against the wall, blew out a breath. "This is an awful lot to take in, Kat."

"I'm sorry."

"I'm not."

"No, I mean, *I'm sorry*. About . . . that night."

The apology he'd longed to hear. He thought he'd feel a sense of satisfaction. Thought he'd feel lighter.

He felt like hell.

He struggled now to recall details he'd missed due to tunnel vision.

"I know something happened," she said in a thoughtful voice. "I know we, he . . . but I don't remember any of it. It had to be the liquor, except I didn't drink more than usual. I know it sounds crazy, but . . . I don't know how it happened."

"*You should have given her the benefit of the doubt.*"

He stared down at her, a cyclone of thoughts and emotions battering his being. "Why didn't you tell me that right off?"

She blinked, her soulful eyes racked with frustration

and hurt. "I tried. But I was upset and confused. I didn't feel well, and you were such a mean bastard. I seized up."

"I know in my heart I didn't do anything wrong."

Rome dragged a hand down his face, cursed himself blue.

Spent, Kat rested her head on his shoulder. "I'm going to hate myself in the morning."

"No, you're not."

"I failed Frankie."

"No, you didn't. The plan's in motion. We just took another angle."

"I don't know if I can do this."

"That's the whiskey talking. You can do it. You're going to take another angle, too."

"Sounds like you've got it all worked out."

She sounded close to nodding off. "I'm working on it, sugar." He wrapped both arms around her, pulled her against his chest. "I should put you to bed."

She didn't answer. She'd already fallen off.

He settled in, thinking she felt good snuggled up against him, thinking Brady was possibly more of a snake than he'd given him credit for. Thinking she'd had good cause to compare him to the bastard.

Just when he'd thought he couldn't sink lower.

CHAPTER 19

Phoenix

"That locket worth dying for?" He made a grab for her neck.

Victoria jerked back.

Tori let loose with a blistering set down.

Victoria saw the fires of Hades burning in the outlaw's eyes. Paralyzed with fear, she did nothing, said nothing.

Tori railed, "Heartless bastard!" and slapped the devil's face.

He struck back, slammed the butt of his gun against her temple.

"Nooooo!" Victoria bolted upright, her throat aching, her ears ringing from the piercing scream. Tori's scream. No, *her* scream.

She heard footsteps. Dark shadow. Dark man. *Him.* This time she swung . . . and hit and hit. "Murderer!"

He caught her wrists. She struggled. *Too strong.*

"Tori, wake up. Calm down."

"Mr. Fedderman?" Her voice sounded scratchy and

weak to her ears. Her eyes hurt when he turned up the flame on the bedside lamp. Only it wasn't the kindly old lawman who sat on the edge of her bed. Another man. A handsome man with intense brown eyes. She tried to focus. Her head pounded. Her clothes . . . Frantic, she swiped her hands over her drenched gown. "So much blood."

"Not blood, honey, sweat. You're soaked through." He grasped her hands, stilled her motions. "Sit tight. I'll fetch you a fresh nightshirt."

Wait, her mind pleaded as she gripped his fingers. The last vestiges of the nightmare receded, and she realized now that she was looking at London Garrett. She didn't trust herself to speak. What if she threw up on him again?

"You're safe here, Tori. Safe with me. Do you believe that?"

She nodded. Not just because her friend had told her so. Because she sensed it. She vaguely remembered swooning after the mortifying boot incident. London had carried her upstairs, laid her on this bed. There'd been a doctor. Exhaustion, he'd said. Influenza, he'd said. "The doctor gave me something to help me rest," she said aloud. There. She spoke. Actual words. Progress.

London nodded. "You've been out for hours. It's well past midnight."

"I'm . . . I'm sorry I woke you."

"You didn't wake me, honey. I'm a night owl. Nature of our business."

Our business. The entertainment business. Her sluggish mind scrambled. According to Tori, London had owned an opera house in San Francisco. He worked with actors and musicians. There was a certain familiarity among their kind. Endearments, she ventured, were common. Still, she blushed. She realized then that she had a death grip on his hands. Strong hands. Kind hands. Hands that didn't smack back. "I'm sorry I hit you. I thought . . . I thought you were . . ."

"The man on the train." He stroked his thumb over the heel of her hand, a gesture meant to comfort. "Did you catch his name?"

The nightmare had faded to black. She couldn't think straight anyway given this man's gentle touch. She shook her head.

"Do you remember what he looked like?"

The devil.

She squeezed back tears. "I don't want to remember. My fault," she blurted.

He slipped her grasp to frame her face. "Nothing that happened on that train was your fault, Tori."

"But . . ." She trailed off, uncertain as to why she'd said such a thing. Just a feeling. An awful feeling that gnawed at her stomach and made her ill. She met London's gaze, wondering how she'd ever thought him dangerous. All she saw was tenderness and . . . *something*. Something that set her blood afire.

"Jesus, honey, you're burning up."

Or maybe it was fever. She confessed to feeling a mite delirious.

He eased away and returned a moment later with a basin of water and a folded cloth. He set the basin on the nightstand, smoothed the cloth over her face—cool, wet, refreshing—and over the back of her neck. "Better?"

Choked up by his kindness, she nodded.

"Fresh nightshirt," he said, rising again.

It took a second for her to realize that he was going though her unmentionables. Or rather *Tori's* unmentionables. Somewhat scandalous, like her wardrobe. Mortified, she wanted to demand he stop, but he was already standing over her, a white cotton frock clasped in his hand.

Surely he didn't think to . . . "I can manage." She pulled the chemise from his grasp. "Thank you."

"Polite *and* modest." His brow furrowed a little before turning. "I'll wait in the hallway."

She didn't understand why her modesty surprised him. Then she remembered she was Tori Adams—entertainer. She flashed on some of her fast friend's stories. Tori was *not* modest.

"I just meant . . . you don't have to take care of me."

He'd already moved to the threshold. His back was to her, but she heard the smile in his voice. "I'm the oldest of five. Three younger brothers, one sister. I've overseen countless theater productions. Actors, dancers, musicians, and variety performers. Not to mention gaming staff. Bartenders, barmaids, dealers. I'm used to taking care of people."

Even so. "I hate being a burden." She'd been a burden to her father. He'd said so a hundred times.

"You're not a burden. Trust me."

She hurriedly exchanged the damp nightshirt for the fresh one, shivering when the air hit her bare skin. She wanted to trust him. She wanted to tell him the truth about who she really was. But what if he turned her out? What if he contacted her father? She shuddered. She couldn't, *wouldn't* risk it. Tying off the ribbon at the chemise's collar, she scooted under the covers. "You can turn back now."

He moved into the room, and the heat returned with him. That *something* in his eyes. The something that distracted her from the awful event that plagued yet eluded her. The something that caused her heart to flutter and her mouth to go dry.

"How about I fix you some catnip tea? Heard tell it has soothing effects."

Tea made her think of this afternoon's catastrophe.

She blushed. "I'm sorry I ruined your boots."

"Polite to a fault." He smiled. "So. No tea."

"No tea."

"Sleep, then."

She swallowed.

"You need to sleep, Tori."

Tori wouldn't give a fig that she was staying in a man's home without a chaperone. *Tori* would speak her mind. "Would you sit with me for a spell?"

"Absolutely."

He pulled over a chair, doused the light.

"Would you hold my hand?" she whispered.

"With pleasure."

The pleasure was hers. His touch was gentle, yet reassuring. She felt safe and cherished. A first. She fought tears, dared to hope. *"You can do this . . . Tori."*

A goodly amount of time passed in silence. Sleep beckoned, but she staved it off long enough to voice her gratitude. "I'm beholden to you for your kindness, Mr. Garrett."

"I'm beholden to you for my future happiness, Miss Adams."

She didn't know what that meant. But she took the sentiment into her dreams.

CHAPTER 20

Tucson

Kat stirred. She didn't open her eyes. She wasn't sure she wanted to face the day. Not without fully remembering the previous night.

The last moments trickled in first. She recalled falling asleep in Rome's arms, remembered a knock at her door, a brief exchange between Rome and Athens. Some time later he roused her, put her to bed . . . and left.

Groaning, she palmed her forehead. Her brain hurt. Not from thinking too hard, but from drinking too much. That knowledge alone would've sickened her, except . . . she remembered every moment. Every action, every thought, every word.

Rome was right. She didn't hate herself.

At long last she'd confronted him about that night. Granted, she'd always envisioned herself of sound mind and body, blasting him for having so little faith in her affections.

163

Cursing him for taking the easy road instead of taking a stand. Instead of fighting. For her. Then again, she hadn't fought for herself either. She'd taken solace in Brady's lies. She'd run.

She massaged her temples, wishing she hadn't fallen back on old vices last night. She regretted pouring her heart out in an inebriated, teary state. But she didn't hate herself. The relief was too immense. She'd finally vocalized her shame and confusion—*I don't know how it happened.*

And Rome believed her.

She hadn't expected that. If it weren't for her pounding head, she'd dance on the ceiling. As it was she could barely open her eyes, let alone kick up her heels. Heavy-lidded, she winced when sunlight pierced her eyeballs, wished so hard for a cup of coffee she smelled it.

"Morning."

Hand to heart, Kat bolted upright. "Dammit, Rome. Stop sneaking up on me."

He'd shaved and changed his clothes. He looked handsome and rested. She tucked bed-mussed curls behind her ears, thinking she looked a fright.

So why was he gazing at her like he wanted to crawl into bed for a tumble?

"Quick response. Prickly mood." He grinned. "Glad you're feeling better."

That smile burned off her sluggishness, reignited an ancient ache. Startled, she forced her thoughts north. "My head hurts something fierce."

"Thought it might." He jerked a thumb over his shoulder. "Brought you something."

She peered around him, noted a small table and a steaming pot. "Coffee." She shoved off the coverlet, nabbed her wrapper from the end of her bed, and pulled it on as she scrambled to salvation. "You're a lifesaver."

"On my best days."

He waited until she sat, then poured for them both and pulled up another chair.

She inhaled the rich aroma. "Heaven," she said, then sipped. "Thank you."

"You're welcome."

Her skin warmed under his watchful eye. She recognized the glint in his ocean-blue gaze as genuine interest. And guilt. And, God help her, affection. Unsettled, she eyed the open window. "Don't tell me you scaled the ledge carrying all this."

"I'm a daredevil, sugar, not a juggler." He slid her room key across the table. "Took the conventional route."

"Anyone see you come or go?"

"Probably."

Silly to be embarrassed. It's not like she hadn't cavorted

with Rome before. It's not like she hadn't already been labeled a fallen woman. But that was before she worried about how her actions would affect someone else. Specifically Frankie. "People will talk."

"That's what we want, isn't it?"

"True." That *was* the point. To ignite gossip. The faster word spread that Kat Simmons was in Tucson and that she'd taken up with Rome Garrett, the faster Brady would show. She drank more coffee to ward off a chill of dread. No, sir, she wasn't looking forward to seeing Jed Brady again.

Rome on the other hand . . . The man was a sight for sore eyes and a wounded soul. Last night something had shifted between them. She didn't fool herself into thinking all was forgiven and forgotten on either side. But there was a definite sense they'd moved beyond. The notion was refreshing, yet unnerving. What now?

Self-conscious, she cleared her throat and broached a point of curiosity. "This is the second morning running I've seen you bright eyed and good-natured, Rome Garrett. Now that I think of it, you were bright eyed last night." She cocked her head. "Haven't seen you bend an elbow once these past days."

"Gave up whiskey over a week ago."

"Why?"

"Made a deal with someone."

She wondered who, but figured he would've offered that up if so inclined. "This a permanent deal?"

"Maybe."

She wondered at his reasons. She wondered a lot of things this liberating, illuminating morning. "You hung up my gowns," she said in sudden realization. "Put away my shoes."

"Guilty."

She blinked as he freshened her coffee. "Why are you being so thoughtful?"

"Penance."

She held her breath.

He blew one out. "I'd like to think that kindness comes natural to me, Kat, but as you pointed out last night, I can be a mean bastard."

"I was—"

"You were being truthful." He scraped white teeth over his full bottom lip, mindful of his words. "You also said I recollect a lot. Reckon I do. But stone sober, some things look different on reflection."

Her stomach clenched. "Rome—"

"You offered up some mighty personal information last night. Figure I can do the same." He reached over and grasped her fingers. "I *need* to do the same."

In that moment, she felt a connection. Not just physical, but emotional. Now her heart pounded in tandem with her temples.

"I fell in love under that faro table, too, Kat."

Thu-dump. Thu-dump.

"With the woman I thought you were. The woman I needed you to be. I fell hard, but I was young and insecure. You heard right," he said when she frowned. "I had two older brothers who'd already made their marks on the world. I desperately needed to leave my brand. Wells Fargo proved the means. Whiskey provided the nerve."

"You're saying your courage comes from a bottle? I don't believe it."

"Just saying it tapped the son of a bitch in me. The part of me that didn't flinch when tangling with outlaws. A crutch that became a habit." He squeezed her hand. "About us. The young and reckless us. You were looking for a protector. Someone to laugh with, live with. I was looking for someone to distract me from the pressures of the job. An independent woman with sass. Someone I didn't have to worry about. *Permanent* was not in my vocabulary, mostly because I didn't figure I'd be long for this earth." He winked. "Not that I'd ever admit that."

"You just did."

"Repeat it and I'll deny it," he teased.

She smiled. "Go on."

"You offered passion and frivolous past times. That's what I latched on to. Your sensual nature. Your irreverence for convention. Your strength. You made me feel good, Kat. About life. About me. But I realize now, as much as I was obsessed with you, I was more obsessed with work, the self-satisfaction, the adulation. I confess I took you for granted. I confess, I was so damned arrogant, I didn't think you'd actually prefer Brady to me."

Her smile had long faded. Her stomach churned. "Preference had nothing to do with it. He filled my head with doubts. About you. About us. He preyed on my insecurities, played to my needs. Brady turned my head . . . but not my heart, Rome. That's why I wouldn't sleep with him. Only . . . I did." She'd never admitted that aloud, and it made her ill to do so. Still, she'd been dodging thoughts of that night for so long, now that it was out, the how and why pressed mightily on her already-throbbing brain.

Unable to hold Rome's gaze, she slipped his grasp and moved to the window. "I was so disoriented when you busted into the room. The fact that I can't remember . . . I've always blamed myself, the liquor, but a thought crossed my mind a time or two. It didn't occur to me until later, after Brady whisked me away, after I'd recovered from your rage . . ." She stared out the window, but all she saw was the sketchy past. "I'm not trying to make excuses, but . . . Do you think . . . Is it possible . . ."

"That he drugged you?" The words seemed to scrape his throat, just as the legs of his chair scraped the floor. She heard him move in behind her. Felt his charismatic and sensual presence. "My mind's been traveling that same road, Kat. Like I said, sobriety has sharpened a few warped memories. Like Brady's fondness for opium dens. The glazed look in your eyes, a look I connected with pleasures of the flesh, could've been due to a heavy dose of laudanum."

"How—"

"Mixed liberally in your drinks. That's one possibility. One drug."

"If that's true, it means I wasn't coherent. It means Brady . . ." She hugged herself against the sordid possibility. "It means he took liberties without my consent."

Rome gripped her shoulders. "Kat."

"Whatever happened," she said, cheeks flaming, "I'm still to blame. If I hadn't encouraged his attention—"

"Don't." Rome swung her around, stole her breath with his intensity. "Don't give that bastard leave."

"But we don't know—"

"Yes, we do. You said it that night."

Throat raw, she whispered, "I know in my heart I didn't do anything wrong."

"That's the truth of it," he said, framing her face. "That's what you cling to, understood?"

Transfixed by his touch, his gaze—strong, yet tender—her knees fairly buckled. *My champion*, her mind screamed. A dangerous notion. A young girl's fancy. She shoved it away. For his sake. For her sake.

For Frankie's sake.

He smoothed bed-mussed curls from her face. "If I had it to do over, I'd take better care to know the real you."

"Likewise," she whispered, half-worried, half-hopeful that he'd end this conversation by ravishing her mouth.

He eased back and offered his hand in greeting. "Name's Rome Garrett. Former Wells Fargo detective. Present Peacemaker. Pleased to make your acquaintance."

"Katrina Simmons," she said, nerve endings sparking as she gripped his warm palm. "Former cardsharp. Current saloon owner." Her pulse raced. Her neck flushed. "Pleasure's mine," she choked out, marveling that a new beginning packed as much sizzle as a passionate kiss.

CHAPTER *21*

San Fernando

Brady spent the night watching for a hip-high version of Kat to make one of her infamous escapes. Would she climb out a window and shimmy down a bedsheet? Would she slip out a door and climb over the whitewashed walls? Sneak out the arched gateway?

She didn't come at all.

Disappointing. But not as infuriating as making his entrance at dawn only to learn Frankie Hart had left the convent.

With Boston Garrett.

All hell broke loose in his head, but he didn't lose his temper. Instead he switched tactics, playing the distraught role of the wronged daddy. *"My sister-in-law wrote me off as dead, but I assure you it was foul play that kept me from my daughter."*

He spun a web of deceit, and Sister Maria fell neatly if not easily into his trap. She didn't provide him with all of the information he'd hoped for, but enough to guide him in the right direction.

An hour later he met back up with the gang. He found them lazing around a campfire, lingering over smokes and coffee.

"Where's the kid?" Elroy asked as Brady pitched him his coat and hat.

"Gone." He finger combed his hair, then buckled on his hardware. "I'm riding for Phoenix."

Itchy scratched and asked, "Why?"

"Because that's where Boston Garrett is heading."

Amos snuffed a hand-rolled cigarette. "I thought you were after Kat's niece."

Brady squinted against the mid-morning sun. "According to Sister Maria, Garrett showed up with a letter from *Miss Murdock* saying she was away on business and enlisted *him* to watch over Frankie until she could come and collect the girl."

"Business being that poker tournament up in Tucson," Boyd ventured. "Wonder how Rome talked his little brother into playing babysitter while he plays cards with the kid's aunt?"

"All I know," Brady said, staving off images of Kat and Rome together, "is that the sister told Boston he couldn't stay at the convent, so he said, fine, he'd take the kid home."

"Casa Bend," said Itchy.

Brady squatted and helped himself to a cup of strong-smelling coffee. "She overheard him talking to Frankie. Heard him mention Phoenix."

"Garrett's home," said Mule.

"Why would a kid need a bodyguard?" asked Elroy out of the blue.

"More like a watchdog," Brady said. "Seems Frankie's got a wild spirit. She's been a thorn in the good sisters' sides for months. Runs off every chance she gets."

Itchy scanned the desolate region. "Kid could get killed wandering around out here on her own."

"Sister Maria said she's smart for her age, headstrong and fearless."

"How old you say she is?" asked Mule.

"Five and a half." Brady clenched his jaw. He'd found a daguerreotype of Frankie in the midst of the bundle of letters. It burned a hole in his pocket just now. He didn't need to look at it to see the little girl's cherubic face and long, dark curls. The spitting image of Kat. Kat, who'd been an only child. He'd done the math. Possible he hadn't been bullshitting the nun when he'd claimed himself as Frankie's daddy.

He had to know.

Mule sleeved the sweat trickling from his hooked nose.

"Whole lotta coincidences at play here, boss. Everything from that skinny bitch and her necklace to Garrett and Kat's niece, all directing you to Phoenix."

"I was thinking the same thing," said Itchy.

Boyd cast a look at Elroy. "I'm thinking trap."

Elroy blanched. "Are you accusing me of being in cahoots with the Garretts?" he squeaked.

"I'm thinking fate," Brady said. His cousin wouldn't intentionally cross him. He didn't have the guts. "And I'm thinking it's best if I ride alone and meet up with you later in Nogales. Don't expect you to risk your necks just so I can attend to a passel of personal vendettas."

Elroy puffed up his scrawny chest. "I ain't leaving you to face the Garretts alone, Jed. You're kin. The only kin I got."

"Maybe not," Brady muttered. He caught Elroy's gaze. His cousin had been with him in San Francisco. He knew Brady had been intimate with Kat. Seeing he wasn't stupid, he put two and two together right quick. He started to speak, but Brady silenced him with a glare. He didn't know the truth of it yet, but one way or another he aimed on hauling Kat or the kid or both off to Mexico. The gang might balk, and though they didn't know it, he was counting on their loyalty to get what he wanted.

The men traded looks.

Amos spoke first. "If we ride hard, we might catch up

with Boston and the kid *before* they reach Phoenix. She's sure to slow him down."

"Probably take him twice as long to make the journey," Boyd put in.

"I'd be pleased if that was the case," Brady said. "I want Frankie and Kat a helluva lot more than that damned locket. Plug Boston when we take the kid. Plug Rome when he follows Kat into my trap." He tossed the remainder of his coffee into the fire. "Yes, sir. Mighty pleased."

"The law thinks we're holed up or riding for the border," said Snapper. "Last thing they'll expect is us riding north."

"Personally," said Itchy, "I wouldn't mind getting the Garrett brothers off our backs once and for all."

"I say we stick together," said Boyd. "Lucky seven."

Brady smothered an arrogant smile, patted his coat pocket and Frankie's likeness within. "Can't tell you what it means in this instance, boys, to have you and luck on my side." He jerked on his Stetson. "Let's ride."

CHAPTER 22

Phoenix

Monday. The first day of the business week. The first day in years London hadn't spent the morning obsessing over one of his siblings' problems or his dissatisfaction with his own life. He'd been too busy pondering the mystery of Tori Adams.

After explaining to a flustered Mrs. Chen why it was necessary for an unmarried woman to sleep in his home, he'd set off on a series of errands. Most of them having to do with Tori.

The woman was an enigma. Her appearance. Her demeanor. Her presence. Why was she here and not at the Gilded Garrett? Why would a veteran performer whom his friend had described as a notorious temptress exhibit such demure behavior? He understood that she'd been traumatized. He understood that she was ill. But his gut told him something was amiss.

Regardless, he couldn't ignore the tender feelings Tori inspired. He couldn't forget the way his heart pounded through the night as he'd held her hand. It had taken all of his restraint not to ease into that bed and pull her into his arms. He couldn't shake the desire to love and cherish till death put a kink in the matter.

Damn. He'd been smitten stupid.

"Here you go, Mr. Garrett. Wrapped like you asked."

London swung his thoughts to the present. He'd been staring blindly at the front page of the local newspaper for God knew how long.

The beaming merchant handed over the package. "I'll have the rest of your order delivered by day's end."

"Much obliged, Mr. Peralta." London slid the card he'd penned beneath the package's red ribbon and turned to leave.

"Always a pleasure doing business with you!" Peralta called.

Especially on days like this, London thought as he exited the mercantile. He'd just spent a good deal of money. Necessities would be delivered. The gift he'd chosen for his houseguest was in hand. Satisfied with the morning's endeavors, he headed for the Last Chance and bumped into Parker.

"I've been looking all over for you, sir."

"I'm right here."

Stone-faced, the bespectacled assistant eyed the shoppers crowding the boards and lowered his voice. "Manning's dead."

Frowning, London crossed to the more quiet side of the street. "Walk and talk, Mr. Parker."

"I received a telegram from a Captain Davis at Camp Grant."

"Go on."

Parker pushed his glasses up his nose, dipped his chin. "As you know Peacemakers don't wear badges."

"They carry a contact name and location in their boot. So, Captain Davis found the information and wired Mr. *Fox* in Phoenix. Get on with it, Parker."

The man cleared his throat. "No specifics. Just that Manning was gunned down at a cantina north of Tubac."

What the hell?

"The wire said there was an apparent shoot-out between Manning and the owner of the cantina."

London slid him a disgusted look. "You're saying some barkeep got the drop on a former Arizona Ranger? A Peacemaker?"

"I'm not saying anything, sir. I'm telling you what the captain said. And the barkeep didn't get the drop. He's dead, too."

London worked his jaw and brain. An insult? A dispute over the bill? Neither made sense. Maybe they'd run across each other before. Maybe the cantina owner was a prior crook. The possibilities, London supposed, were many, and none of them mattered. Bottom line: Manning was dead. "I need you to make arrangements for—"

"Consider it done."

They walked along Washington Street, sharing a mutual moment of silence for a felled agent. London's mind worked double-time. "So, Manning never made it to San Fernando," he mused aloud.

"Meaning Boston is doing whatever he's doing alone. No backup."

London wished to hell he knew what that something was. "Send a telegram to Tucson, attention Sherman Shakespeare. Manning novel no longer in stock. L.G. edition ready to ship on your order. Signed, PMA Publishing."

"Done." Parker peeled off and away.

London strode toward the Last Chance, telling himself not to borrow trouble. Assuring himself Manning's death was unrelated to PMA business and that Boston was fine. Wondering what he was going to tell Tori if he had to ride for San Fernando. He'd promised her that she was safe with him. Now he might have to leave.

Edgy, he pushed through his saloon's swinging doors, surprised to find at least a dozen men bending their elbows and playing cards. Half past noon. Given the competition, normally they fared three patrons this early in the day. He walked over to his on-duty barkeep. "Running a special I don't know about?"

"Featuring entertainment *I* didn't know about." Teddy slid a mug of beer down the bar, nodded to the cowboy who palmed it, then turned back to London. "Word's out you hired a pianist. Word's out she's young, fetching, and available. A rarity in these parts. These men strolled in for a look and a listen."

"She's not available, and she's not performing. She's ill."

"She told Mrs. Chen she's feeling better and that she'd come down for a matinee," he glanced at his pocket watch, "right about now."

"Matinee is canceled." London indicated the patrons. "Spread the word."

"What about tonight—"

"Canceled."

"Dang." Teddy mumbled something about bad business, then made the announcement as London hit the stairs.

Ignoring the disgruntled rumblings, he entered his private apartment and hung his hat on a peg. Just as he neared Tori's door, Mrs. Chen blew out of the room in a huff. Though her black hair was streaked with grey, the Oriental woman could pass for anywhere between thirty and fifty years old. A hard worker, she nary said a word and was always pleasant. Just now she was riled.

"She no listen to me," the petite woman ranted. She jabbed a slender finger at the closed door. "She stubborn.

She should be in bed."

"I'll take care of it, Mrs. Chen. Thank you for helping out."

"I no help. She no let me. I could make better, but she stubborn." She muttered something in Chinese, then threw up her hands. "I go cook now. She need strength to make music."

"She won't be . . ." he trailed off as the woman whizzed past, "making music."

Still toting the package, London turned to knock, only this time Tori stepped out. And stole away his breath. The only reason he knew she was still under the weather was from her flushed cheeks and glassy eyes. Dressed in a provocative indigo gown, her long hair arranged into a loose chignon, she looked like an angel and temptress rolled into one. No cosmetics. No accessories, except for the simple gold locket hanging around her slender neck. Her beauty was natural and unique. Never had he been so physically and emotionally stirred by a woman. Were she to go downstairs now, she'd be hit with a dozen propositions before she ever made it to the piano. The notion rankled.

Don't be a jealous ass, Garrett.

"You're staring," she said, pressing a hand over her pronounced cleavage. "Do I look alright?"

"You look beautiful." An understatement.

"Mrs. Chen was kind enough to lace the, my . . ."

Blushing, she skimmed a hand down her midriff.

He raised a brow. "Corset?"

"It's a little tight, I think. Or maybe the décolletage is too . . ."

"Low?"

She tugged at the neckline.

He smiled. "First time you've ever worn that gown?"

"Yes. No." She looked away. "It's been a while."

Clearly she was self-conscious, which, again, didn't fit with the image his friend had painted of a professional, outgoing, and flirtatious Tori Adams. His gut told him this pretty, shy thing was not who she claimed to be. But why the pretense?

He backed her into her bedroom. "Maybe you'd feel more comfortable in a less revealing gown."

"I don't own a less revealing gown." She glanced at her trunk. "Not for stage anyway."

He laid the package on her bed, crossed his arms. "Guess you didn't notice when you were downstairs yesterday. Last Chance doesn't have a stage."

"Oh." She frowned, wrung her hands. "Does it have a piano?"

"An old upright. But it's out of tune, and three of the keys are broken. Frankly, Tori, I hadn't planned on anyone playing it."

She rushed forward, tugging at her plunging neckline.

"But you hired me—"

"About that—"

"I have proof."

"Excuse me?" He was more surprised by her anxious tone than the odd statement.

She brushed past him, nabbed her reticule from the nightstand, and rooted. "Here." She thrust a folded paper into his hands.

Intrigued, he read, noting the date, recognizing the wording. "The wire I sent offering you an engagement at the Gilded Garrett."

"That's right."

He glanced up. "This isn't the Gilded Garrett."

"I know. But the new owner refused to honor my contract, so I thought . . . well, it was you who promised me a job."

His lip twitched. "You got me there."

"They say I'm a gifted pianist."

"I've heard."

"I know I didn't make a good first impression, and then last night . . ." Her cheeks flushed hotter. "You must think me horribly childish."

He placed the telegram on her nightstand, then turned to find her fingering that locket. The necklace she'd refused to give over to Brady. Either it was worth a fortune or held sentimental value. He'd ask, but he didn't want to force her into talking about the heist before she was ready. "I think you've been through a frightening ordeal. I think you're understandably shaken. I *know* you're unwell and agree with Mrs. Chen. You should be in bed."

"But your patrons—"

"Have been told your performance is canceled."

"But—"

"Why are you in such a hurry to entertain my customers?"

"Because I want to prove to you that I'm worth keeping around."

The woman vibrated with anxiety and a sadness that made hash out of London's heart. "Never crossed my mind to send you away."

"It didn't?"

He clasped her hands and gazed into her troubled eyes. "There a man in your life, Tori? Anyone special?"

"No." Tears filled her eyes. "There's no one. It's just . . . me."

"Not anymore." He pulled her into his arms and kissed her, sweetly, softly. She tasted like peppermint, her lips lush and warm. Given her shy streak, he expected her to stiffen.

She didn't. She wrapped her arms around his neck and—hell's fire—kissed him with a passion that obliterated sane thought. For a moment he thought maybe she *was* who she claimed to be—the temptress who'd delighted men with her talents, on and off stage.

But then he slid one hand to her rear and slipped his tongue inside her mouth.

Then she stiffened.

She gasped and wrenched back, eyes wide with shock. Then he knew.

He hadn't fallen for Tori Adams. He'd fallen for the woman in his arms, an innocent, and he hadn't a clue as to her real identity.

But he'd find out.

He stroked a thumb over her heated cheeks. "Get some rest, honey."

If he didn't leave her now, he'd seduce her. He knew he could, he felt it. Yet that was her strange power over him. Her vulnerability proved her protection. She wasn't ready, in more ways than he might know. He needed some distance, needed to send some wires. He needed to hear back from Athens.

He made it to the threshold before she spoke. "You," she said.

He looked over his shoulder.

She quirked a shy smile. "You're special."

The words pierced his heart. He was usually the one backstage, in the shadows, the one in an office or at home taking care of family needs. In short, compared to his brothers he had always considered himself the boring one. The way she looked at him, the way his heart pounded for the first time in his life, he felt anything but boring.

Yup. Definitely smitten.

CHAPTER 23

Tucson

"Full house." Kat showed her hand, bit back a smile.

Rome delighted in her uncharacteristic excitement. "Thought you said you were rusty."

"Guess it's like riding a horse."

"Some things you never forget." Locked away in her hotel room for the second time today, he gazed across the table at her, thinking they were a stone's throw from her bed. He'd been having thoughts like that all afternoon. Him and Kat. In bed.

Naked.

He winked.

She narrowed her eyes. "I was referring to playing poker."

"I wasn't."

"Stop trying to distract me, Rome Garrett. I won. I get to ask the next question."

"Seems to me you've asked *most* of the questions."

"Can't help it if I'm the better card player."

"Modest, too," he teased.

She smiled full-out and Rome hardened. Christ, she was beautiful. She'd dressed in a stylish gown. The golden satin accentuated her vivid doe-eyes. The neckline dipped just low enough to garner attention. Throughout the day, now and then, his gaze drifted down and over the swell of her breasts. Considering his arousal just now, he struggled to keep his eyes level with hers. Regardless, his blood pumped with desire. It wasn't so much about her physical beauty, he decided, but the beauty of her spirit.

Knowing she was nervous about playing cards later tonight, he'd suggested a few rounds of poker—just the two of them, for practice. As a way of getting to know one another, he suggested they play for information instead of money. For every hand she won, she got to ask him a personal question and vice versa. So far they'd played four hands. He'd won one and had asked about her metamorphosis from gambler to saloon owner.

"*Monopolize on what you know,*" she'd said.

Learning how she'd settled in a remote town, changed her name, and kept life simple—all in order to avoid Jed *Bulls-Eye* Brady—had tripled his admiration of her and doubled his conviction to squash the treacherous outlaw.

Kat had just won her third game. So far she'd asked him

about his favorite reading material and his political views. He had a feeling she was warming up to a more personal interrogation. The price to be paid for wanting to know her better, he told himself. Surprisingly, he didn't mind.

She eased back in her chair and tapped her forefinger to her chin, contemplating her question.

Rather than torturing himself with visions of unlacing her corset and palming what he knew to be spectacular breasts, he thought back on this whirlwind day. Earlier this morning, they'd joined Athens, aka Sherman Shakespeare, for breakfast—their first public outing as a couple. In between animated discussions, they'd spoken softly of the night to come. The new angle involved her not attempting to be the "Kat everyone knew" but being true to herself. She didn't have to dazzle the public with a saucy personality, just with her impressive card skills. She didn't have to flirt with every man—just Rome.

Her relief had been visible.

After breakfast Shakespeare went one way, Rome and Kat another. Disguised as Dwight Dupree, Seth was already circulating. The group's agenda: to fan excitement and gossip about disgraced dime-novel hero, Rome Garrett, and Katrina Simmons, cardsharp extraordinaire.

For their part, Rome and Kat visited various merchants, shopping, gossiping, making and leaving an impression wherever they went. By mid-afternoon, a good portion of the city's populace believed that Rome Garrett and Kat Simmons, daughter of famous gambler Charles F. Simmons, had reunited. Once they started cleaning up at the tables, they'd garner even more attention and, hopefully, publicity. Rome knew all about making headlines. Only this time it was calculated.

He wished he could say the same regarding his amorous treatment of Kat. In public, he'd taken liberties—holding her hand, nuzzling her cheek. He'd stolen a kiss in the dry goods section of Drachman's General Store. Her warm response had struck him weak in the knees. Logically, he knew they were baiting Brady. Emotionally, he felt like the one primed to get burned. If only Kat hadn't blown away his cynicism and anger with her heartfelt revelations.

"I've got it." She swayed forward, brown eyes bright with curiosity.

Rome leaned back in his chair and braced himself. "Fire away."

"Why a crime fighter? Why not an actor or a director? Your mother was a musical actress. Your father, owner of an opera house. Your upbringing had to be less than conventional. I know they died when you were young. I know London inherited the Gilded Garrett and became the patriarch of the family. *He* went into the theater business.

Why not you?"

Rome raised an eyebrow.

"What?"

"Winning one hand affords you one question."

She smirked. "Why a Wells Fargo detective?"

"The glory."

She tucked loose ringlets behind her delicate ears and processed his answer. Two seconds later, she shoved her cards to the middle of the table. "I'm not playing any more until I have a detailed answer. If I don't play, you don't have a chance of winning, and therefore you forfeit any right to question me about . . . whatever."

She-devil.

He smiled. "Detailed, huh?"

"Start from the beginning. Don't leave anything out." She poured herself another cup of coffee, freshened his. Their third pot today. "I'm all ears."

Lucky him. He blew out a breath and decided payback would be a bitch. He wanted to know about Frankie. She'd yet to offer details about the young girl and their relationship. In fact, she'd refrained from mentioning her at all today, yet he *knew* the kid was on her mind. It was why she'd come out of hiding.

"I failed Frankie."

That statement, the heartbreak in her tone, haunted him.

"My father preferred the limelight to family life," he said, hoping his openness would inspire hers. "He spent more time with hired performers than his children. More time with starlets than his wife. He broke my mother's heart. She was the first woman I longed to save."

Kat sipped her coffee, her eyes pleading with him to continue.

"I never had the chance. Not long after my father died, my mother succumbed to an illness. As the eldest, London took charge of caring for the younger siblings. Only I wasn't keen on being looked after."

"Obstinate, even then."

"I've been a pain in his ass for a long time." He hadn't felt bad about that until now. *Well, hell.* "Once Athens proved a reliable caretaker, London started spending a good deal of time in San Francisco overseeing the family's business. On my sixteenth birthday, I started frequenting Percy's Poker Palace, a local bawdy featuring musicians, variety acts, and dancing girls. I didn't burn to perform like Ma. Wasn't driven to stage theatrical productions like my father. But I sure as hell enjoyed the view from the audience. I appreciated the performers' talents. Admired the actresses and girls in the chorus and, like my dog-of-a-daddy, enjoyed flirting with those women."

He eyed Kat, wondering if he'd shared too much.

She tilted her head in interest. "I'm reading you like a book just now, Rome."

"Do tell."

"You're thinking, though you despised your father for being a faithless seducer, you turned out just like him."

He wanted to avert his gaze, but didn't. "I had an affair with a married woman."

"Sarah Smith," she said. "I know."

He grunted. "The whole world knows."

"I don't know about the whole world. You're not *that* famous."

"Noted," he said with a contrite smile.

"But certainly it's common knowledge wherever dime novels are sold, thanks to I. M. Wilde."

Rome had breathed life back into Sarah, the sole survivor of a stage robbery. She'd thanked him with a kiss. Wilde had found out about it and, as of a way of weaving romance into the deadly adventure, had made public the indiscretion that blossomed into an affair. "Guess you read the tale."

"*Showdown in Sintown*," she said. "I've read all of I. M. Wilde's tales. Gifted storyteller. Too bad he gave up writing."

"Wilde didn't give up writing. Just moved on from dime novels."

She raised a brow. "You know Wilde personally?"

"You'll have to win another hand if you want the answer to that."

"Bastard."

He winked and gathered the cards.

"Wait. About Sarah—"

"I'm not proud of what happened, Kat. Not to make excuses, but she seduced me with . . ." He paused and considered his words. "Let's just say aggressive affection and a tale of marital woe."

She arched a suspect brow. "You're joshing, right?"

If he hadn't felt the fool before, he felt downright idiotic now. Still, he wanted to confess all. Kat listened, he realized, without judging. Commented frankly, but rationally. He appreciated her tolerance and candor. Besides, if he was honest about his life, hopefully she'd be inclined to do the same. "She told me her husband was a cold, cheating bastard. Told me they had an arrangement. So long as she stayed out of his affairs, he'd ignore hers. A lie. Obviously."

Kat scrunched her brow. "Even if it were true, why would you want to get involved in something so . . ."

"Tawdry?" He shrugged. "If you ask one of my brothers, they'll say I was thinking with my—"

"I get the point." Kat crossed her arms. "What would

you say?"

"That I thought I was saving Sarah from a cold, love-less existence."

"With hot, meaningless sex?" She bit her bottom lip, but her eyes telegraphed her amusement.

"Believe me, I'm paying for my arrogance and stupidity." He riffled and cut the deck. "I believe I've answered your question and then some."

"Actually you veered off course. Not that I mind. You quenched my curiosity about the Smith scandal without my even asking. But as far as my original question, you left me dangling at Percy's Poker Palace. How did that lead to your becoming a detective?"

"You're relentless."

"I'm sure you'll reciprocate when the tables are turned." Her mouth tilted in a playful smile. "Of course, you'll have to win another hand first."

"I'm aware." He matched her grin. "Hope you're prepared."

"I'll take my chances."

Where's Frankie now? How long has she been in your care? What's she like? "All right then," he said, bracing his forearms on the table. "Let me get this out so I can beat your bloomers off. So to speak."

She leaned forward, eyes twinkling, neck flushed. "So

to speak."

For a moment words failed him. He was hypnotized by her enigmatic presence. Encouraged by her mutual flirting.

He was in deep shit.

He dug down and grabbed hold of his senses. "The year after I started frequenting Percy's, Boston started tagging along. Before long we were drinking beer and stealing time with Calico Queens. If a brawl busted out, we joined in, fists swinging. In general, we were naturally inclined to defend the underdog. Always knew we would end up fighting the bad guys one way or another."

"Sounds to me like you enjoyed playing the part of the hero early on."

"That's a fact." Uncomfortable now, he drank coffee, then rushed on. "The older we got, the more action we craved. We spent more time in San Francisco, but we were bored even there. Hungry for an adventure, we jumped at a chance to hire on with Wells, Fargo and Company as shotgun messengers. Brandishing a sawed-off shotgun, I rode alongside the drivers of the company's stagecoaches, watching for road bandits and protecting the passengers, the U.S. mail, and the coveted Wells Fargo treasure box stored beneath the seat. The padlocked chest contained everything from gold dust to gold bars, from checks to drafts to legal papers. Ruthless thieves killed for that box, and after witnessing one such event, I made it my mission to stop the sons of bitches at all costs. If they rode in hardware-jerked, I didn't think twice about smoking them first."

She shuddered. "Dangerous work."

"Important work." He clenched his jaw. "That's my point. It should have been enough. But it's a thankless job. No meaningful recognition."

"No glory."

"That came with detective work. With tracking and apprehending outlaws. Boston followed in my footsteps, and between our unconventional tactics and outgoing personalities, we garnered attention and praise."

"I. M. Wilde dramatized your adventures, and dime-novel heroes were born."

"Worst thing that ever happened to me." Not that he'd ever admit as such to *Wilde*. "Fame, for someone like me, works like a drug. The more you have, the more you want. The more you believe you're invincible and above it all. In hindsight, I did a lot of things I'm not proud of. Whiskey soothed a smarting conscience."

"But you're not drinking anymore, and you've also done a lot of things you should be proud of." Kat reached over and grasped his hand. "The quest for glory may be shallow, but it was never your sole motivation, Rome. You said it yourself. You have a deep-rooted desire to save women from hurtful or dangerous situations. A natural inclination to defend the underdog. As a Wells Fargo detective, you battled the bad guys. Courageous, selfless work. So you got a big head. So you messed up." Her cheeks burned, and he knew she was thinking about herself, too. "We all mess up."

He marveled at her compassion and cursed himself a thousand times for treating her ill their first time around. He stroked his thumb over her wrist, noted her racing pulse. "To err is human."

She quirked a tiny smile. "You and I just happen to be *extremely* human."

He laughed at that.

She laughed, too, and he had a sudden and exhilarating image of her laughing and playing with a little girl. He could see it now. He could absolutely see Kat raising a child. He set the deck in the center of the table. "Cut. High card gets to ask a question."

"So now you'll have a fifty-fifty chance of winning instead of twenty-eighty?"

He grinned. "Cut."

She did and he did and—hell, yeah—he won.

She rolled her eyes. "Ask away."

"Can I kiss you?"

She blinked, opened her mouth, shut it, then, thirty-God-awful-long seconds later, spoke. "That's your question?"

He'd meant to ask about her niece, dammit, and he would. But . . . "Just now I have a fierce need to kiss the hell out of you. Not 'for show.' Not 'for the good of mankind.' For me." His blood burned hotter when she pressed a hand to her heart. Was it beating as hard and fast as his? "So, yes. That's my question."

"Ask again."

"Can I kiss you, Kat?"

"Yes."

They shoved out of their chairs at the same time and collided. A clumsy, frantic meeting of two aggressive participants.

Hands skimming, grabbing, stroking.

Lips and teeth clashing, meshing.

Tongues dueling.

Her eagerness flamed his actions. He lifted her and pinned her between the wall and his hard, hungry body. He held her beautiful face captive as he satisfied his fierce need. He kissed her long. Slow. Thoroughly. He felt her knees buckle and bolstered his own. He kissed her still, feasting on her velvety tongue, drinking in her strong, kind spirit.

She melted against him, moaning into his mouth, asking for more. He smoothed his hands over her body, wanting her naked and writhing beneath him. Restraint was hard won, his heart pounding with the almighty effort.

Christ.

More pounding. In his head. No. The door. Insistent knocking.

He eased back.

Eyes glazed, Kat rasped, "Don't answer it."

"I say, Miss Simmons," the voice called through the wood, "I'm looking for Mr. Garrett."

"Athens," Rome and Kat groaned as one.

Another rap. "Sorry for the intrusion, but I'm desperate for a word."

"Sounds important," Rome said.

"Go," Kat said.

"Not without regret." He'd yet to move.

She'd yet to shove him away. "Dinner. Later."

"Then the tables. Then—"

"We'll see."

"Fair enough." He brushed one last kiss across her warm mouth then, cursing another knock, swept up his hat and wrenched open the door.

Athens, dressed as Shakespeare, backed up to allow Rome space to breeze by. "This better be good, *Sherman.*"

"It's bad. I received a telegram from London."

Chest tight, Rome led his brother two doors down and ushered him into his room. He shut the door, then turned, heart filled with dread. "Is it Paris? The baby?

What happened?"

"No, no. Nothing like that," Athens said, abandoning the English accent. "Manning's dead."

"Fuck." Rome's lungs whooshed with relief. He punched Athens's shoulder. "Don't scare me like that. Dammit."

"Sorry."

"Fuck."

"You said that. Calm down. What's wrong with you?"

"You just scared the hell out of me."

"You're usually made of sterner stuff." Athens arched his fake bushy brows. "Catch you at a vulnerable time?"

As a matter of fact . . . Rome placed his hat on the bureau. "Just tell me about Manning."

"Gunned down in a cantina north of Tubac."

"By whom?"

"The owner of the place. Apparently they squared off. Both dead."

"That doesn't sound right."

"No, it doesn't. At any rate, London's volunteering to ride to San Fernando in Manning's stead."

"That's where Boston stashed Frankie? This San Fernando?"

"That's where Kat stashed her. It's a convent. A Mexican school for girls. Didn't she tell you?"

"No." He should have asked about Frankie and stolen the kiss. "So Boston's shacked up in a convent with a bunch of nuns and little girls?" He grunted. "Priceless. How's he holding up?"

"I haven't heard from him. I tried to wire him about Manning, but according to the local operator, the telegraph office closest to the convent has been down for days."

"Coincidence?"

"I'm hoping. Mr. Winters said the wires that far south are unreliable."

Rome frowned. "Inconvenient."

"To say the least." Athens rocked back on the heels of his shiny boots. "About London."

Rome noted his brother's tense expression. "You're not keen on sending him south."

Athens took off Shakespeare's pompous top hat and fingered the brim. "It's selfish, but I'd feel better knowing he was in Phoenix looking after Zach and Zoe and Kaila."

"That's not selfish, brother. That's genuine concern. Family comes first."

"But Boston's family."

"Boston can take care of himself. He can certainly handle a five-year-old girl."

"What about Brady?"

Rome worked his jaw. "Brady doesn't know about

Frankie. He certainly doesn't know about the Star Saloon or San Fernando. Kat covered her tracks. Hell, no one knew where *she* was until she reached out and made contact herself."

"You're right," Athens said. "No reason to believe Boston and Frankie are at risk."

Still something niggled. Manning dead. Wires down. "How far is San Fernando from here?" Rome asked.

"A full day's ride."

"Send Seth."

"Need him here in case Brady shows."

"Brady will show," Rome said. "Trust me. When he does, I'll handle him."

"Who's to say Brady will ride in alone? In fact, I know he won't. He never acts alone. The cowardly bastard surrounds himself with a gang to keep him safe."

"Bastard?" Rome poked a tongue in his cheek. "Colorful talk for you, brother. Now who's acting out of character?"

"Never mind that. Just stick close to Kat."

"I plan on it."

"*I'll* handle Brady."

"Over my dead body," Rome said. "You're not a gunman, Athens. You're not . . ."

"What?" The former politician folded his arms, angled his head. "Tough enough? Brave enough?"

"Oh, for chrissakes."

"Ruthless enough?"

Disguised as a foppish book peddler, Athens didn't look like he could take a feisty barmaid, let alone an outlaw. Rome kept the observation to himself. In truth, he'd always admired his gentler brother for his cool head and intelligence. He'd never seen the man throw a punch, let alone draw a gun, but he didn't doubt his nerve. He was one of the strongest people Rome had ever known. As far as he was concerned, his brother had walked through hell and survived. "Who are you really chasing, Athens? Bulls-Eye Brady? Or the ghosts of the bandits who killed Jocelyn?"

Athens held his gaze, clenched his fists. "I should've been the one to track them down."

Rome cringed at the pain in his voice. "They would have killed you."

"Maybe. Maybe not."

"Boston and I are trained to track. When a man jerks his hardware, intent to kill, we're conditioned to draw and fire without a second thought. You would have tried to talk them into turning themselves in."

"Maybe. Maybe not."

Rome blew out a breath. "I'll make you a deal. When the time comes, we'll face Brady together." It was a magnanimous gesture on his part, seeing he wanted to rip off Jed Brady's limbs one by one.

"I'll think about it."

Unbelievable.

Hat in hand, Athens strode to the door. "Are you going to tell Kat about Manning?"

"I don't see any reason to worry her unnecessarily."

After a moment, Athens nodded. "Agreed." He donned the hat, thumped the crown. "See you at the tables." Then he affected Shakespeare's vapid expression and sauntered into the hall.

Rome palmed his forehead, thinking that the moment he gave up whiskey, his world had turned inside out. He thought about Kat two doors down. "And this is only the beginning."

CHAPTER 24

The moment the door shut behind Rome, Kat slumped to the floor.

Ten minutes later and still she sat—knees to chest, head bowed. That kiss had robbed her of her last defenses. So different from any kiss they'd ever shared. A connection she'd never felt before. She credited his willingness to share his innermost thoughts, his yearnings, his regrets. His shame. She'd learned more about him in one afternoon than she had in their entire six-month affair. Although, if she had asked those same questions six years ago, she had no doubt Rome would have changed the subject or waylaid her with sex, because back then she was his distraction from the real world. The uncomplicated, independent woman who didn't need a man to make her feel secure and complete. Or so he'd thought.

The illusion.

The irony was that she'd become the woman he believed her to be in the first place. She'd learned to be independent. She'd simplified her lifestyle. She'd survived without a champion. She didn't need Rome Garrett anymore.

But she sure as hell wanted him.

"I have to tell him."

They'd come to terms with the past and had discovered something beautiful in the present, but they had no future with her secret between them.

He wanted to take her to bed and she wanted to go. She ached to know him in that way again. Only she knew it wouldn't be the same. It would be better.

It would also be dangerous.

She couldn't sleep with Rome, fully exploring the extent of their new emotional connection, only to walk away after they'd dealt with Brady. He felt more deeply, more keenly than she'd ever imagined. He'd bared his heart and she would not crush it. Again. So it meant putting hers on the line. Not in her wildest dreams had she ever imagined winning back Rome Garrett. But here it was, and chances were he would walk away from her again. Only this time, she wouldn't blame him. Her heart would shatter beyond repair, but what mattered most was that he didn't walk away from Frankie, not knowing.

She raised her head and banged it against the wall.

"Frankie isn't my niece. She's my daughter."

She'd never said the words aloud. They scraped her throat raw. It was as though she had never spoken the truth to protect herself from this very moment. Having to face that she'd denied a man his daughter. If that man was Brady, she would live happily with that knowledge. But if that man was Rome . . .

I have to do the right thing, no matter how hard.

She had to tell Rome Garrett that there was a fifty-fifty chance that he was Frankie's father.

♥   ♥   ♥

The Cosmopolitan Hotel boasted a lovely dining area. The menu was limited, but the aromas wafting from the kitchens were heavenly, and Kat trusted whatever she ordered would be delicious. Not that it really mattered. She had no appetite.

The evening ahead weighed heavily on her heart. Part of her ached to blurt out the truth and be done with it, but there was an old practice in the theater that her daddy had shared with her when teaching her the art of poker: *Never share upsetting news with an artist before the performance.* It would be cruel to dump life-altering news on Rome and then expect him to play the besotted lover in public. So she'd decided to wait until after they'd put on their show in the gambling den to tell him about Frankie.

Meanwhile, her stomach gnarled tighter and tighter.

Rome reached for his glass of lemonade. "Something wrong with your food, sugar?"

Realizing she was toying with her mashed potatoes, she set aside her fork and forced a smile. "Just anxious about tonight."

He looked at her with tender regard. "The poker part or the after part?"

"Both," she answered honestly.

He took money from his pocket and laid a generous sum on the table.

Kat furrowed her brow. "What are you doing?"

"Hurrying this evening along."

She noted his plate. "But you didn't finish your steak."

He quirked a smile that pierced her heart. "I'm a mite anxious about tonight myself."

He rounded the table and helped her from her chair, his touch burning through the sleeve of her evening dress. She forced her legs steady as he escorted her past the curious diners and into the lobby. "How long do we have to stay out tonight?"

"Long enough to cause a stir."

She swallowed, fighting hard to affect the persona of a

carefree cardsharp as they stepped into the unusually balmy night. "I can do that."

He leaned in and whispered in her ear. "Be warned, sugar, I'm going to take my time."

"At the tables?"

"After."

Her heart pounded, knowing there might not be an "*after*" once she revealed her secret. But she hoped. Oh, how she hoped.

She tugged at his arm. "Walk faster."

"Why?"

"I'm hurrying this evening along."

He chuckled, but he did walk faster.

The thick, muggy air was charged with sensual tension and the promise of rain. Thunder rumbled, an ominous sound that plucked every fretful cord in Kat's body.

Her pulse accelerated with each step, and her mouth went dry. Though she was very much aware of the potential disaster awaiting her once they retired to their room, her focus shifted suddenly to what would come before. Playing poker with professional gamblers. She scrambled to remember every scrap of advice ever offered by her daddy.

The art of the bluff.

Knowing when to check or raise.

When to hold.

When to fold.

"You all right?" Rome asked, stopping shy of Levin's Gambling Palace.

"I'm nervous," she said straight-out. "No offense, but it's one thing playing poker with you for fun. This . . . What I have to do in there . . . So much is at stake."

The black sky flashed white, then boomed with a clap of thunder. She stared off, distracted by the approaching storm. "Frankie hates thunder," she worried aloud.

Rome turned her to face him. "You know, I'm curious as hell about this niece of yours."

Her stomach pitched. "I'll tell you about her. Tonight. I promise. I just . . ." She glanced into the gambling den. "I need to get my head in the game."

He squeezed her shoulders. "You can do this, Kat."

"I know. I just . . ."

"Close your eyes and hold out your hand."

"Why?"

"Just do it."

She did as he asked, her heart tripping when she felt something cool, round, and familiar pressed into her palm.

"For luck," Rome said. "Not that you need it."

She opened her eyes, choked back tears. "Daddy's lucky coin. You kept it."

"I did."

Even though he thought she'd betrayed him. Even though he'd damned her to hell. He'd kept the coin she'd given him for luck. A coin she cherished. "Some part of you still loved me," she croaked, "even when you hated me."

He stroked his thumb over her cheek. "Told you, Kat. I felt a lot of things, but never hate."

Would he be so forgiving tonight?

She closed her fingers around the coin and squeezed. She smiled up at her fallen hero, envisioned passing the sentimental gift on to Frankie. "I can do this."

CHAPTER 25

Phoenix

A storm raged—both outside and in Victoria's heart and mind. She sat on the plush sofa in London's small but comfortable parlor, bundled in the gift he'd given her this afternoon. She'd been in a daze after he'd kissed her, her first kiss, a kiss she would dream about until the day she died, so she was befuddled when she'd turned to find the package he'd toted earlier resting on her bed. She was even more stymied when she saw the attached card was addressed to her.

Her fingers had trembled as she'd read his perfectly penned script. *Something to brighten your life,* he'd written, *as you have brightened mine.*

Heart pounding, she'd untied the red bow and ripped open the wrapping paper to find a beautiful hand-stitched quilt. Whoever had constructed the quilt had been enormously creative as each block featured varying mosaic designs bursting with cheerful combinations of red, yellow, and green. She was in awe of the workmanship and entranced with the creation itself.

She wasn't sure which stunned her more, that London had bought her a gift or that she'd brightened his life. She couldn't imagine how. Thus far she'd thrown up on his boots, caused him a sleepless night, upset his housekeeper, and disappointed his customers. He couldn't have been referring to her embarrassingly amorous reaction to his kiss, because he'd purchased the gift prior.

She never got the chance to ask him or to thank him, since he hadn't returned to her room for the rest of the day. Her only visitor had been Mrs. Chen, who'd fussed over her, bringing soup and medicinal tea and news that London was busy.

The sun set and still he hadn't come.

She knew he had a business to oversee. Every now and then, laughter and raised voices floated up though the floorboards. A saloon probably stayed open at least until midnight. But what if something other than business had snagged London's attention? What if he'd somehow discovered her true identity? What if her father had miraculously claimed her body and discovered the switch? She didn't think he'd bother sending out a search party, but what if the cattle baron did?

Her anxiety had mounted when the thunderstorm hit. The ferocity of the wind and rain rattled the windowpanes as well as her nerves. Unable to sleep, she'd ventured into this parlor, lit a lamp, and curled up on the sofa with her quilt and a book. No lack of reading material in this apartment. London had shelves of adventures. She was three chapters into *Oliver Twist* when she heard the main door to his apartment open and close.

Seconds later, London walked into the room. She wanted to leap to her feet and throw herself into his strong arms. Instead, she laid aside the book and wrapped the quilt tighter.

He stood on the threshold, hands braced on the jamb. An impressive figure, he seemed to fill the entire doorway. "Hell of a storm," he said. "Figured you'd have a hard time sleeping. I came up to make sure you're all right."

"That's very kind of you." She blushed, embarrassed that he considered her skittish.

"How are you feeling?"

"Much better, thank you. Just a little restless. I hope you don't mind, I borrowed one of your books."

He glanced at the novel and smiled. "Truth told, I'm glad you're making yourself at home. I wanted to check in on you earlier, but it's been a day of calamities."

She noticed now that he looked a little tired, though

it did nothing to diminish his devilish good looks. "Nothing dire, I hope."

He shifted his weight. "Let's see. A misunderstanding between two patrons turned into a scuffle. A delivery was made, only there were several mistakes. I made arrangements for a trip, only to learn I'm not needed. *Situation under control*, my brother wired."

"But that's a good thing, that last thing. Right?" Selfishly she would've been crushed if he'd been called away.

"All things considered," he said with a faint smile, "a good thing."

Sensing there was more to his day, she prodded, "what else?"

He moved into the room and sat in the chair across from her. "My niece, who spends more time with animals than people, mistook a spotted skunk for a cat."

Victoria's eyes widened. "Oh, no."

"I spent a good two hours tracking down every tomato I could find so that Kaila could scrub the kid from head to toe in an attempt to remove the odor. I offered to help with the task, but my future sister-in-law insisted she could handle Zoe. Zach, on the other hand . . ." London's lip twitched. "My nephew stole his first kiss. The girl socked him in the mouth, then tattled. Her father pitched a fit. Since my brother isn't here to have a man-to-man with

Zach, Kaila enlisted me."

Victoria scrunched her brow. "I saw Zach at the Café Poppy. He couldn't have been more than—"

"Nine." He shook his head. "We've got another Rome on our hands."

"Who's Rome?"

"One of my younger brothers. The wild one. The charmer. You've probably heard of him. Wells Fargo detective. Dime-novel legend."

"I don't read dime novels." She hoped she hadn't insulted him. Obviously, his brother was somewhat famous. "I'm sorry."

"I'm not." He raised a brow. "You're full of surprises, honey."

Her face heated and her heart pumped. "So are you." She gripped the soft edges of his gift. "Thank you for the quilt, London. It's beautiful."

"Like the lady wearing it."

She blushed and looked away. "I'm not beautiful. My features are uneven and I'm overly thin and . . ." She trailed off when he shifted to the sofa. Her father's assessment of her endowments, or lack thereof, were chiseled in her brain. Saying them aloud . . . she felt ridiculously self-absorbed.

Seated next to her now, London cupped her chin. "Your features are unique and you have the spirit of an angel. You're beautiful, Tori."

Her eyes brimmed with tears. "I can't do this."

"Do what, honey?"

"Lie. To you. You don't deserve such treachery. I surely don't deserve your kindness."

He thumbed away tears. "You're not capable of treachery. If you were, we wouldn't be having this discussion. Just take a breath and take it slow."

"I'm not Tori Adams."

"I had a feeling," he said, lips curving. "A few things didn't add up. So who are you?"

"I'm going to add to your day of calamities."

"I can handle it. Trust me." He winked and squeezed her hand. "Shoot."

His calm demeanor gave her the courage to press on. "Victoria Barrow."

"The woman killed on the train?"

"No," she croaked. "That was Tori Adams." Overwhelmed with grief and guilt, she spewed her story. How they'd met on the train, their shared first name and love of music. Their physical resemblance and their opposing lifestyles. "I didn't want my life, so she gave me hers." She massaged her pounding temples. "I don't remember how it happened. I just remember the blood and . . . and her generosity. She pressed her reticule in my hands, told me to remember all we'd discussed. She called me Tori and told me I was free."

"So much for slow," London teased gently and she realized she'd been rambling a good while.

She took the handkerchief he offered and blew her nose. "I'm sorry. I just, I needed to tell you before I lost my nerve."

London leaned back against the sofa and pulled her onto his lap, quilt and all. "What are you afraid of, Victoria? Who are you running from? What did Tori mean when she said, *you're free?*"

She swallowed, knowing it was inappropriate for him to hold her like this, but not caring. He made her feel safe and cherished. She rested her head on his shoulder, and mentally embraced the moment. "I'm an only child, daughter of a jeweler from San Diego. My father, Gerard Barrow, wishes I was never born."

London stroked her hair. "I'm sure that's not true."

"He's told me so more than once. You see, he adored my mother and she never fully recovered from childbirth. She died when I was two."

"He blames you."

"It pains him something awful to even look at me." She reached down and opened the locket around her neck to show him the picture within. "See?"

"Your mother?"

220

She nodded.

"The resemblance is striking."

"Her name was Juliet. Papa destroyed anything that reminded him of her. My grandmother gave this locket to me just before she herself died. That was about ten years ago."

"This locket means a lot to you."

"My only cherished possession," she blushed, "except for this quilt."

He tucked her long hair behind her ears, stroked her cheek. "You humble me."

She traced her fingers along an appliqué. "I love it."

"I'm glad. So," he said, his tone suddenly tight, "your father treated you poorly and you decided to run away."

"Actually, he sent me away. He recently remarried, and his new wife didn't fancy my presence. I guess living in the shadows as I'd always done was no longer good enough. I think he wanted me out of his life forever because he promised me to an old acquaintance of his. A cattle baron in Texas."

London frowned. "You were on your way to get married?"

"I didn't have a choice." Cheeks hot, she looked away. "I had no money. No family. And I'm ashamed to say, no gumption to strike out on my own. But then I met Tori and she offered me an alternative. A new life. I'm a gifted pianist, and I had your telegram offering Tori a job." She pushed off of him now, squared her shoulders. "I'm sorry that I tried to dupe you, London, and I'll understand if you turn me out. But I'm not going back to my father, and I don't want to go to Texas. Maybe another saloon would hire me or—"

He cut off her words with a kiss, and this time when she felt his tongue teasing the seam of her mouth, she opened. Lightning cracked and thunder boomed. A storm raged—both outside and in her heart and mind. Frightening and exhilarating in its intensity.

She fought to catch her breath as he eased away. "Do you fancy me, Victoria Barrow?"

"Yes." *More than I dare to say.*

His dark eyes sizzled with intrigue. "Do you fancy an adventure?"

"With you?"

He nodded.

"I do."

He smiled. "Music to my ears."

CHAPTER 26

Tucson

Two hours at Levin's Gambling Palace and Rome was ready to call it a night. Something was wrong with Kat. She played the part of the besotted lover well enough, but when it came to playing cards, her focus was off.

He'd thought by giving her back her daddy's lucky coin, he'd wipe away the last of her doubts regarding her "rusty" skills. He'd expected her to dazzle the ruffle-shirted professionals with their diamond-studded cuffs and quirky superstitions. He'd expected her to rake in a mountain of money. She was more than capable. But she lost more than she won.

They'd played a few rounds together, but then she'd cited the need to shake things up. She moved off to try her luck at another table, and Rome tried not to take it personally. But damn, he could swear she was avoiding him. Was she that nervous about tonight? Had he scared her with that kiss, a kiss that had come from someplace inside of him that he hadn't even known existed? Did she think he expected a night of *hot, meaningless sex*? He expected anything but. He wanted to learn about Frankie. Wanted to know Kat's dreams for the future. He wanted to make love to her and wrap himself around her until dawn.

Maybe *that's* what she was afraid of. Getting too close, too attached. Did she worry that he'd walk away after they trapped Brady?

Of course, that's exactly what he'd initially planned to do. Seduce her and break her heart.

Christ.

"Seems to me you're more interested in your lady than this game, Huckleberry."

Rome shifted his focus to Seth. "No offense, Dupree, but she's a lot prettier than you."

The other men around the table glanced nervously from the former detective to the purported hired gun. Seth played his part to the hilt. He indicated the pile of chips in front of Rome. "I'd say you've won more than your fair share this evening. Why don't you do us a favor and vamoose?"

Rome narrowed his eyes on the man, silently thanking him for the pardon. "Not that I'm taking direction from you, Dupree, but in this case, I have a sudden hankering to make better use of my time." He pushed away from the table, scanned the room for his brother. *Shakespeare* was whooping it up, playing chuck-luck. Rome rolled his eyes, looked back to Kat, and saw an old geezer yapping in her ear. He watched with a sickening feeling as her life's blood seemed to drain away.

At that inopportune moment, a man from his past got in his face—a pretty boy with an ugly disposition. "If it ain't Rome Garrett."

"Step aside, Butch." Butch McCree, a rustler and a two-bit road thief. Rome and Boston had apprehended him and turned him in to the law two years back.

"I did time 'cuz of you." He balled his hands into fists. "I'll never be the same."

"You did time because you held up a Wells Fargo stage. Now move. I won't ask again." Rome spotted Kat rushing for the door. He sidestepped Butch, but the son of a bitch, grabbed him and whirled him around. Rome ducked his punch and landed one of his own.

The bastard slammed into a table, and a brawl broke out between a passel of ticked-off gamblers. Butch came up swinging, but Seth interceded, leaving Rome free to sprint after Kat. Out of the corner of his eye, he saw Athens nabbing the geezer who'd sent her into flight.

He cleared the doors in time to see Kat's skirts flapping in the wind as she raced off on a horse in a torrential downpour. Furious and concerned for her safety, he freed a drenched buckskin from the hitching post and gave chase. Now they'd both risked their necks for stealing another man's horse.

Lightning cracked, spooking Kat's horse and illuminating the scene as the steed reared and she careened into the muddy street.

Rome was on his feet and at her side as she pushed herself upright. "Are you all right?" he shouted over the rain.

"Where's the horse?" She knocked away his hands and pushed to her feet. The horses were trotting back to where their owners had left them. "I have to get to the convent!" She eyed the stable one block up and took off, slipping and sliding in ankle-deep mud.

Heart in his throat, Rome nabbed her by the waist and hauled her onto the boards under a veranda. "What did that old man say to you, Kat?"

"Brady! He was at the Star!" she screamed over the thunder. "He killed Johnson! He's going after Frankie! I have to stop him. *Please* let me go!" Gown and hair sodden with rain and mud, chest heaving, eyes haunted, she looked half-crazed.

She tried to run, but he grabbed her wrist. "It's dark and that's a goddamned monsoon, Kat. You'll get lost or swept away by a flash flood. You'll get yourself and the horse killed."

"But he'll steal my baby!" She wrenched away with a strength that shocked him and darted for the stables.

When he caught her, she fought him, lashing out with fists and words as the sky wept and grumbled. Heart pounding, he overpowered her and hauled her into his arms. He ignored her pummeling fists and made his way through the blinding rain.

He nearly plowed into Seth. Never a fan of Rome's tactics, the lawman motioned to his kicking, screaming captive. "What the hell, Garrett?"

"She's bent on riding to the convent. Said Brady's going after Frankie and seems to think she can stop him."

"Tell him to let me go!" Kat shouted to Seth.

He shouted back over rolling thunder. "Can't do that, hon."

She continued to rail as Rome headed for the hotel.

Seth kept pace. "Athens dragged the bearer of bad news over to the sheriff's office to spew his tale. Bottom line: Brady hit Kat's saloon two nights ago." He touched Rome's shoulder as they stepped onto the boardwalk. "Either Boston escaped with Frankie or Brady's got her by now."

He didn't mention the latter would mean the outlaw had killed Boston to get the kid, because they both knew that's what it would take. Rome had never felt as helpless as he did at that moment.

Kat went limp with exhaustion, and he knew she'd just absorbed the crushing reality. There was nothing she could do.

Rome glanced at Seth. "I need to get Kat dry and warm."

Seth nodded. "Athens is sending a wire to Camp Grant. Soldiers can make it to the convent in a few hours." He sleeved rain from his face, softened his voice. "I know it's hard, but we're better off sitting tight until we learn more."

Throat tight, Rome nodded and carried Kat into the hotel.

The front desk clerk gawked.

Rome didn't offer an explanation, just issued an order. "Send up a tub and hot water."

"But it's late—"

"I don't care."

"It'll cost you—"

"I don't care!" Jaw clenched, he carried her up the stairs and into her room. He kicked the door shut, set her to her feet. She'd gone stiff and silent. Shock? "Talk to me, Kat. Who was that old guy?"

"Skeet Appleby," she said in a scratchy voice. "A regular at my saloon. Said his woman locked him out that night. Said Johnson told him if he washed off his stink, he could sleep in the back room. After Johnson dozed, Skeet snuck back into the bar to snitch a bottle of whiskey. That's when he heard them break in."

"Brady?"

"And his gang."

Rome frowned at her hushed, monotone voice. Definitely shock. He started unfastening the hooks, buttons, and laces of her many layers and pitching drenched articles of clothing into the corner.

"Skeet hid under the bar. All I know is that they were looking for me and Johnson wouldn't tell them anything so Brady shot him. He killed the sheriff, too. Gus was only nineteen."

Rome swore under his breath, wrapped Kat's chilled, naked body in a blanket, and placed her on the bed.

"He found the letters from Sister Maria." Her voice cracked. "He knows about Frankie."

"Hush now." He smoothed her wet hair out of her face, then moved swiftly to answer a knock on the door.

Athens. Not as Sherman Shakespeare, but as himself. Soaked to the bone, he hovered on the threshold, voice calm and low. "Something went awry. I don't know how Brady found out about Kat's saloon, but he did. According to Mr. Appleby, Brady tortured the bartender before killing him. Don't share that with Kat. She considered the man a friend."

Rome processed this and blew out a breath. "Go on."

"He didn't get any information out of the barkeep, but the sheriff told him Kat had taken off with the Garrett brothers for Tucson. As thanks for the news, Brady killed him, too. The murdering thug was set to ride here until he read some letters from a nun, something about Kat's niece. He told his boys he wouldn't have to go after Kat, she'd come to him."

Rome clenched his fists. "Son of a bitch."

"I wired Camp Grant. Heard directly back. Soldiers are on their way."

Rome caught a flash of angst in his brother's green eyes. "You're worried about Boston."

"Aren't you?"

"If something bad happened to him, I'd feel it in my gut." They'd been tight as ticks for too long.

"Sound awfully sure of yourself."

"Like London always says—"

"Don't borrow trouble," Athens finished. He glanced over Rome's shoulder. "How is she?"

"Not good."

Athens worked his jaw. "I'll let you know as soon as I hear something."

Rome shut the door in his wake.

"Is it bad news?" Kat asked in a shaky voice.

Rome sat on the bed and pulled her into his arms. "I want you to stay calm and listen to me."

"But—"

"Do you trust me?"

She bit her lip and nodded.

"Truth is, Brady's had plenty of time to make it to the convent. Us riding in a full day after isn't going to change what's already gone down. Athens wired a nearby fort. Soldiers are on the way." He framed Kat's pale face. "You have to have faith that Boston protected that girl. My little brother has more sand than the desert."

She shivered and he could well imagine her dark, ugly thoughts. "But Brady rides with a gang. Even with that other Peacemaker there, your brother would've been out-numbered. What if Brady got the best of them?"

Rome thanked God she didn't know about Manning. He ignored his own dark thoughts. Boston wouldn't have been in this position if Rome hadn't told him to *get his own damned life*. "Then we wait to hear from the bastard. Apparently Skeet overheard Brady saying he wouldn't have to come after you, you'd come to him. If he's got Frankie, he's not going to hurt her. He's going to use her as bait. He knows you're in Tucson. He'll send word letting you know where they are. I know it's hard, baby, but we have to sit tight."

She stared into his eyes for what seemed a lifetime. Tears fell and her breath hitched. "I have to tell you something."

She was interrupted by another knock on the door.

Rome forced himself to move. "It might be Athens with more news."

It was the bath he'd ordered.

He glanced over his shoulder, saw Kat curl into a ball, her face hidden beneath the cover. Gut clenched, he helped the man tote in the brass tub. Fifteen minutes later it was filled with steaming water, and once again, Rome was alone with Kat.

He stared down at her, his brain pounding from fifteen minutes of fast-paced deducing, his heart racing due to a wild but logical conclusion. He factored in things she'd said and things she hadn't said, her expressions and reactions, and Frankie's exact age. He sat on the bed and placed a hand on her hip. "I remembered right first time around, didn't I, Kat? You're an only child. There is no sister. Frankie isn't your niece." He spoke past the choking lump in his throat. "She's your daughter."

She rolled over and faced him, and though she was no longer crying, her eyes were red and puffy and she looked tortured as hell. "I was going to tell you tonight."

He battled mounting frustration. "Why didn't you tell me before? When you first mentioned Frankie at the ranch? Or the next morning when we walked together? Or, for chrissakes, this morning when I revealed my own stark truths?"

"I'm sorry," she croaked. "You don't know how hard it's been keeping this secret all these years."

He had a hundred questions. He focused on one. "Is she mine?"

"I hope so with all my heart."

"Meaning she could be Brady's."

Fresh tears welled. "The timing . . . I have no way of knowing."

He told himself to breathe, to think. He put himself in her shoes. "That's why you didn't tell me. Because you feared I'd reject her, you. Because of my explosive words and actions when I walked in on you and Brady."

"I thought you hated me. And I couldn't risk coming out of hiding. If Brady found me, if he thought . . . You don't know how he was after he got me away from you."

He didn't want to imagine, but he did. His brain and temper threatened to blow. But it wasn't Kat he wanted to blast. He reined in his emotions and grasped her hand. "Climb into that hot bath. Last thing we need is for you to catch pneumonia."

She shook her head. "At least I'm dry. Your clothes are soaked. You take it."

He tugged her off the bed. "Get in." He peeled off his shirt as she dropped the blanket and stepped into the tub. He'd seen her naked plenty of times before, but he felt as though he were seeing her for the first time. He tried imagining her belly swelled with a child. *His* child. He couldn't grasp the idea that he'd missed out on almost six years of his daughter's life. It was too huge. Too painful.

Then again, no guarantee Frankie was his to claim.

Frankie. A curious name. A feminine play on Frank? Then he remembered. Charles F. Simmons. Charles *Franklyn* Simmons. She'd named her little girl after her father. It pained him to think that gambler had turned out to be the only stable man in her life.

He draped his wet clothes over a chair, then stepping in behind Kat, eased down into the hot water, his front to her back. He felt her tremble and knew without looking that she was crying.

"Please don't hate me," she whispered.

"I don't hate you, Kat." He was too poleaxed to feel anything but malice for Brady and concern for Frankie and Boston. He snatched the provided soap and washed the mud from Kat's hair, bursting with questions about the little girl he'd never met. They'd have to wait. He'd never guessed the woman in his arms could be so fragile.

"How did he find me?" she croaked. "My saloon? I was so careful."

"I don't know, sugar."

She turned her lathered head and met his gaze. "Please

tell me Frankie's safe."

Her anguished expression tore at his already-aching heart. "Frankie's safe." He said it for himself as much as her. He also said a silent prayer for his brother.

CHAPTER 27

Kat woke in the middle of the night wrapped in Rome Garrett's embrace. For a moment she thought she was dreaming. But she could feel the weight of his thigh, the warmth of his skin, the strength of his arms. He was real, but too good to be true.

She remembered now, crawling into bed after he'd warmed her bones and heart with that thoughtful bath. She'd been exhausted—physically and emotionally. Regardless, she couldn't sleep. She couldn't stop thinking about what Brady did to Johnson, what he might've done to Boston, and wondering where he'd taken Frankie. Was he treating her kindly? Was she scared?

Rome hadn't asked permission. He'd just climbed into bed and pulled her into a spooning position. Even though they were both naked, he hadn't come to her bed for sex, but to offer comfort. She knew he had to be reeling from her news, yet he'd treated her with nothing but tenderness. Probably feared she'd shatter if he even raised his voice. Surely, she'd felt that breakable. Even now she had a tenuous hold on her composure.

She sensed he was holding in his disappointment and anger to spare her more distress. Would the negative emotions pour out once they'd found Frankie and she was safe in Kat's arms? Would he look at the pint-sized girl and see shades of Brady? Would he see glimpses of himself? Would he want to be a part of their lives, or would he walk away, this time forever?

"I can hear you thinking, Kat."

She must've been fidgeting. "I'm sorry I woke you."

"Who can sleep?" His voice was husky, his breath hot on her neck. Under different circumstances, she would've been insane with desire. As it was, she was acutely aware of his charisma. "But we need to rest," he said. "We need to be ready for whatever Brady throws our way."

We. Our. Dare she hope there could someday be an *us*? As in *the three of us*? She let that fantasy float away almost as soon as it formed. She had no experience with a conventional family. She'd never even lived with her own daughter—just *the two of them*. She'd not only denied a father a daughter, she'd denied herself motherhood. In a moment of stark self-awareness, she acknowledged that she'd never had a close, long-lasting relationship with anyone other than her father. Was she so afraid of loving and losing again that she'd unconsciously looked for ways to keep Frankie at arm's length?

Kat shuddered at the thought.

The urge was fierce to revisit the path she'd chosen, to assure herself *and* Rome that she hadn't acted selfishly but selflessly. She needed to start at the beginning so she could start living in the present and anticipating the future. A future with no self-destructive expectations or fears. "I need to talk about Frankie."

"Okay."

She turned into Rome, forehead to forehead, and rested her hand on his shoulder. Again she was aware of their lack of clothing, yet she needed to shed even more layers in order to bare her soul.

Once he knew her chosen path, would he condemn her as a horrible person? Feel her pain? Ponder her sanity? "You may not agree with the choices I made," she ventured, "but I want you to know I did what I felt was best for Frankie."

"I'm listening, Kat."

The pressure to choose the right words triggered a bout of nerves. She wet dry lips and braved his judgment. "When I broke away from Brady, I ran as far as my limited funds would afford and landed in Arizona Territory. Near Prescott. I knew an old friend of my daddy's had settled there, and sure enough Mr. Lamour and his wife took me in. When I realized my condition, I confided in Mrs. Lamour that I was with child. I was so scared, so ashamed. But they didn't shun me, Rome. I borrowed Daddy's middle name and went by the name of Katrina Franklyn. I avoided saloons and gambling halls. I helped Mrs. Lamour with housekeeping chores and entertained Mr. Lamour by joining him for nightly games of gin. They kept me safe and sheltered even after Frankie was born."

"They sound like good people."

"They were the best." She swallowed hard and continued. "I felt awkward with Frankie. She was so tiny and I . . . I worried that I'd do something wrong. If you remember I was never very comfortable with children."

"I suspect it's because you were an only child and grew up in an adult world," he said. "As far as worrying that you'd do something wrong, I think that's natural for a new mother."

"That's what Mrs. Lamour said."

"Did she and her husband have children?"

"One son. A soldier. He died fighting the Apaches."

"They were older, then."

"Yes. But overjoyed to have a little one in their home." She scraped her teeth over her bottom lip. "Meanwhile

Jed Brady had become Bulls-Eye Brady, and the papers had started reporting news of his mounting treachery. Mr. Lamour, who sometimes visited the gambling halls, heard whispers connecting my name with Brady's and even softer whispers that the outlaw was interested in my whereabouts. I feared if he learned about Frankie, he'd assume she was his and take her away, so I decided to distance myself from her."

She felt Rome's body tense beneath her hand. Sweat beaded on her upper lip. *This is where it gets hard.*

"I left her in Mr. and Mrs. Lamour's care and relocated to Texas. I dyed my hair red and changed my name to Bertie Franklin. I moved from town to town, played more faro and monte than poker, and won a fair amount of money. When someone likened me to another female gambler, Kat Simmons, I started a rumor that Kat had moved East, where she married a wealthy businessman. The rumor spread, and I remember praying it reached as far as Brady's ears."

"Don't know about Brady, but it caught my attention." Clearly agitated, Rome rolled to his back and raked his hair from his face. "Little did I know."

Kat's pulse quickened. "I know what you're thinking. How could I desert my own daughter? But it wasn't like that. Leaving her was the hardest thing I've ever done. But I truly believed she was better off with the Lamours. A married couple with solid religious beliefs and a fine, stable home. They were generous and caring and so good with Frankie. I didn't want her to grow up like me, Rome, moving town to town, subjected to the seedier side of society. I didn't want her to grow up as the illegitimate daughter of a scandalized cardsharp. Given society's views . . . we'd be ostracized. Surely you can understand—"

"I do understand, I just, dammit, I wish . . ."

"That I'd come to you? The Wells Fargo detective who lived to track criminals, who didn't expect to be long for this earth? The dime-novel hero who craved glory? Would you really have been ready to marry me back then, to take in a child who was possibly fathered by one of your greatest enemies?"

Rome flinched. "Ouch. Jesus, Kat. I don't know. You never gave me the chance to find out."

"I'm sorry." Her cheeks flushed. "I don't know where that came from."

"Obviously, you're still angry with me for not being your knight in shining armor, but merely a human being."

"Ouch."

The subsequent silence cut like a blade. Kat fell back on her pillow, widening the gap between them.

Rome reached over, interlaced his fingers with hers, and tempered his tone. "Tell me how you and Frankie ended up together in Santa Cruz Valley."

Stomach roiling, she gazed up into the dark. *Calm down. Slow down.* "Mrs. Lamour died. It was sudden. In her sleep. Mr. Lamour couldn't cope with the loss, certainly not with a toddler . . . so I returned to Prescott. Learning that Bulls-Eye Brady and the Ace-in-the-Hole gang had recently pulled a string of robberies in Utah Territory, I worried he was drifting closer. I gathered up Frankie, hired a female companion who was good with babies, and paid for passage south on a series of stagecoaches."

"And settled in Casa Bend," he said.

"It was a nothing town in the middle of nowhere. I had enough money to purchase the Star, with a little leftover. I changed my name for the last time—Jane Murdock—and shed my cardsharp ways forever. It wasn't only a matter of guarding my true identity, it was about being a better person, a grounded person—for Frankie."

"How old was she then?"

"Almost three."

"Did you still feel awkward around her?"

His tone was controlled, but she heard the underlying frustration. "You're wondering if I showed her affection." Kat envisioned the little girl who'd stolen her heart—bright, inquisitive, a bundle of giggles and hugs. "The more time I spent with her, the more I never wanted to leave her side."

"But you sent her away, to San Fernando."

She refused to feel bad about it. She still believed she'd done the right thing. *Then show him by staying calm and confident.* "Molly deserted us soon after I rooted in Casa Bend. Said it was too isolated. Nothing about my personal situation had changed, Rome. I was still unmarried, Brady was still a threat, and I still didn't deem myself a proper mother for Frankie. San Fernando's a wonderful school for little girls. A place where I knew she'd benefit from a solid education and the guidance of grounded, wholesome caretakers."

"How did Frankie feel about that?"

"She's an adaptable and easygoing child. At least she was until last year."

"What happened?"

"She turned five." She smiled, remembering how Frankie's face had lit up when Kat had shown up for her special day. Usually, she kept her visits to Christmas and spring, only sending gifts on Frankie's birthday, as the day usually sent Kat into a depression. "She's not a baby any-more, Rome. She's a little girl. A bright, adventurous girl with a mind of her own."

He didn't comment. And even though he still held her hand, she suddenly felt as though she'd just wedged a mountain between them. She tried to put herself in his shoes. He was possibly Frankie's father. He adored chil-dren. He put family above all else. It reasoned that this moment he was feeling irrevocably cheated of Frankie's early years.

She felt ill.

"Sister Maria's last letter cited Frankie as unmanageable." She refrained from mentioning the child was determined to live with family. He'd no doubt twist that knowledge into a hurtful stab. "Reading that letter, I realized that I wanted what Frankie wanted. She wants to be with me."

"Her mama."

Kat fought to keep her voice steady. "She thinks I'm her aunt. I'm not sure how I'm going to break the truth to her, or even if I should. I don't want to confuse her. I don't want to subject her to future ridicule, yet I want to make things right. I want us to live together. To be a family. But that means eliminating the danger in our lives."

"Brady."

She fell silent, her mind clouding over with dark, violent thoughts. The same thoughts that had propelled her out of the gambling house, racing blindly to Frankie's rescue. "I never thought myself capable of killing someone, but if he harms Frankie in any way, if he even scares her—"

Rome startled her silent by rolling on top of her. "First of all," he said, glaring down, "Frankie isn't with Brady. She's with Boston."

"You can't know—"

"Second, I'll handle Brady. I don't want you anywhere near him, Kat."

She stiffened. "I'm the bait."

"Not anymore."

Her blood surged with panic and defiance. She shoved at Rome's shoulders, but he wouldn't budge. "Hiding from Brady is no longer an option," she grit out. "Even if I wasn't worried about Frankie, I can't ignore the lives lost because of that man. The woman on the train. Gus. *Johnson*." Her voice cracked, and she had to fight hard not to cry. Her friend wouldn't want her to mourn his loss. He'd want her to stay strong. To fight back. "I wouldn't be able to live with myself if Brady continued spilling blood, knowing I could've stopped him. I have to put myself out there. Even though our initial plan is dead in the water, I have to follow through."

He dropped his face closer. "Don't counter me on this, woman."

She flinched, even though he didn't yell. His body pressed flush against hers, she felt every muscle in his chest and midsection tense. His restraint was unnerving. She stated the obvious. "You're angry with me."

"I'm angry with the situation."

In the past, their fights had almost always ended in

heated lovemaking. Even though they lay skin to skin, even though sex was the last thing on her mind during this volatile moment, her body trembled in remembrance of their shared pleasure. "Every night," she whispered as emotion clogged her throat.

He eased back. "*What?*"

"Two days ago. You asked if I ever thought about those days. How it was between us before it went wrong." Tears stung her eyes. "I thought about it every night for the last six years."

He stared down at her a full minute, then blew out a breath. "Goddammit, Kat." He rolled onto his back, taking her with him.

She melted against his warm, hard body, fought tears and lost as he wrapped her in his strong embrace. She still felt the mountain of frustration between them, but at least it seemed less daunting.

"You keep knocking me off my feet with one revelation after another. Just do me a favor and go to sleep while I try to find some fucking balance."

Sleep wouldn't come easy if at all, but she welcomed a chance to shut down. Baring her soul had been exhausting, and further talk at this point would be fruitless. Rome needed time to absorb and accept her *revelations*. She couldn't predict how this would all turn out. She was even afraid to hope. For now she clung to Rome's strength and his assurances that Frankie was safe with Boston. As for Brady . . . She aimed on doing whatever she had to do to end his murdering days, even if it meant defying the man she loved.

CHAPTER 28

Riding across the desert in the dark during a monsoon had been plumb crazy. But after Bulls-Eye had vehemently nixed Itchy's suggestion to seek shelter, no one else in the gang had thought it wise to complain. No one wanted to be pegged a coward. No one wanted to tempt Bulls-Eye's wrath.

That included Elroy. His cousin's mood had turned as dangerous as the storm. Elroy knew without asking that he was obsessed with the possibility that Frankie Hart was his daughter. He was obsessed with catching up with Boston Garrett and snatching her away. At any cost.

The gang paid for that obsession somewhere around midnight when Snapper and his horse stumbled blindly into a gully and got swept away by raging waters. Only then had Bulls-Eye relented. With one man down, they took shelter in a sheepherder's home. Elroy almost wished they'd kept riding. He feared for the owner and his young wife's lives. Itchy and Boyd had blindfolded and dragged the sheepherder into the barn, where they'd left him tied up in a stall. His woman lay blindfolded and tied to their bed. Mule had gagged her so the gang wouldn't have to listen to her cries as they raided the couple's kitchen. The men had fired up the cookstove, seeking heat, hot coffee, and vittles.

Elroy's slicker hadn't provided sufficient protection from the heavy rains and now lay abandoned in a heap with his gloves and hat. Soaked to the bone, he sat in the cramped, humble parlor hunkered down in front of the hearth alongside his cousin. He plucked at the wet shirt plastered to his skin, then fanned his chilled fingers in front of the flames.

Rather than his person, Bulls-Eye seemed more concerned with drying out the bundle of letters he'd had in his pocket along with the daguerreotype of Frankie. The man stared at the image, almost as if he were possessed.

Elroy had a bad feeling. A real bad feeling. He swallowed and risked conversation. "See any of you in her, Jed?"

The man angled the photo so Elroy could get a look. "All I see is Kat. You?"

Elroy curled his nine good digits into fists, hoping he answered correctly. "You're right. She's the spitting image of Kat with those long, dark curls and big, dark eyes. But," he squinted and peered closer for effect, "but that smile. Sorta ornery, don't you think? Pegs her as a charmer and a troublemaker. Qualities she could've inherited from you."

"Or Rome Garrett. Or Kat." Bulls-Eye slid him a look. "But I appreciate the observation." He narrowed his eyes on the image. "I'm thinking she's mine. Why else would Kat have gone to such trouble to avoid me?"

Elroy thought it best not to ponder aloud. "No disrespect intended, cousin, but you're risking your life in pursuit of that little gal. Once you have her, once you have Kat . . . What are you gonna do with them?"

"I've got a good deal of money stashed away, Elroy. Figure I'll take my girls south of the border, purchase a comfortable hacienda."

More crazy talk. "What if Kat don't wanna go?"

"I won't give her a choice. If she refuses, I'll make her disappear for real and for good, and it'll just be Frankie and me."

Elroy thought about what his cousin had done to that barkeep's toes, the hole he'd plugged between that young sheriff's eyes, the talk of his killing that woman on the train. He hadn't been thinking on any of that when he'd alerted his cousin of Kat Simmon's whereabouts. He'd acted, thinking he was rejoining a gang of thieves, not the devil's spawn. He'd thought his cousin was his salvation, not his ticket to hell.

He thought about Kat cold as a wagon tire and that five-year-old kid being reared by a man with little to no conscience. And what if Bulls-Eye learned the girl wasn't in fact his, but Rome Garrett's?

Elroy's stomach gurgled with dread and remorse. He shuddered.

Bulls-Eye mistook the cause of his shivering. "Hell's fire, cousin. Move closer to the hearth before you take your death. We're already one shy of our lucky seven."

"Speaking of the gang," Elroy said, voice low. "How do you think they're going to feel about your retiring?"

"Who said anything about retiring? Just aim on planting roots for my family and lying low for a spell."

More crazy talk, in Elroy's estimation. He noted the beads of sweat on the man's brow, the way he kept working his wounded shoulder. Maybe he was comin' down with a fever. "You feelin' alright, Jed?"

"Think I could use some rest." He stood and shrugged out of his slicker, laid it out to dry alongside the bundle of letters. "Think I'll curl up in bed with something warm." He waggled his brows at Elroy, then took off to the room where the sheepherder's wife lay.

Elroy dropped his head into his hands. Yes, sir. He'd done bought a ticket to hell.

CHAPTER 29

Phoenix

The sun had yet to rise, but London was already dressed and shoveling grounds into a pot. Sleep had been futile. Coffee—strong and black—was imperative. He moved about the saloon's kitchen as quietly as possible, not wanting to wake the woman upstairs. They'd had a late night. A night fraught with confessions, affection, and a spontaneous overture.

The adventure he'd proposed to Victoria had been audacious. Totally uncharacteristic. He'd been the grounded one, the prudent caretaker for so long, he'd forgotten the thrill of reckless abandon. Last night, he'd punctuated what had to be the shortest courtship in history with a heartfelt proposition. He'd felt like an infatuated youth as opposed to an experienced man—heart pounding, palms sweating—as he'd waited for Victoria's answer. When she'd asked, in her achingly polite manner, if she could sleep on it, he'd squeezed her trembling hands and calmly responded, "*Of course.*" Inwardly, he'd pitched an impatient, immature fit. "*Shit!*"

Saying good night and retiring to his bedroom had been an exercise in supreme restraint. Anticipating one of her nightmares, he'd been ready to rush to her side. Only she never cried out. Either she was too exhausted to dream or London had managed to obliterate memories of an ugly demise with descriptions of a beautiful beginning. Selfishly, he wanted to believe the latter.

Daydreaming about the second, deeper kiss they shared before saying good night, he stooped to light a fire in the bottom chamber of the stove.

"Good morning."

London bobbled the match, cursed. Amazed at the depth of his distraction, he peered over his shoulder.

Victoria hovered on the threshold. "I didn't mean to startle you."

Laughing, he shut the castiron door and stood. "If Parker were here just now, I believe he'd cry."

She raised a questioning brow.

"He's intent on catching me unaware."

"I spent my life avoiding attention," she said matter-of-factly. "Were Mr. Parker here just now, I'd console him with the phrase: practice makes perfect."

Brow furrowed, he moved to the kitchen table and turned up the flame of the lantern, shedding more light on the lovely lady before him. "I hope you don't think that just because I asked you to remain upstairs yesterday that I expect you to dwell in the shadows."

Her lips quirked. "I remember it more as an order than a request, but I understand the dictate was rooted in concern."

"Why, Miss Barrow, I do believe you're poking fun at me." He grinned. "I like it." She broke eye contact, but her shy smile warmed his heart. He noted that, like him, she was fully dressed. "What are you doing up so early?"

"I couldn't sleep."

That explained how she'd avoided night terrors. It also meant she hadn't "slept on" his proposal. He pushed back his disappointment. "Anything you want to talk about?" *The bastard who traumatized you? Your memory loss?* Between what John Fedderman had told him and bits of information gleaned from Victoria herself, he was certain he could fill her in on specifics, and he would. When she asked or when the time felt right. The last thing he wanted was to push her into facing a reality she wasn't emotionally ready to handle.

She smoothed her palms down the skirt of her blue satin gown, an unconscious tick as if wiping her hands clean. "It's cowardly of me, but I didn't want to sleep and relive that awful altercation on the train. I didn't want to see that man's face or Tori's blood. I didn't want to grapple with the sickening feeling that, if not for me, she'd still be alive."

"Victoria—"

"I know I need to face what happened, but I didn't want to do it last night." She braved his gaze. "I didn't want to ruin what turned out to be the most special day in my life. The quilt. The kisses." Her breath hitched. "Everything you did. Everything you said." She palmed her forehead. "I sound like an idiot."

She sounded smitten. Her sincerity torched his blood. His inflamed heart battered his ribs. He was worse than smitten. *He* was in love. "I wonder if you realize the magnitude of the compliment you just paid me, Miss Barrow."

"I only speak the truth. I've never known anyone like you."

"Nor I you." He approached and lightly grasped her forearms. "I believe you are the most gentle and polite person I have ever met, Victoria. In case you're having the same thoughts about me, I need to disabuse you of that notion. You do bring out my tender side, but mostly I'm bossy and unbending and on occasion can be an infuriating SOB. Ask my sister or any one of my brothers."

"I guess that comes from being the oldest," she said,

laying her palms tentatively to his chest. "The caretaker, as you said."

"Taking charge comes naturally, yes. I just want you to know there are different facets to my personality." He studied her with interest. "What about you? Are you always so lamblike?"

"I'm not always this . . . fragile. The events of the past two weeks shook my world. But even when I am at my best, I am of a quiet nature." She scrunched her brow. "Certainly I must be boring compared to the women you usually . . ." She worried her bottom lip. "Wouldn't you rather spend your days and nights with someone more exciting?"

He smiled at that. "You are exciting. You make me feel things I've never felt before. I haven't had a sane, typical thought since you walked through my swinging doors."

"Thus the crazy notion we should marry."

"No crazier than your marrying a family acquaintance—which, given what I know of your father, doesn't bode well—a rancher three times your age, a man you've never met. *We've* met, Victoria, and we fancy one another." He smoothed dark waves from her pale, arresting face and experienced almighty lust and affection. "We make a good match. I feel it in my gut, and even though it's not obvious by looking at this ramshackle saloon, I'm a very successful man because of my dead-on intuition."

"When you look at me like that," she said in a breath-less voice, "I feel pretty and . . . wanted."

He brushed his lips over hers. "I'd like to make you feel a lot of things, Victoria. Things I'd rather show you than name. But that involves taking you to bed, and I'd prefer to put a ring on your finger first."

Her whisper-soft, "Yes," caressed his heart.

He was almost afraid to voice his hopeful assumption. "Yes, you'll marry me?"

"Tori Adams offered me a new life when she directed me to your door. I'm thinking . . . I'm thinking we were meant to be."

"Serendipity."

She framed his face with her tiny hands and smiled. "I don't need a fancy wedding, London. I'm awful anxious for our adventure. For the intimacies you want to show me," she said, cheeks flaming. "Whenever you're ready—"

"I'm ready."

"But your family—"

"My brothers are away on business for God knows how long, and my sister is a day's ride away and near to birthing her first child. If you're ready, honey, I'm not waiting."

"What about your niece and nephew? Kaila? They're here, and they're family."

London narrowed his eyes. "Zoe might still smell like

skunk."

"I don't care."

He kissed her, a happy, hard smack on the lips. "You're going to fit right in."

They blew out of the kitchen as one, then separated. "Where are you going?" she asked as he targeted the swinging doors.

"To spur our adventure. Where are you going?" he asked as she lit for the stairs.

"To prepare for a life in the sunshine."

❤ ❤ ❤

Tucson

The monsoon subsided as the night crawled by, but a storm of emotions battered Rome well into the dawn. Murky light peeked through the closed drapes, casting the hotel room in a grayness that matched his mood.

Kat had fallen into a restless sleep, wrung out from worry and exhausted from her long and emotional walk down memory lane.

Rome wondered if he'd ever sleep again.

The woman in his arms had ravaged his heart and mind with her harsh truths. He'd listened and absorbed. He'd reined in his shock and disappointment. He understood why she'd made certain choices, but wished she would have afforded him options as well. He wished she would have contacted him when she learned she was carrying. He wanted to believe he would've done the right thing, though he acknowledged, given his mind-set back then, he might've harbored resentment. He might've done more harm than good, marrying her with distrust in his heart, distancing himself if the child turned out to have Brady's dimpled chin and grey eyes.

Then again, maybe they would've worked through their troubles to forge a true family bond.

He'd never know.

Throughout the sleepless night, he'd told himself to leave go of that regret. Told himself to focus on the present. Difficult, what with the chaos ravaging his senses. He didn't know what to think, what to feel. But the idea of Kat going one on one with that son of a bitch Brady gutted his insides. Though her confession had shaken him deeply, he still worried about her welfare, as well as the child's. He would be concerned for any child, but knowing Frankie could be his daughter intensified his feelings tenfold. Twentyfold. In fact, he'd shut down that part of himself hours ago, believing that, in the event Brady did somehow kidnap Frankie, the only way he could handle the situation was with cold control.

As for Kat, with her warm body clinging to his, ignoring his feelings for her proved impossible. Her complexity intrigued him. He harbored profound affection for the vulnerable girl and a new appreciation for the woman who'd survived financial and emotional turmoil. When his own life had taken a turn for the worse, at least he'd had the love and support of his family. Aside from Mr. and Mrs. Lamour, and her dead friend, Johnson Pratt, Kat had faced the world alone.

He gazed down at the woman sleeping in his arms, thinking she possessed not only an inherent sensuality, but also true grit. Given her beauty and intelligence, she could have snagged a man of her choosing and married, lending her daughter a name, respectability, and, hopefully, protection. The notion had niggled throughout the night. Why hadn't she taken the sensible and easier path?

A light knock stole his attention. Pulse quickening, he slipped away from Kat and had his britches on and his arms shoved in the sleeves of his damp shirt by the time he reached the door. He opened it a crack, saw Athens, and waved him inside. His body surged with adrenaline. "Tell me."

Athens stopped just over the threshold. He glanced over Rome's shoulder to where Kat lay sleeping, then averted his eyes and tempered his voice. "Just received a telegram from Camp Grant. All is well at San Fernando."

Rome blew out a breath, his heart lighter but not free.

"Boston arrived as planned," Athens whispered. "But Sister Maria sent him away . . . with the kid. I don't have specifics. Only that Boston mentioned taking Frankie home."

"To Casa Bend?"

"To Phoenix."

"What the hell?"

"I was hoping you could tell me."

Because they'd worked side by side for so long, Rome knew Boston better than any of his siblings. Athens was counting on his insight. "If he'd suspected Frankie was in immediate danger, he would've sought refuge at Camp Grant. If they simply needed a place to stay until Brady was snagged, he could've hunkered down in a nearby hotel."

"Exactly," Athens said. "Why cart the kid four days north? To Phoenix? More specifically—into the Garrett fold?"

He's protecting one of our own.

"He must've suspected," Rome thought out loud.

"Suspected what?"

He wasn't ready to discuss the possibility that he'd fathered Frankie. He needed to live with the notion awhile longer. Not knowing for sure put a twisted spin on an already-uncomfortable situation. "Never mind." He bit the inside of his cheek, jawing on more *whys*. *Why had*

Sister Maria tossed them out? Why didn't Boston inform Athens of his intentions? "I know the telegraph office nearest to the convent was down, but Boston could've wired you from other towns along the way. Odd that he'd keep us in the dark."

"I agree, but maybe he deemed it imperative to avoid civilization. A lone man traveling with a small child? Bound to raise brows and questions."

Bound to instigate talk. Boston wouldn't want to draw attention.

Athens's expression darkened. "There's more. A couple of days after Boston hit the trail, Brady arrived at the convent, claiming to be Frankie's father."

Rome's body vibrated with seething hatred. He didn't care that the man's boast was possibly true. No way, no how, would he allow that bastard to pull an innocent little girl into his life. Frankie belonged with Kat. And Kat, goddammit to hell, belonged with him.

"Rome." Athens leaned in, voice grim. "Brady knows where Boston's headed with the kid."

Fuck.

"If he doesn't catch up with our brother and Frankie before they reach Phoenix, there's a remote possibility he'll strike on our home turf."

"Meaning Zach, Zoe, and Kaila could be in harm's way."

"Along with Boston, London, and Frankie." Athens shoved his hands through his hair. "I sent wires to three Peacemakers, all within a couple days' ride, pulling them off their current cases and sending them to Phoenix. I'd notify Josh, but I don't want to pull him away from Paris. Although I should at least make him aware of the situation."

"Probably. But if Paris and Emily caught wind of the potential danger to family, you know they'd insist on Josh riding to Phoenix and no way in hell would they stay behind."

Athens nodded. "Noted."

"London, however—"

"Seth's wiring him while I'm briefing you. A coded message with essentials only and a directive to alert Marshal Clancy. No details, just advising him to be on the lookout."

"You really want to bring the local law into this?"

"Foolish not to. Clancy can deputize a small legion. Visible guns on patrol may be enough of a deterrent to buy us the time we need."

Rome quirked a grin. "My brother, the strategist."

Athens grunted. "The sooner we hit the trail, the better. I don't want to leave Kat behind and unprotected, but at the same time—"

"I won't slow you down."

Rome turned to find his tousle-haired bedmate already partially dressed. He turned back to Athens. "Meet you out front in ten minutes."

Athens left and Rome walked over and wrenched open the curtains, shedding light on Kat and her ministrations. He assumed she'd heard most or enough of his conversation with Athens. He imagined her anxiety, but she looked calm as you please as she stepped into a split skirt and riding boots.

"Give me five minutes to pack essentials," she said.

"What about all of your gowns?"

"Do you really think I care?"

Stupid question. "Kat." He grasped her shoulders, bid her attention.

"If you leave me behind," she said, serious as an undertaker, "I'll make the journey alone."

He didn't doubt her word. What's more, he understood her determination. "If you ride with us, I want your promise you won't act without my consent. No more rushing blindly into a storm. No more solo heroics."

"I could easily pull a poker face right now. I could promise you the moon. I could bluff and make you buy it, because I'm that good. Is that what you want from me, Rome? A lie?"

Normally, her hard tone and steely glare would have whipped him into a confrontation. But he recognized the tactic. *Cold control.* He also recognized the futility in trying to reason with her just now. Not to mention the wasted time.

"I'll secure you a fast mount from the livery." He snatched his holster from the table. "We're riding out in ten."

"If you're banking on me being late, you'll lose."

CHAPTER 30

Phoenix

For a man who thought he'd never wed, London couldn't marry Victoria fast enough. Her father didn't want her, but the cattle baron might. When the truth came out that she'd survived the train robbery, would the man seek her out? If so, and if he tracked her to Phoenix, London wanted to be in a prime position to send him packing.

There was also Bulls-Eye Brady. Rome and Kat were out there taunting the bastard. If all went according to plan, they'd catch the outlaw. Next step: trial. Victoria was the eyewitness Athens needed to hang the man, literally. Whether or not she chose to testify, London wanted her under his protection. Legally.

He did what came naturally. He took control.

Despite Victoria's thoughtful nod to his family, he didn't inform Kaila, nor his niece and nephew. London didn't want to waste time explaining his actions. He'd set things in motion, prepared and willing to deal with the impending fallout with his family. For once, he'd put his own needs and wants first. He'd roused a jeweler and a Bible-thumper and, by sunrise, Victoria was his bride.

"How do you feel?" he asked her as they exited the minister's home arm in arm.

"A little dazed." She shook her head. "I can't believe it. We did it."

Her nervous laugh warmed him like the desert sun. He smiled down at his wife. *Wife.* He could scarcely believe it himself. "Shadow dwellers, no more."

He'd admired Victoria plenty during the brief ceremony, but even so he couldn't drink his fill. She'd changed into a cheery yellow day gown, creatively utilizing a paisley shawl and brooch to camouflage the revealing neckline. Decorative combs held back the sides of her hair, the bulk of her shiny waves swinging just above her waist. London thought her the most beautiful woman on earth—inside and out.

Heart full, he smoothed his thumb over the simple gold band he'd placed on her finger when they'd said their vows. "How would you like to spend the first day of our adventure, Mrs. Garrett? Shopping for a new wardrobe? Looking for a place to call home?"

"We have a home," she said as they walked the boards of

Jefferson Street. "Your apartments above Last Chance."

"Always meant that to be temporary. Now I have a reason to hurry things along." Although he liked the idea of keeping Victoria close, he didn't want her living above the saloon. She deserved better, and he wanted better for her. He also wanted privacy. Thoughts of getting her naked, often, put a hitch in his step.

She stopped in front of Thomas Howe's carpentry shop. At first London thought she wanted to peruse the merchant's handmade furniture. Instead, she gripped the lapels of his frock coat, tugged him closer. "So much is happening, so fast," she whispered. "Would you mind if we spent the day alone together? I'm more intrigued by the things you promised to show me, you know, intimately speaking, than with shopping."

Well, hell. His heart and shaft throbbed. He framed her face, aching to kiss her dizzy. *Later, Garrett. Behind closed doors for chrissakes*. "It pleases me to know you're curious, and even more that you let me know."

She blushed, and he knew this conversation had run its course.

He scooped her into his arms and carried her across the muddy street, smiling and dipping his chin in greeting to the merchants who were opening doors for business. "Just married," he said to seamstress Nattie Burns. The news would spread like wildfire. Fine by him. It would shelve talk regarding the unchaperoned woman sleeping in his home. No doubt Victoria's reputation had already taken a beating. As his wife, the whispers would stop.

Once on the opposing boardwalk, London set his bride to her feet but hastened her pace. The Last Chance and a morning of lovemaking waited two blocks ahead. "Business affairs keep me bound to Phoenix just now," he said, trying to focus on something other than seducing a virgin. "But as soon as I'm able, I'll take you on a honeymoon. Anywhere in particular you'd like to visit?"

"What's it like where your sister lives?"

"Paris and Josh live near the Superstition Mountains. Rugged territory mostly populated by miners. Not the most romantic place for a bridal tour."

"Maybe not, but I'm curious about your family."

He couldn't imagine the loneliness of being an only child. Worse, an only child raised by one parent, a father who bemoaned her existence. "You'll meet my family soon enough, honey. Be warned, they're a colorful bunch."

"Like Zach and Zoe and Kaila." Another smile. "I can't wait."

Once again his thoughts turned to lovemaking. Beyond the physical ecstasy to an extended emotional bond. For the first time in his life he actually envisioned himself with a passel of kids. It occurred to him that he was happiest when he had a brood to care for. It had been a long time since his siblings had needed him in that fashion, and now that he was no longer managing a large opera house and hoards of mischievous performers . . . well, hell, no wonder he'd been so damn bored.

Nearing the saloon, he spied a buckboard in front. The driver looked familiar. *It couldn't be.* But then the tall, Stetson-wearing man hopped from the driver's throne just as a slender blond woman dressed in boyish clothes swung out of the back and the two of them helped a very pregnant half pint to the ground. *It was.* "What the hell?"

Victoria squeezed his hand. "Who is it, London?"

"My sister."

So much for boredom. So much for a morning of love-making.

♥ ♥ ♥

The first hour of dawn had passed in a blissful sleep-deprived blur, and Victoria had hoped for even more bliss, bliss of a deeply intimate nature. She'd been floating on air, detached from reality, living a life she'd only fantasized about—marrying a charismatic, handsome man, marrying for love. The crash to earth was sudden and sobering. This wasn't a fantasy. This was real. She'd just married a man she barely knew. A man with a large, loving family. A family who would question her place in his life.

If the pregnant young woman was London's sister, Paris, then the broad-shouldered man handling her with kid gloves must be her husband, Josh Grant. The tall young woman with the blond braids and wire-rimmed spectacles had to be Paris's best friend, Emily. Emily, if she remembered correctly, was married to Josh's best friend, Seth Wright. What would they say when London introduced her as his wife? What would *she* say?

Victoria wanted so badly to be accepted, yet given her history, she anticipated the familiar—rejection. Her heart, fluttering with joy mere seconds ago, thudded slowly and painfully in her chest. Self-conscious, she wished herself invisible as they neared the animated trio.

London spoke, or rather, snapped first. "What the hell, Grant? Paris has no business traveling over rugged territory when she's this far along."

"Exactly what I told her," the man grit out, sliding his wife a peeved look before glaring at his brother-in-law. "Don't tell me how to care for my wife, Garrett."

"Wouldn't have to if you showed some common sense."

Josh stepped forward, and Paris stepped between them. The dark-haired sprite with the freckled nose smacked her brother's chest. "Stop picking on Josh. He refused to bring me, but then Emily and I came up with this plan and he overheard us and—"

"Enough said." London frowned at his sister.

"At least I got her to agree to my stipulation," Josh said.

"I'll be staying in Phoenix until the baby's born." Paris's tiny smile indicated she wasn't displeased.

"I'm not going to risk bouncing and jostling you around a second time," Josh said, tugging at her messy braid. "If the kid's anything like you, she'll come kicking and screaming into the world in the middle of the desert just to give me grey hair."

"Not to mention," Paris said while stealing a glance at Victoria. "He's not fond of our new town doctor. Doc Barry's a little on the young side."

"Doc Barry," Josh said, "drinks too much."

Victoria marveled at the frank and heartfelt family discussion. She also felt out of place and longed to withdraw into the background. A difficult habit to break. She felt London squeeze her hand as if reading her mind and sensed he was about to introduce her. She braced herself, but the tomboyish blond woman beat him to the task.

"Hello, my name is Emily." Silent until now, she extended her hand to Victoria. "You must be Tori Adams. Mr. Fedderman told us about you when he came to visit

Josh." She indicated her companions, including London. "They don't mean to be rude. Long trip. Unexpected arrival. Everyone's worried about someone or another. Still, no excuse for skipping introductions."

So much for being invisible. Victoria clasped the woman's hand. "I hope Mr. Fedderman fares well," was all she managed. How was she going to explain about her true identity? They'd think her a liar before they even got to know her.

"John's fine," Josh said with a friendly smile. "Sends his regards. Apologies for our poor manners, ma'am." He smiled and Victoria thought him handsome and kind, though not nearly as handsome and kind as London. "Joshua Grant," he said, removing his hat in greeting. "This is my wife, as you've probably guessed, Paris."

"I get carried away sometimes. Mouth runs ahead of my brain. My apologies as well, Miss Adams," Paris said, brown eyes sparking with curiosity. "Nice to meet you."

"Pleased to make your acquaintance," Victoria said, skin burning when the woman glanced down and saw her fingers interlaced with London's. Victoria tried to slip free, but London held tight.

"Let's take this discussion inside," he said. "We're gaining an audience."

Though only an hour past sunrise, the town was starting to come to life. Early birds took note of the commotion in front of the Last Chance. London had pegged his family as colorful. An understatement. In addition, people were no doubt whispering about the saloon owner and the immoral entertainer sleeping under his roof. Unless gossip had already spread about their impromptu wedding.

Victoria felt faint from the unwanted attention, but she stiffened her spine, a shadow dweller no more. "Have you no luggage?" she asked after a glance at the buckboard.

"We're staying at Emily and Seth's house," Paris said.

"Their place sits on the outskirts of town," Josh put in. "Swung by there first. Didn't tally and rest though. Appreciate the opportunity to get Paris out of the sun and off her feet."

"I was off my feet for the entire journey. Stop fussing."

"Stop being a pain in the neck," Josh said.

Emily snorted.

"You do realize you're asking the impossible," London said as they moved into the saloon.

Josh smiled and kissed the top of his wife's head. "I do."

Feeling like an intruder, Victoria desperately wanted to escape by doing the hospitable thing and offering to make breakfast. Only London had yet to announce their marriage. Stepping in as hostess would be premature. Her discomfort mounted by the second.

"What happened on the train," Paris blurted, once

London locked the front doors behind them, "must've been awful, Miss Adams."

"I can't imagine," Emily said, her eyes mirroring Paris's concern. "We read about it in the newspaper, but the story was even more chilling when relayed by Mr. Fedderman."

Victoria's pulse galloped as glimpses of the robbery came to mind. *Three men, two wearing bandannas that disguised the lower half of their faces, burst into the passenger car. "Your valuables or your life!" one called. "Your choice."* Sweat broke across her upper lip as she reached beneath the shawl to finger her locket.

"Paris," London said, sounding annoyed. "Why were you so all-fired determined to come to Phoenix?"

Frowning, Josh eased his wife into a chair. "She thinks the family's falling apart."

"I don't think it," she squeaked, hands splayed across her big belly, "I know it. Seth joined a posse intent on tracking the gang that robbed that train, a gang led by Bulls-Eye Brady."

The name sent a chill down Victoria's spine. *"You should be ashamed,"* Tori railed, *"terrorizing old men and defenseless women. That locket is worth a hell of a lot more to my friend than you, Mr. Big Shot Bulls-Eye. Leave her be!"*

"Rome and Boston should be helping Seth," Paris said, grabbing hold of Emily's hand. "God knows they were hot on Brady's path more than once, but instead they're drinking and brawling and disappointing a whole lot of good people. Emily would sleep better if they were riding with Seth, and so would I, because it would mean they'd recovered from the scandal, business as usual."

"And surely Miss Adams will rest easier," Emily said, with a thoughtful nod to Victoria, "when the Ace-in-the-Hole gang are brought to justice."

"A person would have to be blind," Paris said, "not to see that you don't harbor warm regards for Miss Adams, London. I would think—"

"About that," London said.

"—that you would want Brady squashed like a bug as soon as possible."

"Calm down," Josh said, squeezing her shoulder. "Fretting isn't good for you or the baby."

"Did you hear that?" Paris asked her brother. "I'd fret a whole lot less if you were out there doing what you usually do, London. Why aren't you out there lecturing the devil out of Rome and Boston? Knocking their stubborn, self-destructive heads together?"

"I told her things are under control," Josh said with a cryptic glance at London.

"I'd like to believe that," Paris said, with a sympathetic glance to Victoria, "but I don't. I have a bad feeling. Even Athens is acting squirrelly. He's head over heels in love with

Kaila, but he's dragging his heels walking her down the aisle. He's obsessed with work again, only instead of politics he's stuck on hunting down murderers like Bulls-Eye."

Another chill. Another vision.

"Thank you kindly for your money, miss. I'll take that pretty necklace, too."

"No. Please. It's the only thing I have of my mother's."

"I'm telling you," Paris said, "when Athens heard that a woman had been killed in that train robbery, it reminded him of how Jocelyn died and pushed him into a vengeful state."

The grey-eyed devil cocked his gun. "That locket worth dying for?"

Tori struck out in Victoria's defense, and the outlaw struck back. Hard.

"My fault," Victoria whispered, wiping her hands down her dress. *The blood. So much blood.*

"Mercy!" Paris exclaimed, pushing to her feet. "Are you all right, Miss Adams?"

"Maybe we should change the subject," Emily said.

"Maybe you shouldn't have brought it up," Josh grumbled.

"Victoria," London said softly, stilling her hands.

Tears blurred her vision, her head spun. "If only I'd given him my locket," she cried. The guilt was crushing, unbearable. She felt London catch her as her knees gave way. "Tori would still be alive."

CHAPTER 31

Pima County

Kat's muscles screamed. She hadn't ridden this hard for so long . . . ever. But she didn't complain. She'd walk through a hail of bullets to secure Frankie's safety. *Whatever it takes.*

The miles and scenery blurred as they rode north, leaving the perennial green valley and the rugged Rincons in the dust. The bold Santa Catalina mountain range had looked daunting, but the well-traveled stage road proved an expedient route. Superior horsemen, the men pushed their mounts hard, but as promised, Kat didn't slow them down. No one spoke, but every now and then, Rome spared her a look and his gaze spoke volumes. *He cares.* Even though she'd shocked and disappointed him, he was concerned for her well-being and state of mind. She continually broke eye contact, not wanting to succumb to the tender feelings he inspired. If she softened, she'd fall apart.

Her imagination proved cruel over the hours, torturing her with scenes of Brady killing Boston and stealing Frankie. She didn't want to think he would harm a little girl, but she had no reason to believe him incapable. His treachery had progressed over the years. He'd started off cheating fellow gamblers of their funds, something Kat hadn't realized at first. Something she couldn't stomach when she found out. Sure, she was a gambler, born and raised. But skilled, not dishonest. Her father had never indulged in shifty tricks of the trade, confidence games, and gaffed equipment, so she'd been appalled when Brady suggested they work the circuit as a couple utilizing disreputable tactics. Between that and his mounting possessiveness, she'd known within days that she'd made a dire mistake in letting him whisk her away from San Francisco. Brady continued to shower her with practiced charm, but she no longer wanted his attention. His touch left her cold, and she managed to avoid his bed for multiple, concocted reasons. Only after awhile he mistook her refusal as playing coy, playing games. The more she resisted, the more he rallied. He even offered to marry her, then he insisted. His persistence only heightened her desire to flee.

Then she'd witnessed his first killing and fleeing had become time sensitive.

Kat shoved away the memory. It inspired guilt and

regret. She didn't want to feel. Anything. Good or bad. She focused on the horizon beyond the rocky pass, on the rhythmic pounding of hooves. She kneed her mount faster and leaned into the wind. If only it could blow away her many mistakes.

A gunshot rang out, echoing between the narrow canyon walls. Then another. Seth's horse went down, and Kat felt herself being plucked from the saddle. A blurred moment later she hit the ground hard, pinned beneath Rome.

"Don't move," he said. "I mean it, Kat. Don't even twitch."

Twitch? She could barely breathe. But her thoughts churned plenty. *Brady.*

"Seth," Rome barked.

"I'm alive."

"He's hit!" Athens called. "It's bad!"

"Not that bad," Seth snapped. "Get the hell off of me, Garrett."

Another shot rang and pinged off of a nearby rock.

Squashed to the ground, Kat couldn't see, but she could hear.

"Goddammit, Garrett. Keep your head down," Seth ordered. "Roll behind that boulder and stay there."

"Your shoulder—"

"Leave him be, Athens," Rome called, "and do as he said."

"But he's hurt," Kat whispered.

"Wright's a tough son of a bitch," Rome said close to her ear. "Don't fret."

Tall order.

"Rome," Seth called low.

"Yeah."

"Straight across. Northeast ridge. Formation shaped like a teakettle."

"Yup."

"Watch."

Kat tried to look, but Rome forced her head down. "Got it," he said to Seth.

"I see it, too," said Athens.

Kat vibrated with frustration.

Rome slid off of her. Belly to ground, he offered her a single-action revolver. "Know how to use this?"

She nodded and took the gun.

"It's loaded with five cartridges." He dumped a handful of ammunition into a kerchief and passed her that, too. Then he shifted her slightly and pointed out the teakettle formation. "Whoever's shooting at us is behind that rock."

"You're talking like it's one person."

"It is."

"How can you know?"

He grinned. "It's what I do."

If she didn't know better, she'd suspect he was enjoying

this. Maybe he was. The danger. The action. The act of protecting—her—and avenging—Seth. The act of felling a miscreant. "But Brady always travels with his gang."

"If it was Brady, I would have taken that bullet," he said. "Not Seth."

"Then who?"

"I aim to find out." He looked to his left.

She looked, too, but she couldn't see anything aside from cacti and boulders.

"Seth. You thinking what I'm thinking?"

"Probably. But I'm going to need a rifle."

"Noted. Wait for my mark."

"Don't do anything reckless, Rome," Athens gritted out.

"Only way I know, brother." He looked to Kat. "On my word, fire at that rock. Two rounds only, spaced a breath apart."

Sweat beaded her brow. "I'll never hit him at this range."

"Just looking for a distraction, sugar." He slid a .45 from his holster. "Ready, boys?"

They affirmed and Kat aimed.

"Now."

She squeezed the trigger. Cocked, breathed, and fired again. She heard simultaneous shots—Seth and Athens—and returned fire from the ridge. She glanced over and saw Rome dodging bullets as he hotfooted it to the felled horse and his own horse, liberating Winchesters from their scabbards. Her mouth went dry with fear, her pent-up breath whooshing out when he tossed a rifle to Seth, then rolled out of sight.

She heard Rome plotting with his brother and Seth, though she couldn't make out their words. The anticipation was unbearable. Fingers trembling, she reloaded. She wasn't convinced the assailant wasn't Brady. Maybe his men lay in waiting.

"That rifle won't do you any good, Garrett," the shooter called, breaking his silence and sending a chill through Kat. Not Brady. But a gang member, maybe? Obviously someone who knew Rome and held a grudge against Seth. "I've got the advantage all the way around, Wells Fargo man."

"That you, McCree?" Rome bellowed.

"You should have dealt with me last night face to face when you had the chance, you son of a bitch!"

Kat's skin prickled with dread. She didn't know any McCree, but she knew this wasn't good.

"Why'd you shoot my associate, instead of me?" Rome asked. "Like you said, you have the advantage."

"'Cuz he broke my fuckin' nose!"

"Guess I should've done worse," Seth grumbled.

"Hell's fire, Wright," Rome said in a teasing tone.

"Didn't you know Butch is fussy about his pretty face?"

Kat's temper rivaled her fear. How could they joke? Seth could be bleeding to death. Any one of them could be next.

"You hangin' in over there, sugar?" Rome called from his position.

The endearment at this particular time was not appreciated. On the other hand, his casual manner smacked of confidence, and she surely took solace in that. "Happy as a flea in a doghouse," she grumbled.

Someone laughed. Someone closer to her than Rome. Seth, she thought. "Just listen for my cue, Kat, then empty your bullets into that rock." Definitely Seth.

She wished she could see him, any of them, but she was hunkered down behind a small boulder with cacti, brush, and rocks obscuring all but the road they'd traveled and the opposing higher ground. One wrong move and she risked getting shot by that maniac, Butch McCree.

"I suffered unspeakable injustice in that prison, Garrett. Swore if I ever met up with you and your brother, I'd settle the score!"

"Probably noticed, Boston isn't with me, McCree. Why don't we postpone this party until he can face the music with me?"

Kat noticed a slight difference in Rome's voice. She

couldn't put her finger on it. Was he nervous? She'd never heard him rattled, so maybe that would account for the picayune variance. At the same time she noted movement behind her. A blur. She thought she caught a glimpse of a brown frock coat. Athens? What the devil was he doing?

McCree noticed, too. Bullets ricocheted off the rocky wall to her back. She heard a yip, and her gut roiled thinking he'd winged Athens or worse. She turned, but the gentler Garrett brother was nowhere to be seen.

"Your friend's a damned coward, Garrett. Ran off and left you with a wounded man and a useless woman!"

"Only half-right, you bastard," Kat said to herself. She cocked her gun and aimed. If she saw a clean shot, maybe she could at least nick him.

Rome yelled out a disparaging remark about McCree's mother, instigating a verbal row.

Kat was no prude. She was used to Rome's foul language, but he stunned her with a string of lewd insults. Had he gone *loco*? Seth was wounded. Maybe his brother, too. She pondered taking action herself and squirming over to help Seth. Did Rome plan to *talk* McCree to death?

Just then Seth said, "Now," and she did as directed and let loose. She fired shot after shot, and when the chambers emptied, she reloaded. Her ears rang from the exchange of fire. She wasn't sure if she was hitting anything, but apparently Seth and Rome were making good use of those long-range rifles. Rock shattered and rained down on Butch McCree.

She prayed with all her might for one of their bullets to hit home. She ran out of ammunition and noticed suddenly the absence of gunfire. She heard a shrill whistle, saw a hat waving in surrender. Saw a man—Athens?—haul a limp McCree from his hiding place. She couldn't believe it. *"Athens?"*

She felt a hand on her shoulder. She whipped around, gun pointed.

"Whoa." *Athens* held up his hands. "Just wanted to make sure you're all right, Kat."

She blinked. "How did you . . . Weren't you . . ." She looked at the teakettle ridge and back. Athens was wearing Rome's duster and Stetson. So that meant Rome . . . "But I heard Rome shouting at McCree."

"That was me."

"But you sounded like him." *Almost like him.* "And talked like him." *Exactly like him.*

"Inherited a gift for acting, remember?"

"But I've never heard you talk like that before. So . . ."

"Earthy?" He sleeved sweat from his brow. "Doesn't mean I don't have earthy thoughts."

Kat was stunned.

"Seth's hurt bad," he said.

That got her moving. She scrambled alongside him, her heart lodging in her throat when she saw the lawman propped against a boulder, the rifle at his side, his shirt soaked through with blood. "Jesus."

"Looks worse than it is," he said, head lulling.

"You've gone sheet white, Seth." She pointed to his poor dead horse, fearing the owner was close on his steed's heaven-bound hooves. "See what you can find in those saddlebags, Athens. Something we can use to bandage the wound. We need to stop the bleeding."

She ripped Seth's shirt to get a better look. So much blood.

She heard the sound of an approaching horse, Rome's voice. "I should've killed the bastard, but considering McCree's view on jail, knocking him out instead seemed the sweeter payback. He's gonna be pissed as hell when he comes to behind bars."

Kat looked over her shoulder and saw Rome dismounting, leaving an unconscious McCree draped over the saddle. "Seth's in a bad way, Rome."

"The hell you say." He neared and crouched next to the pale, sweating man. "Damn, Wright."

Seth licked dry lips. "Did it go through?"

Rome shifted him slightly, inspected his back. "No." He glanced at Kat, then Athens, who passed over one folded shirt, then ripped another into strips. "This bullet's got to come out."

Kat felt ill. "How do we—"

"Best to get professional help." Rome applied pressure while Kat wrapped and tied off the bandage. "There's a town, Fulton, just through this pass and an hour east. Can you make it that far, Seth?"

The man grunted. "Screw you, Golden Boy."

Rome's lip twitched. "Right. You're a tough son of a bitch."

"Got something worth living for."

Emily, Kat thought, heart sinking.

"How did McCree get the jump on us?" Seth asked.

"Don't know," Rome said. "Didn't ask."

The miscreant groaned, and Athens glanced over at the bound man. "What are we going to do with that piece of dung?"

"Leave the goddamned horse killer for the coyotes," Seth said though clenched teeth.

Fond of his own horse, Rome commiserated, only he didn't want to risk the chance of McCree somehow escaping. He looked to Athens. "*Or* you turn him into the authorities in Fulton."

"You mean *we*."

Rome shook his head. "Kat and I need to press on to Phoenix. Boston and Frankie should be there by now."

"Unless Brady caught up to them first," Kat said, throat tight.

"He didn't," Rome said in a tone that brooked no argument. "But there's a chance he's hot on their tail."

"He's right," said Seth to Athens. "Time's ticking."

In more ways than one, Kat thought, hoping Seth was as tough as he professed.

"Dammit, Rome."

"I didn't plan this, Athens."

"Fate," the PMA director griped, "is not my friend."

Kat didn't know what he was talking about. She didn't ask. She was too busy helping Rome haul Seth to his feet.

"You'll have to double with me for a spell, Kat," Rome said as they maneuvered the weakening lawman onto her mount.

She didn't comment. She didn't care. What mattered was that Athens got Seth to a doctor and that she and Rome rode hell-bent for Phoenix.

"Not a word to Emily," Seth grit out as the others saddled up. "If either of you wire London, leave off mention of me. I don't want her to worry."

"Just get yourself stitched up," Rome said, hauling Kat up behind him, "and get your asses home." He reined in close to his brother. "Never thought I'd feel comfortable partnering with anyone aside from Boston. You just shot that notion to hell. My brother, the Peacemaker."

Kat swallowed hard as the two brother gripped hands.

"We'll catch up soon as we can," said Athens. "Do whatever you have to do to keep Frankie and the family safe, Rome."

He tugged down the brim of his hat. "Whatever it takes."

Kat held tight to Rome as he spurred his mustang north. The last time she'd ridden double with him, they'd been young and selfish and in love with the idea of one another. Now there were no more illusions. And without Athens and Seth, no backup. Just the two of them against a man they both hated. Just the two of them fighting to keep the Garrett family and a little girl safe. Question was, when the smoke cleared, would Rome embrace the future Kat had her heart set on? Would he embrace Frankie?

Overwhelmed, she rested her forehead against his shoulder. So much for not feeling.

CHAPTER 32

Phoenix

"You go now," whispered Mrs. Chen. "She sleep. I watch."

London had spent the morning holding his wife in his arms, assuring her that she was not to blame for Tori Adams's death. A sensitive soul, Victoria blamed herself for what she perceived as a moment within her control. London argued otherwise. Sensing his wife was logical and grounded, he had faith she'd come to terms. Acknowledging and accepting the tragedy was the only way she could move on.

It took him a while, but he finally convinced her to take the medicine the doctor had prescribed two days prior. Something to calm her. She'd barely recovered from the influenza. She hadn't slept the night before. She'd experienced a life-altering morning. No wonder she was exceptionally fragile.

Now she slept, and Mrs. Chen was right, he needed to go. He needed to update his family on her well-being, as well as their relationship. He'd promised to meet them at Athens's house. That had been three hours ago. He could almost hear Paris fretting even though she was halfway across town.

He stole a last look at his sleeping bride before shrugging on a frock coat and finger combing his hair. "I appreciate your kindness, Mrs. Chen. I won't be long, but if you need me sooner, I'll be at my brother's."

The petite woman responded by shoving him out the door.

That coaxed a smile out of him, as did thoughts of the future. His future with Victoria.

Focused on squaring things with his family, London hurried down the stairs and outdoors. He'd sent Teddy home the moment he'd shown up for work and closed the saloon for the day. On a flexible schedule, Parker came and went as needed. He was always a step ahead and typically knew London's mind. London had half-expected the man to show up at dawn, magically anticipating London's need of facilitating a quick wedding. So far today, no Parker.

The afternoon sun burned off remnants of last night's storm. The town buzzed with activity. Citizens, some on horseback, some afoot, greeted him as he made his way to Washington Street. Aside from the casual "*How do you do,*" he fielded "*Congratulations,*" and "*Is it true?*" Word of his nuptials had already spread.

He hastened his steps.

Athens's home stood on the outskirts of town. Utilizing shortcuts, he'd easily walk the distance in under quarter of an hour. He jogged onto Central Street and plowed into Parker. The collision knocked the assistant's spectacles askew and shocked London. "Hell's fire, man. What happened to sneaking up on me?"

Parker passed him a telegram.

B ON WAY TO PHOENIX WITH PRECIOUS CARGO. SNAKE IN PURSUIT. SOUTHERN PLAYERS FOLLOWING. NEED BACK-UP CHORUS. ENLIST LOCAL STAR. SHOWTIME. - S. WRIGHT

London read the note a second time before commenting. Last he'd known, Boston was at San Fernando. Was the *precious cargo* a nun? More likely he had Kat in tow—precious to Brady, the *snake*. *Southern players* being Seth, Athens, and Rome. Only how had Kat ended up with Boston and not Rome? *Local Star* being the local badge, Marshal Clancy. *The chorus*, his deputies. Details were murky. One thing was clear. Trouble was coming to Phoenix. But when? "This just came in?"

"I couldn't shake the feeling that something was

wrong. I kept stopping by the telegraph office. Nothing. Nothing. Then this." He jerked off his hat, jabbed his fingers through his short, fair hair, then slapped the hat onto the back of his head. "The message actually came over several hours ago. There was a mix-up. As this news is of a sensitive nature, I didn't make a fuss, but oh, how I wanted to strangle the new telegraph operator."

"Discretion was indeed wise, Mr. Parker. Let's practice some now, shall we?" He tugged the man into a deserted alley, needing privacy to corral his own thoughts.

"I apologize, sir," Parker said at a lower volume. "I'm perplexed and concerned. Why would Boston lead Bulls-Eye Brady and his gang to Phoenix? Zach and Zoe are here. Miss Kaila."

Victoria.

"I worry about the safety of all good citizens, of course, but I have grown especially fond of the Garrett children. I despise the thought of them being exposed to a gang of murdering outlaws."

"As do I."

"But, selfishly, I am also eager to face and thwart the Ace-in-the-Hole gang." He hitched back his coat allowing London a glimpse of a pearl-handled six-shooter. "Instead of going into the field, the action is coming to me."

The same action London had craved only a few days

before. Only his yearnings had taken a detour the minute Victoria walked into his life. Still and all, he couldn't shake that word *serendipity,* and he couldn't ignore the drive to protect those he loved.

He gestured to Parker's holstered gun. "Know how to use that piece?"

"Practice every day, sir. At the risk of sounding boastful, I always hit my mark."

"Glad to hear it, Mr. Parker, because as of now you're on active duty."

Bernard Parker, personal assistant to PMA director, Athens Garrett, removed his spectacles, minimizing his scholarly air. He readjusted his hat to a menacing angle. Rolled back his shoulders, adjusted his stance. His tailored jacket suddenly seemed a size too small. The transformation from pencil pusher to Peacemaker was remarkable. "Whatever you need," he said, "I'm your man."

London assessed the situation. "I need a ghost."

♥ ♥ ♥

Pinal County

Mule and Elroy led the dwindling pack. Brady and Boyd rode a few paces back, with Itchy bringing up the rear. They'd eased the lathered horses into a walk, aiming to take it slow and easy for a while instead of stopping full-out. The more distance they put between themselves and the sheep ranch, the safer they'd be.

They'd left the woman alive and tethered to the bed. They'd chased off the couple's two horses and a mule, ruining her chances of riding off and alerting the law should she manage to free herself. She could always walk, but she'd be walking for miles. Killing the bitch would have been the wiser choice, maybe kinder should she not wiggle free and should nobody happen along, but no one, including Brady, had had the stomach for it.

He wasn't himself today. They'd been riding since the crack of dawn. Felt like weeks to Brady. He felt like shit. The night before, his shoulder had pained him so bad that instead of screwing the sheepherder's pretty wife, he'd collapsed on the bed in a wash of feverish sweat. He'd lain next to the whimpering woman, wishing she was Kat. Instead, he'd fallen asleep and dreamt of her.

In his dreams, she came to him willingly. The cock teaser stripped slowly, then begged for it. For him. In his dreams, she was fully conscious, not doped up on liquor and laudanum. In his dreams, she gave as good as she got.

A shotgun blast had obliterated his sweet ecstasy. He'd bolted upright, and upon hearing return fire, hauled ass.

By the time he'd reached the ruckus, Mule was sheathing a smoking .38 and the sheep man was facedown in the sand, pushing up daisies. Amos was sprawled on the warped veranda, his chest ravaged by a shotgun wound. Somehow Sheep Man had freed himself and come gunning to save his wife. The idiot had been outnumbered. Just like the young maverick who'd pulled a revolver on Brady during the train robbery. The stupid things men did to save women.

Only they didn't always save them. Sometimes they deserted them. The way Rome Garrett deserted Kat six years ago. Booze-blind and twisted with jealousy, the arrogant Wells Fargo detective had taken the scene at face value. Much to Brady's delight and Kat's devastation. All Brady had suffered was a black eye. She'd suffered a broken heart.

The more he thought on it, he was having a hard time believing she'd forgiven Rome. So why were they back together? Did she have ulterior motives? Did she aim on working her wiles to make the man pay? Why come out of the woodwork after she'd spent so many years in hiding? She had to have read about the train robbery. Had to know Brady was in the territory.

Like Mule had said, too many coincidences. Possible he could attribute this sudden paranoia to the fever. Or maybe it was because the gang was now two men shy of their lucky seven and his superstitious streak was mightier than his obsession with Kat. What if it was all a lie? What if there was no Kat? No Frankie? What if it was an elaborate scheme meant to lead him into a trap? A trap masterminded by the Garrett brothers in a bid to regain the public's favor and their legendary status. Snagging Bulls-Eye Brady and the Ace-in-the-Hole gang would certainly land them a write-up in the dime novels.

Temper simmering toward boil, Brady caught Boyd's attention.

The man reined his horse closer, kept his voice low. "Don't take this the wrong way, boss, but you look like hell. Is it your shoulder?"

"Yes," Brady said through clenched teeth. "It's my goddamned shoulder." He forced himself to sit straight, not wanting to appear as weak as he felt. "Didn't anticipate this, given the bullet went clean through and we patched up the wound quick and true."

"Think we need to find a doctor?"

"I don't think it's infected. I think it's a combination of making use of my arm too early, the hard riding, and getting drenched last night. Aggravated my wound and contracted some sort of fever. It'll pass, but I could use something for the pain."

"I got a bottle of whiskey—"

"Laudanum."

"Your recreational stash—"

"Gone. Something else, Boyd. What if you and Mule were right? What if we're riding into a trap? Everything that transpired the past few days, maybe it's part of an elaborate setup. What if Kat's still working the riverboats? What if there is no Frankie?"

"What about the daguerreotype?"

"Looks like a young Kat. Maybe it is a young Kat."

Boyd shifted in his saddle. "All right. Let's say we're being set up." The seasoned outlaw tugged at his hat brim, eyes forward. "Maybe you don't want to hear this, but this chase was started by one man."

Brady fixated on his stick-thin cousin riding just ahead. "I swan Elroy gets more twitchy by the day. I don't think he has the guts to cross me, but I've been wrong about a person a time or two." Maybe Elroy was being paid off, or maybe his motivation was revenge. Brady *had* mangled his hand. He'd kicked him out of the gang, leaving him to fend for himself. From the looks of him, he'd had a helluva rough year. "Gila Gulch is a couple of hours north. I want you and Elroy to ride ahead, buy me some laudanum. They have a doc there. A general store with a telegraph. Give him enough rope to hang himself. See if he tries to get word to anyone. Or maybe he'll try to make a break."

"All right."

"I know a bad-egg rancher up that way who'll give us shelter a night or two. Meanwhile, I'm sending Itchy ahead to Phoenix. Let him nose around. I want to know if there's a little girl. Want to know if he sees Kat."

"Kat's in Tucson with Rome."

"Maybe. Maybe not. Ain't clear on what's fact and fiction just now. Are you?"

"Nope. All right. So Itchy noses around in Phoenix. Say he doesn't see Kat or the kid."

"Regardless, I want a full rundown on where the Garretts live and work. I don't aim on riding into a trap, but I don't intend to turn tail. One way or another we're going to get those bastards off our backs once and for all."

Boyd scratched at his whiskers and settled into the notion.

Brady secretly hoped that Kat and Frankie weren't a figment of a scheme, but in fact the real thing. Maybe his obsession *was* stronger than his superstitious streak. "You with me on this, Boyd?"

"Why the hell not? Hate to think Snapper and Amos bit the dust in vain." He spit in the dirt. "Never did like the Garretts." Grinning, he spurred his horse to the front line.

Phoenix

"You got *hitched*?"

Paris's shocked squeal rang in London's ears. Hers was the only vocal response to his news. Kaila furrowed her brow. Emily splayed a hand to her heart. And Josh, the cocky bastard, grinned. Zach and Zoe were in school so he wouldn't glean their reaction until later.

After dispatching Parker to act as his eyes and ears at the north end of town, as well as invisible bodyguard to his niece and nephew, he'd enlisted Teddy to watch over the saloon, citing a threat from a pissed-off patron. Secure in the knowledge that his sharpshooting barkeep would protect Victoria and Mrs. Chen with his life, he'd then hotfooted it to his sister and their extended kin.

The only thing he intended to share with the women just now were the facts pertaining to Victoria. He needed to reveal a helluva a lot more to Josh, but in private. He also needed to touch base with Marshal Clancy and to return to the Last Chance and his wife as soon as possible.

Not wanting to waste time, he'd started with *Tori's* arrival in town, segued into revealing her true identity, and ended with, *"We were meant to be together, and I didn't want to wait."*

Seated in Athens's comfortable parlor, his family, those in town at any rate, stared at London in awe.

"Coldcocked by love. Wish I could say I feel sorry for you, Garrett." Josh thrust out a congratulatory hand. "I'll settle on, welcome to the club."

Until this moment, London had harbored lingering resentment toward the lawman who'd tricked his sister into marriage. Now he understood that love made a man reckless. He gripped his brother-in-law's palm, bonding them in a new and interesting way.

"I can't believe it," Paris said.

"Why not?" said Emily. "You hadn't known Josh but a week and you two tied the knot."

"That was different."

"Different circumstances, maybe. But at heart, the same motivator. Love at first sight," Emily said. "Why wait? Seth and I didn't."

"Why, indeed?" Kaila said with a wistful smile.

All eyes flew to the sophisticated and beautiful Englishwoman. They all knew her mind. It had been love at first sight for her and Athens, yet he hadn't committed to a wedding date. Unless "*soon*" counted, and London was pretty sure it didn't.

Paris started to say something, but Josh stopped her. London was glad. No sense filling Kaila with false hope. Athens had to be the one to set things in motion.

"I just wish," Paris said, turning back to London, "that

I could have been there." Her brown eyes filled with tears. "My big brother got married, and I missed it."

"Ah, hell, honey," Josh said, putting his arm around her shoulders. "Don't cry."

"We all missed it," Emily said. "Honestly, London."

He narrowed his eyes. "I don't recall being invited to either of your nuptials."

"That was different," they said in tandem.

London bit back a laugh. Laughing just now would land him in a peck of trouble.

"Not to mention," Kaila said. "Poor Victoria missed out on a traditional wedding."

"She didn't want a traditional wedding," London said.

Emily crossed her arms. "Maybe she just said that."

"Yeah," Paris said, then blew her nose into Josh's kerchief.

Was it possible? Had Victoria been too shy to voice her desire for a church wedding? London didn't think so, but he did see an opportunity to keep the women distracted for the next few days. "How about I make amends by allowing you to plan a belated reception?"

Paris quirked a watery smile. "You mean, with music and dancing?"

"Flowers and presents?" asked Emily.

London smiled. "Think you could manage it by the weekend?"

"As this is a family event, perhaps we should wait until your brothers can attend as well," Kaila suggested.

London caught Josh's eye. "I have reason to believe they'll all be home by week's end."

"Even Seth?" Emily asked.

"Even Seth."

Knowing the county sheriff rode with Athens, Kaila's tense shoulders wilted with relief. Her face beamed. "I'm going to bake a cake the likes of which you have never seen or tasted."

London stood. "Plan away, ladies."

The room exploded with feminine chatter, and the two men faded to the foyer.

"I take it you heard from Athens," said Josh.

London passed him the telegram.

The lawman read, cursed. "All right. We get the ladies into town, turn them loose on the shops, then we break away and visit Clancy."

London nodded. "Wish we had specifics."

"Can't believe Brady would risk showing his face in this town. Or any major town, for that matter. Wanted posters are rampant."

"Seems unlikely to me, too," London said. "But I'm thinking we should prepare for the worst."

Josh nodded and glanced at the three laughing women. "And hope for the best."

CHAPTER 33

Pima County

Rome sensed the moment Stargazer started to tire under the weight of two riders. This particular breed was fast and sturdy, but even mustangs had their limit. The horse was in need of water and rest and, truth told, he and Kat would benefit from the same.

He knew just the place.

The late afternoon sun played hide and seek, ducking in and out of white clouds. The temperature was mild, but Rome's skin sizzled. Kat had been riding flush against him for several hours. He was intensely aware of her touch, her scent.

To make matters worse, he couldn't stop thinking about the way she'd handled his Colt without a second thought, the way she'd braved the McCree shoot-out and tended to Seth's wound without a whimper. Her courage and grit worked as an aphrodisiac as surely as her beauty and form.

Instead of focusing on wrangling an outlaw, all he could think about was tangling with Kat. He was hot and hard and goddamned miserable. He needed to walk it off or sleep it off or act on his urges. Salvation, temporary though it may be, for horse and man, waited around the bend.

The Flapjack Ranch didn't deal in cattle or sheep, but people. It was a stopover for travelers on their way north to Phoenix, or beyond to Prescott or Flagstaff. For those destined west to Yuma or east to Globe. One could purchase a meal or a bath, bunk down for an hour or a night. Stagecoaches swapped out teams, and generally the owner set aside a few horses for trade or sale. The facility was centrally located, and rustic but clean, and Rome and Boston had made use of it on occasion. Sensing food and water and a familiar location, Stargazer whinnied and strained for the upcoming stables.

Kat, who'd been resting her head on Rome's shoulder for the last several miles, straightened as they neared the humble, but sizable ranch house. "Why are we veering off course?"

"We're taking a break."

"Why?"

"Because we've been riding for hours."

"I'm not tired."

Liar. "Maybe not, but Stargazer is. He needs looking after." He glanced over his shoulder, noted the shadows beneath Kat's eyes, the weariness in her shoulders. She was exhausted. He suspected she'd slide off, if she didn't have such a tight hold on his waist. Her hands rested innocently above his holster buckle. All the same, those feminine fingers riled lustful thoughts.

"We'll be better equipped to handle any adversity if we're equally rejuvenated," he said, trying to blot out images of her naked body. "We've got a ways to go, sugar."

She tugged down her felt hat to shield eyes that swam with concern. "I know you're right. It's just, the sooner we get to Phoenix . . ."

"Look at it this way. Brady and his pack will need to stop now and then as well. Can't ride a dead horse."

The reference put her in mind of another man. "I hope Seth is all right."

"I expect he's already stitched up and giving the doctor hell for making him lie still for a spell. You can bet Athens is chomping at the bit to ride out. We'll see them soon enough. No worries."

"I'm afraid that's a foreign concept to me."

A casual statement, but one that stabbed his gut. He squeezed the soft hands clasped around his middle. "We'll have to do something about that."

She didn't comment. Probably because she couldn't imagine life without some worry or another. He wanted to amend that. He wanted to abolish her financial hardships and emotional unrest. He wanted, he thought with a self-deprecating smile, to rescue her. Some things never changed. Yet he knew in his gut this situation was unique. This wasn't a save-the-day-then-move-on mission. This smacked of a 'til-death-do-us-part collaboration. Instead of pitching the notion, he let it simmer. The idea seeped into his bones, diluting the past and whetting his appetite regarding the future. *"Life's what you make it,"* he could hear London say.

In his mind, Rome wiped the slate clean and drew a family portrait. Kat at his side. Frankie on his knee. In his mind, the little girl possessed Kat's beauty, his fire, and their shared survival instincts. He wallowed in the fantasy, because it kept his mind from straying into darker territory.

They arrived at the Flapjack Ranch and the proprietor, a tough old buzzard known for his frank talk, greeted them at the ramshackle stable. "You're traveling in prettier company these days," Vern said as he took Stargazer in hand.

Rome slid from the saddle and helped Kat dismount, his hands lingering at her waist. "Got me a new partner," he said. "A life partner. Kat, this is Vern Slater. Vern, this is my wife." He squeezed her side, a silent dictate to play along.

"Didn't read about *that* in the newspaper," Vern said as he led Stargazer to an open stall.

"Just got hitched this morning. Heading to Phoenix to break the news to my family before word gets out. Speaking of," he said, playing a wild card, "my brother pass this way?"

"Yup. Boston was here day 'fore yesterday." He snickered. "He's got a new partner, too."

"A little girl?" Kat asked in a breathless voice.

"Yup. Frankie," he said as he loosened the saddle's cinch. "A real cutie, but ornery as the dickens. The Missus and I were sorry to see them go. Kept us entertained, that's for sure." He looked up from his work, narrowed his eyes on Kat. "Say, she a relation of yours, Mrs. Garrett? Thinkin' on it, Frankie's your spittin' image."

Rome saw her struggling with a response. *Niece or daughter?* He freed her of the decision. "Frankie is Kat's daughter. Boston took her ahead to allow us some private time."

"You'll be wanting to ask Aida about a private room, then," Vern said with a gleam in his eye. "Bunking with other guests won't do."

Kat tensed and Rome knew she was thinking about Brady. "You accommodating many folk just now, Vern?"

"Nope. Not a one. But the Overland stage is set to arrive this evening. Folks with money to spare usually request private lodgings. We only got two such rooms, but you're beatin' them to the draw."

"We won't be staying the night," Kat said.

"But we'll be staying a few hours," Rome said. "We'll take the room. I'll speak with Aida." He nabbed their saddlebags, then touched the brim of his hat. "As always, much obliged, Vern."

"Did you hear that?" Kat asked in a hushed voice. "Boston and Frankie were here, alive and well, and only a day and a little ago."

"And they'll arrive alive and well in Phoenix sometime today."

"If Brady doesn't catch up to them first."

He clasped her hand and squeezed. "I told you. No worries."

She shot him a look that said, *That'll be the day*.

He just smiled because *that day* would come, hell or high water. He'd see to it.

She frowned. "Why did you tell Mr. Slater we're married?" she asked as he hustled her toward the house.

Because, mentally, he'd already slipped a ring on her finger. Because she'd been melded against him the last few hours, unwittingly stoking fires he couldn't douse. "Because a good story spreads like wildfire, and right now every newspaper west of the Mississippi seems hungry for gossip involving the fallen dime-novel hero." He grunted thinking how far and surreal that life seemed just now. "I'm thinking it will work to our advantage if Brady hears or reads about us tying the knot. Might be just the thing to draw his attention away from Frankie, *if* that's even where it's focused, and back to you and me. Truth told, Kat, we don't know if he's ahead of us or behind us, or if he pitched it all and vamoosed for Mexico."

"He killed Johnson in an effort to learn my whereabouts. He tracked Frankie to the convent." She glanced away. "He won't leave without getting even with me, Rome. I can feel it."

"He'll have to get through me first, sugar." That coaxed a tentative smile out of her, but he could still feel her fear. He wanted to obliterate thoughts of Brady. He wanted her to trust him, body and soul. "I confess I had another motive for telling Vern we'd wed," he said, by way of distraction. "I don't want to let you out of my sight. I don't want separate beds, and the Slaters are respectable folk."

"It's the middle of the afternoon. We have a potential crisis on our hands. Who can sleep?"

He clasped her hand and hurried her inside. "Who said anything about sleep?"

❤ ❤ ❤

Dressed in a clean chemise and pantaloons, Kat wore a trail in the already-threadbare carpet, pacing the small and simple guest room as she waited for Rome. Mrs. Slater had been overjoyed to welcome newlyweds to the Flapjack—especially Rome, whom she'd never thought would settle down—and though they'd both begged off food just now, the woman had insisted they wash off the trail dust before lying down to rest. Grimy from the canyon shoot-out and sweat-soaked from the hard ride, Kat had been grateful for the washbasin of heated water and the bar of lilac soap. She'd also been grateful that Rome had washed up elsewhere, allowing her the privacy to strip down.

Silly to be nervous. He'd seen her naked before. The night before, in fact. They'd bathed in the same tub. He'd washed her hair, soaped her body. They'd slept together in the raw. But sex had not played into the scenario.

Even now she had a hard time believing he'd interrupted their frenzied trek to Phoenix for a toss in the sheets. That's why she was clothed and pacing instead of naked and waiting in bed. Surely, she'd misunderstood. Surely, he'd meant though sleep was impossible, rest was a must. Yes, that was it.

She took a calming breath and sat on the edge of the bed just as a barefoot Rome walked through the door. He placed his boots and saddlebags in the corner, straightened, and made knee-buckling eye contact. So much for calm breathing.

He'd shaved. He'd donned a fresh shirt, though he

hadn't bothered to tuck it in or fasten the buttons. He looked handsome and intense and deliciously rakish. The ornery gleam in his eye told her she'd been dead wrong about the *rest* and dead on about the *sex*. She sprang off of the mattress as though it were a bed of nails.

"You look nervous, Kat," he said, while pulling his shirt over his head. "Not like we haven't done this before."

Her gaze was riveted on his muscular torso. Desire sparked throughout her body, igniting lustful thoughts. She wanted to stroke her hands over his chest, trail her fingers over his chiseled abdomen. She wanted to dip below the waistband of his britches and to palm the beast that had once rocked her to shuddering orgasms. It had been so long. Instead, she backed away. "This is insane, Rome."

"Why?"

"Mr. and Mrs. Slater are within earshot." It was a stupid thing to say. There were so many other good reasons. Reasons having to do with emotional connection and long-term commitment. Yet, her brain and body seemed stuck on the short-term pleasure.

He quirked a brow as he approached. "You aim on being loud, sugar?"

"No. I mean, it's just not proper." Her back bumped up against the wall.

He braced his hands on either side of her head, leaned

in. "I expect Mr. and Mrs. Slater deem it right proper for newlyweds to make love."

Regret stabbed her gut, even as he nipped her earlobe and stole away her breath. "But we're not newlyweds."

"They think we are and, for what it's worth, they had chores to attend to. Outside."

She started to say something, but the words garbled in her head as Rome seared her neck, jaw, cheek, and brow with sensual kisses.

"You're so goddamned beautiful, Kat."

She braced her hands on his shoulders to keep her balance. Her voice came out a breathy croak. "Why are you doing this? Why now?"

"Because you're in my blood. Because I can't think straight. Because I've never wanted a woman as badly as I want you right now."

"Even after all that happened."

"Because of all that happened."

She had no response. It didn't matter. It's not as if she could speak with his tongue making quick and thorough work of her mouth. A deep, scorching kiss that spread through her body, awakening every nerve ending. A kiss that ignited the primal need to join as one.

Hands still braced on the wall, he eased back and nipped her lower lip. "Say the word and I'll stop."

Breathless, she stared into his devastating blue eyes, telegraphing her mutual desire. She might regret this tomorrow, but today, this moment, she wanted to burn in Rome's arms. Retaining eye contact, she stroked her hands down his chest, trailed featherlight fingers down his rock-hard abdomen. She released the buttons of his britches, but before she could dip her fingers inside, he gently nabbed her wrist.

"If you touch me now, sugar, I'll lose it."

The intensity of his desire brought tears to her eyes. "Make me remember, Rome, and make me forget."

Understanding sparked in his eyes as he leaned in for another kiss, only this time his hands glided over her curves. In doing so, he ridded her of her unmentionables. She was vaguely aware of it, lost in the throes of a passionate kiss. Only after he'd lifted her and laid her on the bed was she starkly conscious of her nude state.

Rome drank his fill as he pushed his britches down his muscular thighs. For a moment she worried that he might not like what he saw. Her shape had changed. First the pregnancy had filled her out, and then, later, she'd thinned from physical labor and a tendency to eat less due to depression and worry. Sans cosmetics, she'd never felt more self-conscious. But then his lips curved into a small wicked smile, vanquishing her inhibitions.

The longer he looked, the more aroused she became,

the more bold. She moved her hand over her breasts and down her belly, admiring his body as well. He'd bulked up with age. She noted a scar on his shoulder. And though he'd retained a head of sandy blond hair, the thin line of hair that trailed south down his belly had darkened. Her gaze landed on his hard, thick shaft just as her hand slipped to the apex of her thighs.

Suddenly, he was on top of her, kissing her, his hands working magic on her sexually deprived body. She felt hot and languid and deliciously starved for attention. She ground her pelvis against his, but he merely pressed her back against the mattress, intent on taking his time.

Her mind was mush when he finally broke the kiss, and words tumbled out without thought. "I just want you to know . . . I need you to know . . ."

He smoothed her hair from her face, his palm warm and comforting, his gaze shining with desire and compassion.

"I haven't been with anyone," she blurted, "since . . ." She refused to say his name, because to her he didn't count. "It's been six years."

He held her gaze for a long moment, then dropped his forehead to her brow. She felt the sinewy pressure of his body flush to hers, though he spared her the bulk of his weight. "Kat."

She held her breath, bit her lip.

"When you were pregnant with Frankie or even after she was born, why didn't you marry for protection?"

"What?"

"With your beauty and intelligence, you could have besotted any man, a good man, an influential man. A walk down the aisle would've provided respectability, financial security, and protection from Brady. Why didn't you take that route, Kat?"

She spoke from the heart, past the damnable lump in her throat. "I'll only marry for love."

His voice was gruff with emotion. "Do you love me?"

Heart full and aching, she didn't have it in her to bluff. She threw down her cards. "I do."

He responded with a kiss that seared her soul. A kiss that seemed to go on forever, but then suddenly he was worshiping every pulsing inch of her body with his skilled mouth and hands.

She shuddered with multiple orgasms.

He made her remember.

Then, when she was writhing with insatiable need and calling out his name, he plunged inside of her.

And made her forget.

CHAPTER 34

Phoenix

By late afternoon, eight civilians had been deputized by Marshal Clancy. All told, that made eleven men patrolling the streets of Phoenix. So as not to panic the residents, most of the men wore their badges under their coats or vests.

Because the Peacemakers Alliance operated out of Phoenix, and because Seth and Clancy went way back and Seth had vouched for the man's honesty, Athens had trusted the local marshal with the knowledge of PMA's existence. Once London and Josh had shown the man the telegram and filled him in on what little they knew, Clancy agreed that, even though Brady and his gang might not show, they needed to take an active stance. Hence the deputized patrol.

Privately, London and Josh agreed to keep the women in the dark regarding Brady's possible visit until they'd spoken with Boston and substantiated the realistic threat.

Given the wording of the telegram, they expected him tomorrow, the day after at the latest.

As far as protecting the ladies, Josh had a handle on Paris and Emily. Down the road, Parker kept watch over Kaila, Zach, and Zoe. *"Don't worry,"* the man had told London. *"They'll never know I'm around."* At last, Parker had found practical use for his stealth skills.

Marshal Clancy and his deputies were also aware of the elevated danger to those associated with the Garretts, so London felt fairly at ease regarding his family's safety when he returned to the Last Chance. What concerned him this moment, as it had through the day, was Victoria's state of mind.

He found Teddy seated at a table playing solitaire, a rifle at the ready. After confirming he hadn't encountered any trouble, London thanked the man and sent him home. He locked down the saloon, then hastened to his apartment.

He expected to find Victoria bedridden with grief, so he was delighted to see her in the sitting room, alert and making use of his stationery. She sat at his desk, so engrossed in her writing that she didn't hear him come in. Mrs. Chen was equally absorbed, hunkered on the sofa, brow furrowed as she attempted to read one of the novels in his collection.

"Ladies."

They both started. Mrs. Chen popped up to her slippered feet. "I go now." She left the book and brushed past London. "She fine."

His gaze locked with Victoria's. Heat pooled in his loins. *Damn.*

She set aside the fountain pen and hurried over. "Will you sit with me, please? I need to speak with you."

He grasped her hand and led her to the sofa.

She looked up at him with those bewitching, pale green eyes. "I'm sorry I fainted in front of your family."

"They're sorry they triggered bad memories."

"I'm not." She scraped her teeth over her lush lower lip. "It's not pretty, what happened on the train, and I wish I'd handled the situation differently. But I'm glad I remembered, because now I can somehow put the awful matter into perspective. I slept on everything you said, London."

"And?"

She held up two tri-folded missives. "I wrote letters to my father and Mr. Blevins, the man I was supposed to marry," she clarified. "I told them both that I had, in fact, survived the robbery and had, of my own choice, taken charge of my life. I mentioned," she said, expression now fierce, "that should they try to find me and coerce me in any way, my husband would wallop them." As if hearing the vehemence in her tone, she blew out a breath and lowered her voice. "Was I remiss?"

He laughed and thanked God for serendipity. "No, Victoria. You were not remiss."

She passed him the letters. "Will you please mail these for me?"

"With pleasure."

"Thank you. Something else."

He set the letters on a side table, pleased with her surprising bold streak. "Let's hear it."

"Tori Adams offered me her life. I want it. Part of it, anyway," she said when he raised a brow. "I want her name."

"Tori Adams?"

"Tori Garrett."

London cocked his head in thought. All this emotionally battered woman had needed was a nurturing atmosphere. He imagined her blossoming with each passing day, less inhibited, more vibrant, yet always polite. Not wholly Tori Adams or Victoria Barrow, but a unique blend. "Tori Garrett." He smiled. "It suits you."

"Honestly?"

"Honestly." London brushed his thumb over her cheek.

She blushed and cleared her throat. "One more thing."

He hoped it had something to do with the intimacies they'd discussed this morning. Christ, how he ached to make love to his wife. "Yes?"

"Although I can't change what happened on the train, I can, hopefully, avenge Tori's death."

His smile slipped. "How so?"

"Paris mentioned that Emily's husband is riding with a posse in an effort to catch Bulls-Eye Brady and his gang. If they do catch them—"

"Not if," he said, wanting to assuage her fears, "when."

"*When* they catch them, the outlaws will go to trial, yes?"

"That's how it should work. Yes."

She took a breath, straightened her spine. "I want to testify against them. I'm not positive I'll be able to identify the ones who wore masks, but I can definitely identify the man who . . . who . . ." She blinked back tears. "He has to pay for his crimes, London. He needs to be locked away for a long time. Forever if possible."

He admired her courage and determination, and he believed she'd follow through—it's what he'd initially hoped for—but he worried about her sensitive side. "*Tori.*"

Her mouth curved at the sound of her preferred name. "Yes?"

"Justice is harsh and swift in these parts. If Brady's found guilty, your testimony won't send him to jail, but to the gallows." He clasped her hand and smoothed his thumb over her knuckles. "Can you live with that?"

She fingered her locket then met his gaze. "I'll have to. The alternative, him somehow going free or escaping . . ." She shuddered. "Knowing he was out there terrorizing people when I could have stopped him. *That* I couldn't live with."

He shook his head, smiled. "Is it any wonder I fell in love with you?"

She blinked. "You love me?"

He realized then that he hadn't actually put into words what he'd felt at first sight. He cupped her delicate face. "The moment you walked through my door, you changed my world. You stir me. You touch my heart as no woman has ever done. I can't explain the sensation. It just *is*, and it spurs yearnings and desires completely foreign to me."

"Oh, London."

He thumbed away tears of joy and continued to speak his heart. "I want to wake up next to you every morning. I want to have children with you. Grow old with you. Yes, I love you, Tori Garrett. And I want nothing more than to show you, in a physical sense, husband to wife."

She touched his face in kind, her eyes shimmering with curiosity and affection. "I've been afraid to speak it. It seemed too soon. It happened so fast, and it's overwhelming and beautiful and frightening." She caught her breath, smiled. "I love you, too, London Garrett. I ache to know you in the intimate way a wife knows her husband. I wish we didn't have to wait until tonight," she said on a sweet sigh.

Smiling, he stood and swept his blushing bride into his arms. "We don't."

♥ ♥ ♥

Pima County

Sated from their passionate lovemaking and emotionally exhausted, Kat had fallen asleep in Rome's arms. For the first time in years, she'd slept peacefully. No nightmares. No dreams. Just healing, all-consuming blackness.

When he woke her, she felt disoriented. At first all that registered was his intensely handsome face. She smiled a little, remembering how he'd made her forget.

"You make me feel like I'm the only man on earth when you look at me that way, sugar."

"You're certainly the only one who matters to me." Her voice sounded hoarse, as if she hadn't used it in a spell, and it was a sappy thing to say, but she couldn't help herself. After so many years of holding in her true emotions, it felt good to speak her heart.

"You're killing me, Kat." He smoothed her hair from her face. "Under different circumstances, I'd keep you in this bed for a week straight."

She heard a hint of urgency in his tone and noticed, suddenly, that he was fully dressed. Her heart fluttered with alarm. "What time is it?"

"Time to move out."

She palmed her forehead and focused. The room was awash with shadows, and the air was cooler. "How long was I asleep?"

"A few hours." He kissed her on the forehead. "I'll meet you at the stable. I said our good-byes to our hosts. Make use of the back door unless you want to be waylaid by Aida, who was damn insistent about our staying for supper." He kissed her again, this time on the mouth. "Make haste, sugar."

Supper?

The door shut behind him, and she scrambled to dress. She peered out the window, cursed when she saw the stagecoach. Mrs. Slater had mentioned they were expecting a southbound stage around six this evening. Why had Rome let her sleep so late? How would they make up for lost time?

She shoved her feet in her boots, tugged on her brown slouch hat, and heeded his advice. Hearing the chatter of a half-dozen voices, she circumvented the kitchen and the aroma of fried chicken and blew out the back door. She still felt as if she only had half her wits about her when she hit the stable.

Rome was just adjusting the stirrups of a saddled giant. The frisky beast pawed at the dirt and snorted. "Only horse Vern had to spare just now. Spirited bastard."

So this is how they'd make up time. No longer riding double. Heart thumping, she neared the grey gelding. "I can handle him."

"I'm sure you can." He took her elbow and steered her to his mustang. "But I'd feel better if you'd take Stargazer."

She started to argue but again sensed urgency. "You heard something about Brady, didn't you?"

"From the coach's shotgun messenger."

"A Wells Fargo man?"

Rome turned her to face him. "There was an incident at a sheep ranch, and he heard about it when they made a mail drop in a town four hours north of here."

"What incident?"

"A hired hand came in from the range and found his boss shot dead. Found the boss's wife tied to their bed."

Kat's breath caught and tears stung her eyes.

Rome pulled her into his arms. "It's all right. She's alive and unharmed. Just scared and upset. Apparently the gang took refuge in her house during the storm. They blindfolded her, so she didn't see anyone. Heard talk though. Seems Brady's lost two of his gang members—one in the storm, one by her husband's hand."

On shaky legs, Kat clutched the back of Rome's duster and buried her face in his shoulder. "Given she was a witness, I'm surprised they let that woman live."

"So am I," he said. "Although Brady probably wasn't counting on her being discovered so quickly. Thing is, word's out he's in the region. Pinkertons and Federal Marshals will be on the scene in the next couple of days. Wouldn't be surprised if Wells Fargo sends a couple of men. The man's days are numbered."

Kat pushed off and stared up at Rome. "Unless he moves fast."

"Real fast." He kissed her—swiftly, sweetly—then helped her mount Stargazer.

"Don't worry, baby," he said as he swung into the saddle of the grey. "Just ride."

In tandem, they spurred their horses and hit the road at a gallop. Assuming they had a chance to catch Brady before he caught up to Boston and Frankie, Kat leaned into the wind and concentrated on keeping up with Rome and his spirited steed. She envisioned a future with no worries. She thought about the lucky coin tucked in her skirt pocket and rode.

CHAPTER *35*

Phoenix

Victoria stared out the window adjacent to London's bed. From their second-story position she could easily see the night sky, a sky filled with twinkling stars. She imagined Tori Adams winking down at her. She was not only free, she was blessed.

Wrapped in her husband's arms and her treasured quilt, she kept reliving her wedding day over and over. Mostly, the parts after London had carried her to bed.

She'd heard lovemaking was painful the first time. It was. But only for a heartbeat. London had attended her body so lovingly and thoroughly, she'd been out of her mind with scandalous want by the time he'd entered her. He'd prepared her mentally and physically, so she knew what to expect. His kisses stole away her fears and her shocked gasp as he broke through her virginal barrier. Yes, there was pain, but then, because he'd combined tenderness with passion, any discomfort was soon replaced with indescribable pleasure. Pleasure she wanted to experience over and over again.

"You're asking for trouble wiggling against me like that, Tori."

She smiled, liking her new nickname, liking the sound of London's sleepy voice so close to her ear. She turned in his arms. "I'm sorry I woke you," she said, combing her fingers through his thick, disheveled hair. She studied his moonlit face, thinking him the most devilishly handsome man in the world. Her body pulsed with desire. "But since you're awake, do you think we could do it again?"

His mouth curled into a lazy smile. "We've done *it* twice already and for extended periods of time, honey."

True. In between they'd slept and later he'd served her dinner in bed. He'd told her how his family wanted to throw them a wedding reception and she'd assured him she didn't mind. She thought it was sweet. She'd asked about his brothers, and he'd explained how they were all part of a special law-enforcement team. He'd mentioned playing a small part, and she'd said, "*How exciting,*" to which he'd replied, "*Not so much.*" Then he'd segued into talk of making babies, and they'd ended up making love a second time. He'd been a little less gentle and she'd burned even more.

Just thinking about it heated her blood. She pressed up against him and wiggled.

He groaned and smoothed his hand over her bare hip. "Don't you feel tender down there?"

"A little," she confessed.

He leaned in and kissed her mouth, her forehead. "Tomorrow morning's soon enough."

She stilled. "But—"

"All right, then. Have mercy on *me*. You wore me out."

"I find that hard to believe." His body was a work of art. Like one of the sculpted statues she'd seen in a museum. Granite sinew. For a big man, she'd been stunned by his agility and impressed with his restraint and stamina.

He smoothed his hand over the side of her face, tucking her head into the crook of his shoulder and neck. "It's been a long day. An eventful week. It's long past midnight, honey. You need to sleep."

"I can't."

"Nightmares?"

"No." She snuggled closer. She thought about how he'd obliterated a lifetime of unhappiness in a few short days. All she'd ever wanted was to be appreciated and loved. London made her feel all that and more. "My mind and heart, they're full and racing. I never dreamed I could be so happy. Part of me thinks it's too good to be true. What if something or someone ruins it? What if I go to sleep and wake up and we never happened? What if—"

His wickedly delicious tongue swept into her mouth and burned away her worries. Too soon, he eased away.

"Put those notions out of your head."

She ached with desire. "I can't. Maybe you should distract me some more."

"What would you suggest?" he asked in a playful voice.

Suddenly shy, she shrugged. "Can't you think of something?"

He smiled and started kissing his way down her body.

She gasped, then froze. Was that the front door closing? Then the floorboards creaked. "Someone's—"

London covered Victoria's mouth and motioned her to hush as he eased out of bed. Who the *fuck* was in his apartment? An image of Brady exploded in his head. He had his pants on and a gun in his hand before his wife took her next breath. Probably because she was *holding* her breath. He squeezed her hand and whispered in her ear, "Probably nothing, but stay put. I'll be back."

She nodded and he moved swiftly and silently across the room and through the door.

Body vibrating with anger and purpose, London peered down the pitch-black hall. Suddenly the door to the guest room—the room Victoria had previously slept in— opened, and a silhouetted figure stepped out.

London advanced, gun cocked. The other man reacted simultaneously. Lightning quick, they were both staring into the business end of a Colt .45.

"Fuck."

"*Fuck.*"

"Why the hell did you draw on me, London?"

"What the hell are you doing creeping around my apartment?" London glared at Boston, wanting to hug him and smack him at the same time. "Did you just ride in? Are you all right?"

His little brother shushed him. "She's sleeping."

London poked his head into the guest room. Moonlight shone through the window illuminating a tiny, bundled-up girl. She looked about Zoe's size. Was this the precious cargo Seth had mentioned in the telegram? "Who is she?" he whispered.

"Kat's *niece.*"

"Huh." Rome had once mentioned Kat being an only child. Boston's expression promised a juicy tale. Before he could inquire, another door creaked open.

"London?" Victoria inched into the hall, wrapped shoulder to toe in her quilt. Her waist-length hair looked tousled and sexy as hell.

"Who's *that?*" Boston asked.

London slammed the back of his hand to his ogling brother's shoulder. "My wife."

"No shit."

London shut the door to the guest room, nudged his brother to the sitting room. "Pour us a whiskey. I'll be right in." He turned then and moved to Victoria. *Tori.* "I thought I told you to stay put."

"I couldn't. I couldn't stand by, frozen with fear, again, and let something awful happen."

He wasn't sure how she'd expected to protect him, but he appreciated the thought. Noticing she was trembling, he pulled her into his embrace, and kissed the top of her head. "It's all right. It's just my brother."

"Which one?"

"Boston." He maneuvered her back into their room and into bed. "I need to speak with him. Try to get some sleep."

He left before she could argue, anxious to glean insight on the Brady case, curious about Kat's *niece*. He reached the sitting room, now glowing with the muted light of a lantern. His youngest brother sat on the sofa, looking wrung-out. His clothes were dusty and wrinkled, and his expression was haggard. He offered London a glass of whiskey and they both drank.

Boston scratched his head, making his recently cut hair stand on end. "You got *married?*"

"I did."

"When?"

"This morning."

"Well, hell." Looking a tad put out, he stretched his legs and crossed them at the ankle. "Do I know her?"

"Only of her." London succinctly relayed Victoria's story. Boston absorbed the information, clearly angered by

Brady's tactics and sympathetic to Victoria's plight. "Talk about a string of odd coincidences."

"Too many coincidences. I'm thinking fate."

Boston downed his whiskey, shot London a bemused look. "Married. Never thought I'd see the day."

That made two of them. London refilled their glasses. "Tell me about the little girl."

"She's a damned pistol, but smart and cute as hell."

"This pistol got a name?"

"Frankie. Frankie Hart. Kat claims she's her niece. Said the kid's parents are dead and she's now responsible for the girl."

London scratched his forehead. "Could've sworn Rome said Kat was an only child."

"That crossed my mind, too. Gave me pause. In addition, Kat's changed. Doesn't look or act anything like the vibrant flirt we knew. Plus, some things she said . . ." He shook his head. "The whole thing didn't sit right with me. Then I met Frankie."

"And?"

He scraped a hand over his dark stubble, leaned forward, and lowered his voice. "She looks like Kat. Exactly like Kat. A pain in the ass one minute and a charmer the next. Exactly like Rome. I did the math, London. I could be wrong, but I'd lay money."

Rome and Kat had been an intimate item for six months. It was possible. "Although . . . given the timing and her relationship with Brady, it's also possible—"

"Possible," Boston said. "But I'm laying odds on Rome. After ten minutes in the kid's company, I'm thinking you'll agree."

"Back up a minute. I'm operating on minimal information supplied through two coded telegrams. Why were you at a convent?"

"That's where Kat stashed Frankie. A girls' school. Kat worried if our plan backfired Brady might retaliate by striking out at the kid. She agreed to Athens's plan with the stipulation that we protect Frankie. Athens sent me. Little did I know the kid was a pain in the good sisters' wimples. Sister Maria essentially told me to hit the road . . . with Frankie."

"Why didn't you hole up in a nearby town?"

"Because the only way I could get the minx to cooperate with me is if I promised to deliver her to family."

"But her aunt was in Tucson and you couldn't take her there."

"So I told her about *my* family. Turned the trip into an adventure so she wouldn't be scared. Told her Kat would meet up with us as soon as she could."

London blew out a breath. "That could be as soon as tomorrow."

"What are you talking about? The plan—"

"Somehow blew to pieces." London retrieved Seth's telegram from his desk.

Boston read the note, then leaned back against the sofa

with a frown. "The only way Brady could've known I was headed here is if he heard it from Sister Maria. Which meant he somehow found out about San Fernando. Which meant he went there in search of Frankie."

"Why would he do that?" London asked. "Unless he came to the same conclusion as you."

"So he thinks that little girl belongs to him and he's coming to take her."

London glanced in the direction of the room where Frankie slept. "Seems that way."

Boston swayed forward and braced his forearms on his knees. "I can't believe that bastard would risk showing his face in this town. You know him. I know him. Not to mention his face is plastered on Wanted posters throughout the region."

"Maybe he'll send in a gang member," London said. "Trouble is, we don't know what *they* look like."

Victoria appeared on the threshold. "I might."

London and Boston stood.

Even though it was three in the morning, ever modest, she'd thrown on a gown and a shawl. "I'm sorry. I didn't mean to eavesdrop. I just . . . I thought you might like some tea or coffee."

"That's all right, honey," London said, moving to stand next to her. "This is my youngest brother, Boston."

She extended a hand in greeting. "Pleased to meet you. I'm—"

"My sister-in-law. I know." He ignored her hand and gave her a hug. "Welcome to the family."

"Thank . . . thank you." She was blushing profusely when she eased away.

London bit back a smile and placed his hand at the small of her back.

"About Bulls-Eye Brady's men," she said in a soft voice. "I only saw two of them and they were wearing masks over the lower halves of their faces. But I think I'd know their eyes, their voices. And maybe the manner in which they moved."

"Good to know," Boston said.

"Absolutely," said London.

She looked up at him, eyes wide with curiosity and compassion. "Where's the little girl I heard you mention?"

"In the guest room."

"I'm going to make sure she's warm enough. Excuse me."

Boston stepped in next to him and they watched her go. "Sure is polite."

"Sure is."

"Caring, too."

"And pretty."

"Brave to put herself out there like that."

"You have no idea."

Boston slid him a look. "Must scare the shit out of you."

"You have no idea."

CHAPTER 36

Florence

Riding through the night had been a challenge. Kat had dozed off a time or two in the saddle, but Rome had stayed alert, watching for trouble, keeping them on track. Now the sun teased the horizon, and the horses had reached their limit.

Rome wasn't sure if it was sleep deprivation or his damn sentimental streak, but instead of stopping at a mission they'd passed a couple of hours back, he'd pushed them farther north to Florence, a verdant town on the southern bank of the Gila River. Seth's former jurisdiction. The town Paris had duped Josh into believing was her destination when she'd run away from home last year. Due to circumstances Rome still didn't believe, they'd ended up having to share a room at the Elliot House, one of the town's hotels. Thinking Josh had compromised Paris, Seth had hauled in a Bible thumper in the middle of the night, forcing an in-room shotgun wedding.

Rome had been pissed at Josh a good while, until he realized how much the man loved his little sister. He'd never known two people *more* in love, except maybe Seth and Emily, who'd also married quickly. Maybe he was superstitious after all, because he couldn't shake the desire to share his sister's good fortune by seeking out that same Bible thumper.

He also booked them into the same hotel. The Elliot House. The innkeeper introduced himself as Mr. Loss. Rome recognized the name—Paris had told the story dozens of times—and took it as a good sign, an even better sign when the room he requested—room number 9—was available.

He'd signed the register *Mr. and Mrs. Rome Garrett*, thinking it was merely a projection of the truth, and hustled Kat up to the room. "You get some rest, sugar. I'm going to walk the horses over to the livery. They need food and water and—"

"Rest. I know. You can't ride a dead horse. Speaking of—"

"I'm sure Seth's fine." Damn. They were beginning to finish each other's sentences. That was a good sign, too, right?

Kat pulled off her boots and flopped on the bed without argument. "Hurry back so you can get some rest, too, Rome. We can't stay long. We're still a good sixty miles from Phoenix"

"I know."

He hurried along, tended to the horses. He ignored curious glances. *Yes, I'm the man you saw sketched on the cover of numerous dime novels. Yes, I'm the one you read adventurous tales about.* Only he wasn't. This was Rome Garrett stripped bare. No pretenses. No illusions. Just a man. A man in love.

He pondered wiring London, only he didn't have anything of value to share. London was the one with the premium information. Did Boston and Frankie arrive safely? Any sign of Brady? Rome wouldn't be in Florence long enough to receive a return wire. At least he didn't think so. On the off chance, he stopped by the telegraph office.

DOG AND CAT STILL ON WAY. DID B AND CARGO ARRIVE? ANY SIGN OF SNAKE? RESPOND POSTHASTE. —DOG

Former dog, he thought as he left the mercantile in search of a specific preacher. It occurred to him that he'd been two-thirds true to his word to Him. He'd given up philandering and whiskey. But as far as thinking of Kat . . . Hopefully the Almighty was prone to giving leeway. He couldn't stop thinking of Kat because he loved her. Surely he could be forgiven that.

He located Preacher Davis and roused him. *Yes, he knew it was barely dawn. Since when was there a decent hour for eternal happiness?* He talked the Bible thumper into accompanying him to the Elliot House, pausing when they reached the door marked 9.

The preacher clutched his Bible to his paunchy middle and stared at the door. "I'm experiencing an odd sense of déjà vu."

"You married my sister to her husband in this same room last year."

"Ah, yes. At the insistence of Sheriff Wright. Speaking of, you have no witness."

"I'm thinking you and God count plenty. I just need you to wait here in the hall for a bit."

"Why?"

"I need to brace Kat."

"You mean you didn't discuss this with the young lady first?" He tugged at his banded collar. "Listen, son, this is highly unorthodox."

"Kat and I are unconventional folk. Give me five minutes, Preacher."

The man frowned. "By all rights I should still be in bed."

"Four minutes." He entered the room and strode to the bed. "Kat. Baby. Wake up."

"Ten more minutes," she mumbled.

"I've only got four." He pulled her into a sitting position. "Kat."

Her eyes flew open. "I'm awake. I'm ready. Let's go."

He sat next to her. "That's good, sugar. I'm ready to go, too. But there's something we have to do first."

She shoved her tousled curls from her face. "What?"

"Get married."

She blinked him into focus.

"I've got a preacher waiting in the hall, and he's kind of grumpy so—"

"I can't marry you."

His insides froze. "You said you'd marry for love."

She nodded.

"You said—"

"I love you, Rome." She raked her hands through his hair, laid her forehead to his. "With all my heart."

"Then what's the problem?"

"Frankie."

"How so?"

"What if you see her and . . . see Brady?" She dropped her hands to her lap, glanced away. "I couldn't bear it if you turned your back on her. On me."

He interlaced his fingers with hers. "I won't."

"How can you be sure?"

"I just am."

She met his gaze, eyes shimmering with tears. "That's not good enough."

"I need it to be good enough. I need you to trust me. Listen." He cupped her face and spoke his heart. "This is about you and me. We're the foundation. I love you, Kat. Frankie is a part of you. So by extension, without even meeting her, I love her, too. No matter what. Do you understand what I'm saying? I don't want you to think I stayed because of Frankie or fled because of Frankie. I want you to know that I married you because I love you. *You.*"

She massaged her chest and squeezed back tears. "I can't think straight when you say things like that."

"I don't want you to think. I want you to feel." He quirked one of his devilish smiles. "Come on, Kat. I thought you had an adventurous streak. Call me. Take a leap of faith. All in."

She blew out a breath and quirked a shaky smile. "All in."

He kissed her, tenderly at first, and then with bone-deep passion. He checked himself when he lost track of time, bounded off the bed and wrenched open the door. "Come on in, Preacher."

Kat had never given her wedding day extended thought. After her fallout with Rome six years ago, she'd pretty much given up on the idea of marriage, period. The few times she had dared to imagine, the ceremony had been simple, but she'd never imagined anything like this. Married in a hotel room by a preacher who looked like he'd been dragged out of bed and coerced into the proceedings.

No witnesses. No certificate. Was it even legal? It certainly didn't seem real. Kat had stated her vows in some sort of daze. She wasn't sure if the floating feeling was due to euphoria or lack of sleep. If it weren't for the gold band on her finger, she'd chalk the episode up to a dream.

No sooner had Preacher Davis pronounced them man and wife when a knock came at the door. Rome moved into the hall, the preacher shook her hand and wished her luck, and suddenly she was standing alone contemplating her brush with insanity. For surely she'd been two cards shy of a deck to marry Rome Garrett in the midst of a crisis.

"You all right, Kat?" he asked as he reentered the room. "You look a little shaky."

"I'm just . . . Did we just . . ."

"We did."

She fingered the gold band. "So I'm . . ."

"My wife." He kissed her forehead, pressed a telegram in her hand. "Read this."

She shook off her shock to focus on the words. A note from London. "B and cargo home safe and sound," she read aloud. "No sign of the snake." Her knees gave way.

Rome caught her and guided her to the bed.

She felt faint with relief as she sat on the edge of the mattress. Her heart thudded against her ribs, and her voice came out a strained croak. "Frankie's safe with your family."

"*Our* family." He took the wire from her trembling hands and read on. "Two PMs arrived this morning. Local law on alert. Security high. Watch your own back." He pointed out the last line. "This part's for you, sugar."

She focused and read. "Tell Kat the kid's happy, but says hurry up." She swallowed and looked at Rome with misty eyes. "That's her way of saying she misses me."

He smiled and traced his thumb over her cheek. "Then we best *hurry up*."

For the first time she noticed the weariness about his eyes. She tugged at his hand, urging him to sit next to her. "You've slept even less than I have, Rome. You rented this room, and you didn't even make use of the bed."

He pocketed the telegram, then clasped her hand. "Didn't rent the room for rest. Rented it for a wedding. Call me sentimental."

"I don't understand."

"Or maybe superstitious."

"I still don't understand."

"Remind me later to tell you a story about my sister."

Her lips quirked. "All right." Her smile slipped when it registered that Paris was now her sister-in-law and that Rome's brothers . . . She'd married into a big family. Frankie was with most of them now. Because of a lack of male influence, Kat imagined her idolizing Boston and London. She'd probably already bonded with Zach and Zoe, and if Kaila was as nice as they all made her sound . . . No wonder Frankie was *happy*. She'd gotten her heart's desire—to be with family.

Feeling queasy, Kat pressed a hand to her stomach. Now instead of aching to be in Phoenix, she dreaded it. She believed Rome when he said he'd love Frankie, no matter what. At least she believed he'd try. But what if he couldn't? What if she had to walk away, just her and Frankie? Just the two of them. Would Frankie be able to forgive her for ripping her away from the only "family" she'd ever known?

"What the hell, Kat? You look like you're going to pass out." He pressed her back onto the bed. "I know it's been a taxing journey. I just didn't realize how much of a toll it took on you. I'm sorry, sugar."

"I'm all right. Just . . . overwhelmed."

"Lie still. We can afford an hour or two." He stretched

out beside her and maneuvered her into a spooning position. He stroked her arm and spoke close to her ear. "Frankie is well protected. Peacemakers and local lawmen are patrolling Phoenix. Even if Brady doesn't hit town, he's as good as caught."

"He's always eluded the law in the past. What makes you think this time will end differently?"

"Because he's letting his personal feelings muck up his judgment."

She wondered if the same could be said for Rome and herself. "You make it sound like it's all over."

"On the contrary, sugar." He kissed the back of her neck, caressed her ringed finger. "It's only just begun."

CHAPTER 37

Gila Gulch

For a spell there, Brady had worried his luck had run out. Train robbery gone awry. Gunshot wound. The gang two men down from lucky seven. But then he'd sought out an old acquaintance, a power-hungry cattleman with helpful ties, Newt Gaffey.

Turned out Gaffey was not only willing to give Brady shelter, but also to be his eyes and ears in Phoenix. Not him personally, but two of his men. A couple of bad-egg cowboys who could circulate without raising suspicion. All Brady had to do was pay them handsomely for their trouble.

As for Gaffey, the only reward he wanted was to see the Garretts crushed. Two weeks past, Rome had killed his right-hand gunman, Wild-Man Dan. Boston had intimidated the local marshal, a man on Gaffey's payroll, and London, along with the county sheriff, had dared to ride onto his ranch and issue a thinly veiled threat.

"No one crosses me without paying the consequences," he'd

said, to which Brady responded, "*I knew there was a reason we got on.*"

Shacked up in an abandoned adobe on the outer fringes of Gaffey's property for the second day in a row, Brady played cards with Boyd to pass the time. The laudanum had dulled the pain in his shoulder, but the fever persisted. Brady was cranky and anxious, wondering what was going down in Phoenix. "The suspense is killing me."

"Gaffey seemed confident of his men's abilities," said Boyd. "You showed them the image of the kid, described Kat. You offered them a staggering reward should they help Itchy and Mule deliver one or both to you. I'm thinking since they haven't returned by now, they're waiting until nightfall to act. I'm thinking in a few hours you'll be receiving a delivery."

"Hence the suspense. Kat? Frankie? Or both?"

Boyd eased back in his chair, rolled a cigarette. His silence grated.

"What?"

"If it's the kid . . ."

"Spit it out."

"I'm all for obliterating the Garretts. Don't begrudge you wanting to square things with your woman. But dragging a little girl along with us?"

Brady shuffled the dog-eared cards. "Just need to get her over the Mexican border."

"That's a good long ride, Bulls-Eye."

"I'm aware. Don't worry. I'll make it worth your while."

"I believe you. Just saying. Long ride."

"I got that."

"Every lawman in the Territory will be on our tails."

"Think of it as a challenge."

Boyd fired up his smoke and studied the hand Brady dealt him.

Brady gnashed his teeth. "Something else on your mind?"

"Elroy. Don't think he'll be coming back."

"He'll be back. You rode into Gila Gulch with him yesterday. He didn't try to run off or contact anyone. You vouched he kept to himself while you purchased food supplies and that one measly bottle of laudanum."

"That's all we could lay our hands on."

"Like I said, I need more. That and whiskey."

"You should've sent me."

"You and your steady gun hand are more valuable here. Besides, Elroy was getting on my nerves, pacing like a nervous Nellie." In addition, Brady wanted him to pick up a gift for Frankie. He didn't feel comfortable asking that of Boyd. Didn't want the man to think he was soft. But, dammit, he couldn't leave go of the possibility that he'd fathered a child with the only woman who'd ever possessed his heart. He massaged his chest, rolled his sore shoulder. Desperate not to think on Kat, he focused back on his cousin. "He'll be back. He ain't got nowhere else to go."

❤ ❤ ❤

Phoenix

"Just about now, I'd welcome a disturbance of any kind," Josh said. "A drunk using that cactus as target practice. Paris going into labor." Cheroot stabbed between his fingers, he blew out a stream of smoke, rolling his eyes when feminine voices rose in disagreement, then just as suddenly burst into laughter.

London's lips twitched as he lazed against one of the veranda's posts. Boston had run upstairs to check on Zach, Zoe, and Frankie, while London and Josh had stepped outside for some fresh air.

"They window-shopped half the day," Josh went on, "and spent the other half of the day at the Café Poppy sampling pastries and cakes and they *still* can't decide on decorations and refreshments."

"Stop bellyaching, Grant. At least they're happy and distracted. If they weren't chattering about the wedding reception, they'd be worrying about Athens and Seth."

Josh crushed his cheroot under the heel of his boot. "Hell, *I'm* concerned about those two. Why the devil were they delayed in Fulton?"

"Since Athens didn't elaborate in his telegram, your guess is as good as mine. He said they'd be here as soon as possible. Said Rome would explain."

"And we're expecting him . . ."

"Any minute now? Tomorrow morning?" London gazed out in the dusk, hoping they'd arrive like Boston and Frankie, safe and sound, under the cloak of night. "Like I said, they wired from Florence. Guess it depends on how hard they're pushing or if they run into any trouble."

"Trouble being Brady."

"He's out there somewhere, biding his time, scheming. I don't know. But he didn't set foot in Phoenix today. And you heard Marshal Clancy. No reports of any suspicious activity. What's more, Tori kept her eyes peeled and she didn't spot any of the gang."

"That wife of yours," Josh said. "For a quiet one, she's sure got a boodle of gumption."

"That she does."

"Gets on real well with Frankie, too. They were practically joined at the hip today."

London raised a brow. "You driving at something?"

Josh shrugged. "Just that it might be nice if my kid

had a cousin close in age."

"I'll keep that in mind." He glanced at the lawman. "Anxious for that little one to come along, Josh?"

"Anxious for it to be over with."

London clapped a hand to his brother-in-law's shoulder. "Paris is tough and ornery, and she's going to sail through this just fine. Her and the baby both."

Just then Boston joined them on the veranda.

"Kids okay?" London asked.

"Zach's reading a dime novel, and Zoe and Frankie are playing with Sparkles."

"Sparkles?" Josh asked.

"Zoe's imaginary friend," London said.

"She's a tree fairy," said Boston.

Josh grinned. "Ah."

"So, Frankie can see Sparkles?" London asked.

Boston spread his hands. "Apparently. Which makes those two girls fast friends."

Josh narrowed his eyes, sniffed. "Smell that?"

London tensed at the familiar acrid scent. "Smoke."

Boston stepped into the street, looked north. "This ain't good."

London saw it, too. An eerie glow coming from the center of town.

Teddy came barreling down the street. "London. Come quick," he heaved. "Last Chance is on fire, and I think Mrs. Chen is inside."

"Parker!"

The ghostly Peacemaker appeared out of nowhere. "Sir?"

"Go in the house. Watch over the women and children. Do *not* let them try to come and help."

"Yes, sir."

London took off at a sprint, Josh and Boston on his heels. His barkeep ran alongside, as they utilized shortcuts. All he could think about was Mrs. Chen. He'd sent her home hours ago. "Teddy!"

"Yeah?"

"How do you know Mrs. Chen is inside?"

"Some cowpoke told me he saw her go in."

Josh grabbed London's arm as they reached the scene. "Hold up."

London spotted the line of men already working to douse the flames that had spread to the shop next door. This was bad. "What?"

"Remind you of anything?"

London noted the bucket brigade, the chaos. He flashed back on fighting another fire. Last year, when Josh's opera house had almost burned to the ground. Oh, Christ. "It's a distraction."

CHAPTER 38

Gila Gulch

"Could you hurry up, mister? It's past closing time."

Elroy glared across the mercantile at the impatient proprietor. This errand was difficult enough without the old goat rushing him. "Need to pick out one more item. I'm pert near done."

The man grunted. "You said that twenty minutes ago."

Ignoring the curmudgeon, Elroy turned back to the business of choosing between one of two rag dolls, a painted pony, and a storybook. The more he pondered what to buy for the little girl, the sicker he got. The longer he tarried. His saddlebags were stuffed with bottles of rotgut and laudanum. His cousin was unpredictable as it was, but drunk and drugged? How the hell was he going to care for a five-year-old kid? And what if that kid turned out to favor Rome Garrett?

Dammit.

Elroy didn't want to go back to that shack. He didn't want no piece of this. He wanted to vamoose, far from his crazy cousin, far and away from the Garretts, but he couldn't stomach deserting the kid. Her cherubic face was burned in his brain. He wished Jed never would've shown him her image. 'Course there was no guarantee Itchy and Mule were going to lay hands on Frankie, that's if she was even in Phoenix. But the possibility gnawed at his innards.

He cursed the night he walked into the Star Saloon and laid eyes on the long-lost Kat Simmons. Gut knotted, he settled on the brown-haired rag doll with the frilly blue dress just as the bell above the mercantile door tinkled.

"I'm closed for the night, lady," he heard the owner call.

"I just need something to settle my stomach. I'll be two minutes," she said.

"You've got one! You, too, mister."

Elroy spun and knocked into the she-devil who'd launched this nightmare. His lungs seized as his brain scrambled for a way to get him out of this hellish debacle.

She backed up a step, swallowed. "I know you."

He could tell she couldn't place him just yet. He'd changed a lot since she'd last seen him in San Francisco. Then again, so had she.

"You were in the Star." She studied his face, sucked in a breath when realization dawned. "Oh . . . my . . . God."

Elroy glanced over her shoulder, then met her frightened gaze. "You riding with Garrett?"

She shook her head. "I'm alone."

"Find that hard to believe. What are you doing in Gila Gulch?"

"I'm on my way to Phoenix."

"To see your little girl?" He leaned in, voice low. "You've got my cousin all twisted up, Miss Simmons. If you want what's best for Frankie, you'll come with me."

She glanced at the rag doll clutched in his hands.

He could see her wheels turning, thinking her kid was in Phoenix, thinking Elroy wasn't an immediate threat. "Brady sent two of his own men along with a couple of hired thugs to steal away the kid. Reckon you're the only one who can talk him into making for the border without her. Reckon he'd do just about anything to be with you."

She licked dry lips, nodded. "Let's go."

"Hey, mister," the shopkeeper said as they hastened to leave. "You owe me for that doll."

"I'll get it," Kat said and slapped a half-eagle coin on the counter on their way out.

"You overpaid me," the man called.

"Your lucky night," she said, and Elroy prayed that applied to him, too.

Phoenix

They hadn't been gone but ten minutes, but a miscreant with a plan and a gun didn't need much time to wreck havoc. By the time London slammed through the door of his brother's house, the damage had been done.

Parker lay at the bottom of the stairway, bleeding and unconscious.

Boston sailed up the stairs.

London tended Parker, wadding one of the women's discarded shawls and pressing it to his wound. He saw his sister and Emily, but Kaila and Victoria were missing, along with the kids. He yelled up the stairs. "Boston!"

His brother yelled down. "They're all right!"

Josh knelt next to his wife, checking for wounds as she moaned in agony. Emily held her hand and stroked her brow. "They didn't hurt her," she said, "but the shock . . . I think the baby's coming."

"Three men," Paris said in a stilted voice. "Mr. Parker shot one, but he . . . Then the other two . . . Ohhhh!" She clutched her stomach. "Josh!"

"I'm here, honey. Christ almighty, a man should be careful what he wishes for." He glanced over his shoulder.

"How's Parker?"

"Breathing," London said. "But it's bad. Took one in the gut. He needs a doctor."

"Paris, too," Emily said to Josh.

"I'm not leaving my wife."

Paris slugged him in the arm. "Get the doctor. Please! No, wait. Don't leave me, Josh!"

London glared. "Get the goddamned doctor, Grant."

Cursing, Josh bolted out the door as Kaila came running down the stairs, holding Zach's hand.

Boston followed, holding a weeping Zoe in his arms. He averted her face as they passed Parker, then set her on the sofa.

The little girl sleeved away tears. "What's wrong with Aunt Paris?"

"Nothing, sweetie," said Kaila. "She's having a baby. We need hot water," she said, hurrying to the kitchen.

Zach tore away from her and neared London. "Is Mr. Parker okay?"

"He'll be fine, Zach. Go sit with your sister."

"I can help." The boy knelt down and nudged away London's hands, using his own to retain pressure. "You and Uncle Boston need to catch those men. One came through our window, Uncle London. I shoved Zoe under the bed, but I couldn't help Frankie. It happened so fast. She was kicking up a fuss, though. Maybe she broke free."

London's stomach dropped. "Maybe so." He squeezed his nephew's small shoulder. "You did good, boy." He glanced up the stairs and back to the parlor. "Where the hell's Tori?"

Emily's eyes overflowed. "They took her."

London's heart stopped. The world stopped. Time froze, and all he could see was *her*. All he could hear was *her*. He'd promised to keep his wife safe, and now . . .

"London."

He blinked away Victoria's haunted face and focused on Boston. His brother had pulled him to his feet.

"We'll find her," he said. "Both of them." He squeezed London's arm. "Frankie and I talked about a lot of things on our journey. One of them was tracking."

❤ ❤ ❤

Gila Gulch

Rome hadn't aimed on stopping in Gila Gulch. He'd made an enemy out of Marshal Burke and that rancher, Gaffey. Last thing he needed was a delay when Phoenix was a spit and a holler away. But the spirited grey had gone lame, and Kat wasn't feeling well. He needed another horse, and she needed some medicine. She assured him it was just nerves and exhaustion, and he believed her. Still, he wished he hadn't allowed her to leave and visit the mercantile on her own while he bartered for a new horse at the livery. What if she fainted? Not to mention Brady was still unaccounted for. He'd slipped a pistol in her duster so she wouldn't be without protection. He knew she'd use it if provoked. Still . . . The longer he was away from her, the more his gut clenched. "Shouldn't have left her alone."

His concern escalated when he reined his new mount in front of the mercantile. Where was Stargazer?

An old man was locking the store's door. He turned and saw Rome. "I'm closed."

"My wife. Came in to buy some medicine. Dark, curly hair. Split skirt, brown duster."

"Didn't buy no medicine. But she did overpay me for that man's rag doll."

Rome fisted his gloved hand. "What man?"

"Don't know his name."

"Can you describe him?"

He rattled off a brief description.

Not Brady, Rome thought with relief, but it could have been one of the gang.

"He was in here yesterday, too," the merchant went on. "Him and another stranger stocked up on food and laudanum.

Tonight he dawdled in the children's section, looking at toys. Settled on the rag doll." He flipped a gold coin in the air, caught it. "Like your wife said, my lucky night."

Senses primed, Rome slid from the saddle. "Can I see that coin?"

"You gonna give it back?"

Rome offered him a ten-dollar gold piece, twice what the half-eagle was worth, monetarily anyway. "I'll trade you."

The man whistled, made the trade. "My lucky night, indeed."

Rome palmed the half-eagle, his worst fear confirmed. Kat was in trouble. She wouldn't part with her father's lucky coin otherwise. This was her way of signaling him. "You say they left together?"

"Walked out together, yes."

Rome indicated the street. "See which way they went?"

"Nope." And with that the old man loped off.

Rome crouched and examined the dirt. He easily identified Stargazer's tracks. He'd had those horseshoes especially made. He thanked God for the full moon rising. He needed all the light he could get. He swung into the saddle, settled into old ways. He'd earned a name tracking criminals. According to the dime novels, he and Boston were the best. "Strong and steady, sugar. Don't worry. I'll find you."

♥ ♥ ♥

Strong and steady, Kat told herself as she followed Elroy through the desert. Gambler's advice, compliments of her daddy. Advice she'd once shared with Rome. Funny how often that phrase applied to life in general.

As scared as she was, now was not the time to fall to pieces. Instead she kept replaying everything Rome had once told her about tracking. She knew he was the best. She trusted he would find her. Eventually. She worried because it was dark, so she tried to leave clues when Elroy wasn't paying attention. At first, she used the few coins she had in her pocket, dropping one in the sand every now and then. In the same way the sunlight had glinted off of McCree's rifle in the canyon shoot-out, she hoped the coins would shimmer in the moonlight. When the coins ran out, she pulled a ribbon from her hair and draped it over the arm of a cactus. When they made a hard jog west, she pulled off her wedding ring and slipped it onto a fat thorn of a saguaro. Eye level, a shiny band twinkling in the moonlight.

Rome will see it, she told herself. *Strong and steady.*

She also told herself that Brady's henchmen would fail in their attempt to steal away Frankie because she was in

Boston and London's care, and like Rome, they were fierce protectors. She told herself that she'd be able to bamboozle Brady. She'd manipulate him with a wink and a smile. She'd lie through her teeth and make promises she had no intention of keeping. When it came to creating an illusion, once upon a time, *she'd* been the best. She'd distract him from Frankie. She'd buy Rome and the law time. She'd do what she'd set out to do in the first place. She'd condemn Brady to hell for eternity. Only then could she truly live.

Whatever it takes.

Elroy pulled his horse up short.

"Why are we stopping?" she asked, stomach churning.

"Look yonder," he said, pointing due west. "See that flickering light?"

She squinted across the plain. "Yes."

"That's the adobe where Brady's holed up. Itchy and Mule might still be out, but Boyd and Brady will be keeping watch. I'd ride in real slow-like if I was you, hands up. Might wanna announce yourself as you get close. Elsewise, they might shoot you." He thrust the rag doll into her hands. "Take this just in case."

In case of what?

"And here. Take these, too." He draped his saddlebags over Stargazer's rump.

"What's in there?"

"Whiskey and laudanum. Jed'll be real pissed if he don't get his laudanum."

Her stomach heaved. "Where are you going?" she asked, feeling a surge of panic when Elroy reined his horse south. It's not like she trusted him, but she at least remembered him as being a decent sort.

"I don't want no part of this. I'm real sorry, Miss Simmons, but I've eased my conscience by bringing you this far. I was worried about the kid. If Brady's hired men did manage to snag her, I know you'll protect her. Just remember," he said. "Jed loves you."

Kat managed to wait until he'd had ridden off and then leaned over and retched in the sand.

CHAPTER 39

"I have to pee."

"Again? What's wrong with you, kid?"

Victoria also wondered about Frankie's bladder. She supposed it was nerves. The poor thing had uttered that frank plea at least four times since they'd been snatched from Phoenix. Victoria refrained from comment because each time they stopped it slowed them down. That was a good thing. She believed with her whole heart that London and Boston would rescue them. She *had* to believe. She needed to be strong. For Frankie. For herself. She wasn't ready to give up her new life. A life with London Garrett.

They'd been taken by three outlaws, only Mr. Parker had mortally wounded one of them. That left two. They wore masks and went by the names Smith and Jones. Victoria hadn't recognized either one of from the train robbery, but that didn't mean they weren't part of Bulls-Eye Brady's gang. Frankie was riding double with Smith. Victoria, who'd since been blindfolded, had the displeasure of doubling with Jones, a man who smelled as if he hadn't bathed in a year.

"Oh, gosh," Frankie squealed. "I think it's coming out!"

"Dammit to hell," Smith barked.

"Please, don't curse in front of the child," Victoria said.

"Why are we stopping again?" Jones complained. "Tell her to hold it in."

"Easy for you to say. She ain't sitting on your lap."

"Look," said Jones. "Here comes that Itchy fella."

"Good. They're his problem now."

Victoria couldn't see anything, but she could hear and smell and feel. She heard Smith and Frankie dismount. She felt Jones slide out of the saddle, then jerk her to the ground.

"I have to pee."

"Then pee, dammit!" Smith bellowed. "Right there behind that bush."

"Don't watch."

"I ain't gonna watch, but if you run, kid, swear to God, I'll shoot your mama."

"Swearing to God isn't nice," Frankie told him.

"Pee!"

"And she's not my mama," she grumbled before shuffling off.

Victoria marveled at the girl's spunk. She didn't sound

one bit frightened. How could that be? She heard a horse approach. Must be the Itchy person.

"Where have you been?" he complained. "I've been waiting at the designated . . . Where's Mule?

"Dead," said Jones.

"Damn. Well, at least you got . . . Oh, no."

She heard his boots hit the ground. It was all she could do not to quake. She recognized his voice. One of the train robbers. She heard him strike a match, felt the flame close to her face. "This ain't Kat Simmons."

Jones tugged at her hair. "What are you talking about? She fits the description, and she was with the kid all day."

"Where *is* the brat?" asked Itchy.

"Taking care of business behind that bush." Smith spit. "You *sure* this ain't the right woman?"

Victoria felt the blindfold being pulled off. She braced herself for the shock, locked her knees when she did, indeed, recognize one of the gang members. She almost wished the moon weren't full and shedding significant light. His tooth-less smile made her stomach turn.

"Another one of them damned coincidences. If this don't beat all." He leaned in close, looked down her décolletage. "You ain't Kat, but Bulls-Eye's gonna be happy to see you all the same." He fingered her locket. "Yup. Real pleased."

"Hey," said Jones. "What's taking the kid so long?"

Smith called, but she didn't answer. He cursed, and Victoria closed her eyes and prayed. *Run, Frankie, run. Run fast and hide.*

"No kid, no pay," Itchy said.

"You go this way," Smith said. "I'll go over there."

"Take the locket and give it to your boss," Victoria told Itchy as the other two left. "It's gold, as you can see. Maybe you'd want to keep it for yourself. Please, let Frankie and I go. We won't tell—"

"Forget it. I'm taking you both to Bulls-Eye. When he's done with you, think I'll have a taste." He skimmed a finger down her neck.

She thought about Tori, her husband, Frankie . . . and something inside of her snapped. Victoria slapped away his hand with a force that shocked her.

"Bitch!"

"Touch her and I'll shoot you where you stand."

Victoria's gaze flew beyond Itchy's shoulder and connected with London's. He'd come out of nowhere, and he was holding a gun to Itchy's temple. Her heart lodged in her throat. He looked so fierce, so . . . wonderful.

"Back away, honey."

She did as he asked. "Frankie's out there."

"Boston's got her." He cocked the gun, focused on Itchy. "You just called my wife a very nasty name, Mr. Itchy."

Victoria's pulse skipped. "That's all right."

"No, honey. It's not." He tapped the outlaw's head with the barrel of the gun. "Apologize."

"Sorry," Itchy squeaked.

"I'm sorry for scaring you, Mrs. Garrett," London prodded.

Itchy repeated the apology verbatim.

London glanced at Victoria. "Sound sincere to you?"

She nodded.

"Apology accepted," London told the outlaw then shoved him to the ground. "Move and you're dead."

A half-dozen men moved in, two of them dragging along Smith and Jones. Victoria was stunned.

"A couple of Peacemakers and a few of Clancy's deputies," London told her.

Realizing she and Frankie were truly safe, Victoria's locked knees finally gave way.

London caught her in his arms, dropped his forehead to hers. He groaned, no longer fierce but vulnerable. "I've never been so scared in my life."

"Me, neither." She swallowed hard. "We're not going to have many adventures like this one, are we?"

"God, I hope not." Then he kissed her, magically obliterating all the ugliness.

"Did you find my clues, Uncle Boston?"

"I sure did, Sweet Pea. You done real good."

Victoria eased back from London, just as Frankie and Boston came out of nowhere. Mostly they were silhouettes, a big man and a tiny girl, hand in hand.

"I kicked and screamed when that bad man nabbed me," she said. "Caused a real ruckus like you told me to do."

"Zach said."

"And I did the tinkle thing, too," she announced, sounding enormously proud.

Boston laughed. "Drove them batty, didn't it?"

"*Real* batty. Can we go home now?"

Victoria whispered to London. "Frankie left clues? That's how you found us?"

"Apparently, Boston gave her lessons in tracking as part of their adventure. Told her exactly what to do if a stranger ever stole her away."

"No wonder she wasn't scared. She's very smart," Victoria said.

London nodded. "And ornery. No wonder the nuns couldn't handle her. She's going to drive Rome nuts."

"That makes you happy?"

"Oh, yes." He tugged her toward one of the horses. "Speaking of Rome . . . and Kat . . . I'm sending you and Frankie home under the protection of two Peacemakers. The rest of us are going after Brady."

"But you don't know where he is."

"Itchy does."

Her heart pounded with pride and fear. She grabbed the lapels of his black duster and yanked him down to eye level. "Please, don't get yourself killed."

"Wouldn't dream of it." He smiled. "I've got you to come home to." He brushed his mouth over hers. "Plus, my sister's having a baby."

CHAPTER 40

"Wait outside, Boyd."

"If Elroy blabs to the law about our whereabouts like he blabbed to this woman—"

"I'm sure he thought he was doing me a favor by sending Kat my way," Brady said. "Don't think he's stupid enough to blab to the law. Although," he said, looking pointedly at her, "like I said before, I have misjudged a person a time or two."

Although her insides twisted with rage and fear, Kat held Jed Brady's angry grey stare. No tell. No tilt.

"Just want you to know, boss," Boyd said, his thumbs brushing the butts of his holstered revolvers, "if I ever run across Elroy—"

"Shoot him with my blessing," said Brady. "Now go on and keep an eye out for Garrett."

Kat stood against the wall, near the door, her arms

crossed over her queasy middle. She'd known this confrontation would be hard, but she'd overestimated her acting skills and underestimated Brady's wickedness. It rolled off of him like a putrid smell. She didn't know how to play him because she couldn't read him. She went with her gut and bluffed. "I told you, Jed. I ran out on Rome."

"And ran to the better man?" He cocked a dark eyebrow. "That's what you want me to think, right? This is where you tell me how he done you wrong, *again*. Where you try to convince me that you made a mistake running out on me six years ago. How you've been hiding from me because you didn't think you were good enough for me, or some equally perfumed lie. When your real objective," he said, drawing near, "is to distract me from my daughter."

"She's not—"

"Let's cut through the bullshit." Brady braced his left hand on the wall, next to her head. "I read the letters from Sister Maria. I have your daguerreotype of Frankie. Charles F. Simmons had one daughter: you. Frankie isn't your niece; she's your daughter. I figured some numbers, and it's probable she's mine."

"More probable she's Rome's," she blurted. *Tilt.* She couldn't help herself. She hated this man. Hated what he'd done to her and to people like Victoria Barrow. "Even if Frankie is your blood, she's not you in spirit, Jed. She's good. She's innocent. Let her be. Don't make her pay for what you perceive to be my crimes."

"Perceive?" He leaned in. "*Perceive?*"

His anger was overwhelming. Kat struggled not to tense or cower. She scrambled to assess her opponent. His right arm hung limply by his side. His unbuttoned shirt sagged open, revealing a bandaged shoulder. It was cool outside and inside, and yet he was sweating. She took solace in the assumption that he was not feeling one hundred percent and thought about the pistol in her pocket.

"You teased me. Seduced me. Strung me along," he growled. "You made me feel like I made a difference in your life. Like I *mattered.*"

"I'm sorry." She blurted that, too. Because she *was* sorry. Because he was right. She was not wholly innocent even though she'd had her reasons for stringing him along.

He grabbed a fistful of her hair. "Not sorry enough."

Tears blurred her vision. "You're hurting me, Jed."

"We're a long way from even, sweetheart. You think I'm a fool? I know you set me up. Don't mean nothing that you rode in alone. Garrett tracked you. It's what he *does.* He's out there, somewhere." He leaned in close, his mouth curling into an evil smile. "But I'm in here. And this time . . there'll be no laudanum."

Six years' worth of anger and shame welled up, blinding

her with its intensity.

He tried to kiss her, but she thrashed her head side to side, struggled when he pawed at her breast. *Not again. Never again.*

She heard a bang. A slam. Glass shattering.

She felt Brady's hands fall away, felt him back off.

She opened her eyes and saw him staring at her in disbelief. Saw him clutching his middle with bloody fingers.

She felt a hand on her shoulder. *Rome.* He stood in the doorway, his gun trained on Brady.

She smelled an acrid scent and looked down. Smoke curled from the singed hole in her duster pocket. Her fingers ached from her tight grip on the handle of the pistol that had shot Bulls-Eye Brady.

"My wife don't cotton to being raped, Jed."

The outlaw's watery eyes turned on Rome. The words sank in, and he went for his revolver.

Three shots echoed from different directions, and the bullet-ridden man slumped against the table, scattering the deck of cards.

Rome holstered his smoking piece. Kat glanced left and right, saw Seth Wright and Athens Garrett at the broken windows, guns in hand.

Seth angled his head. "Now that's what I call cashing in your chips."

"Bull's-eye," said Athens.

"It's over," Kat whispered. She knew she should feel bad for taking a life, but all she felt was relief. No more running and riding. No more fear.

For the good of mankind.

For Frankie.

They could finally be together.

Rome caught her in his arms just as her legs gave way. "Don't faint on me now, sugar. You still need to introduce me to my daughter."

His daughter.

"*This is only the beginning.*"

Overwhelmed, she choked back sobs as Rome guided her out into the fresh air. She caught a glimpse of Boyd sprawled facedown. Dead like his boss. Moonlight illuminated a pack of men riding hell-bent for the adobe. Kat feared it was the rest of the gang, but Rome didn't seem concerned.

"Posse," he whispered in her ear.

Seth and Athens moved in on either side of her.

Dazed, Kat tried to make sense of their presence. "How did you know I was here?"

"Had the good fortune of running into Elroy," said Athens.

"His bad fortune," said Seth, massaging his bandaged shoulder.

"I found you the hard way," Rome said. "Only you made it easy, sugar."

He pressed her daddy's coin in her right hand, then slipped her wedding band on her left ring finger. Her heart swelled with wonder and love. Whether their nuptials had been legal or not, she was bound to this man forever and beyond. She ached to voice her feelings, but the sentiments lodged in her constricted throat.

Rome winked as if knowing her mind, wrapped an arm around her waist as the posse thundered in. "Appreciate the gesture, brothers," he said to the two lead riders, "but you're late for the party."

"Did some dancing on our own," said Boston Garrett.

Kat tensed. "Is Frankie . . ."

"Fit as a fiddle and ornery as hell," he said with a grin.

Relief rejuvenated her spirit although her stomach roiled when the other men peeled off to survey the area and London Garrett slid from the saddle. She'd been a pain in his side when she'd spent her nights gambling at his opera house. Would he forgive and forget? Accept her as Rome's bride?

For the moment, the eldest Garrett focused on the director of the PMA. "Everything okay?" he asked.

"Case closed," Athens said.

All eyes turned to the lawyer-turned-lawman, and Kat wondered if his brothers sensed what she sensed. That, in ridding the earth of a rapist and murderer of women, he'd somehow slain his own demons. He could and *would* protect those he loved, and those loved by others. A Peacemaker with peace of mind.

London squeezed Athens's shoulder. "A victory, personally and professionally."

Athens blew out a breath, then smiled. "Time to move on." He looked to Rome. "What about you?"

"Eat my dust," Rome said with a cocky grin. "Made peace with my past and embraced the future." He pulled Kat closer, a possessive, protective gesture that stirred her blood. "We got married this morning."

Pulse racing, she waited for London to protest, but his mouth merely twitched with good humor. "Lot of that going around." Instead of elaborating, he nudged Rome and motioned to Boston, who still sat atop his mount. "Speaking of making peace . . ."

"Sorry for being a horse's ass," Rome said straight-out.

"Can't help what comes naturally," Boston said, backing the comment with a forgiving smile.

Kat was too exhausted to ponder what they'd fought about, but couldn't help but bask in the warmth of brothers reuniting. *Family.*

"If you Garretts are done making nice," Seth said with a disgusted grunt, "I'd like to get home to my wife."

"Speaking of wives," Athens said. "I'll expect you all to be there when I take Kaila as my bride."

Rome raised a brow. "Got a date in mind?"

"Soon. Like tomorrow."

Seth chuckled. "Emily and I will be there."

"Better make it this weekend," London said. "Paris will be pissed if she misses another wedding, and she's laid up right now having a baby."

Rome smiled. "Well, hell."

London winked at Kat. "Welcome to the family."

She wanted to thank him, but her voice seized up again. She squeezed back tears, but they fell anyway.

Thankfully, the other men moved to their horses, allowing her a moment to collect her wits.

Blue eyes sparking with compassion, Rome thumbed away her tears and pulled her into his arms. "Let's go home, Mrs. Garrett."

"Home," she croaked, feeling as if she'd just won the mother lode of all jackpots. A happily-ever-after ending with her champion and her child. Too much to absorb. Too good to be true. Would her luck turn muddy when Rome laid eyes on Frankie?

"Strong and steady," he said with a tender smile, then kissed her and, for this moment at least, burned away her worries.

CHAPTER 41

Rome had Kat double up with him on he ride home. He wanted to hold her in his arms. He needed to hold her. He'd been scared shitless knowing she was in that adobe with Brady. He'd rushed in to save her, only she didn't need saving. His wife had more grit than any woman he'd ever encountered. He knew she was shaken from her standoff with that bastard, but damn, he was proud of her. He'd told her in a million different ways until she'd fallen asleep in his arms.

Even though it was late when they arrived in Phoenix, Athens's house was alive with activity. Kaila and Emily nearly ran over Rome in order to get to Athens and Seth. And a young woman he'd never met, but knew to be his new sister-in-law, launched herself into London's arms.

Kat had a death grip on his hand. He knew she was overwhelmed. He knew she was nervous about him meeting

Frankie. Hell, *he* was nervous. But mostly because he was afraid of the little girl's reaction. What if she didn't like him? In all his born days, he'd never been worried that a female wouldn't like him. Damn. He'd been less nervous facing down a passel of desperadoes.

"Thank God," Josh said, coming around the corner. "Men."

London laughed. "Houseful of women too much for you, Grant?"

"Zach and I have been hopelessly outnumbered."

"Paris okay?" Rome asked.

He grinned. "Come on in here and ask her yourself. While you're at it, you can meet my daughter."

"Another girl," Zach complained as he barreled down the stairs, Zoe on his heels. They threw themselves into Athens's arms. "Papa!"

Family, Rome thought, his heart full. He leaned in and kissed Kat's temple just as a dark-haired girl came loping down the stairs. *Frankie.* She looked like Kat. Exactly like Kat. Long, dark curls; big brown eyes. That impish smile.

His heart thudded in his chest when she cried out, "Auntie!" and raced into Kat's arms.

"I found us a family, Auntie! Can we keep them?"

"Oh, sweetie." Kat hugged her close, kissed her head. She blew out a breath, then gazed up at Rome with tears in her eyes. "There's someone I want you to meet, Frankie."

"We'll be in with Paris," London said, and suddenly it was just Rome alone with mother and daughter.

Pulse galloping, he stooped down to eye level with Frankie. He didn't see Brady or any of himself in her, but she was his alright. He wouldn't have it any other way.

She studied him with her big brown eyes. "Are you my Uncle Rome? Uncle Boston told me all about you. Said you're something special."

Rome swallowed a lump in his throat. "He did, did he?"

"He said you need a life, and he's thinking I could give you one."

Rome grinned and scratched his forehead. "*How* old are you?"

"Five and a half."

"Going on ten," Kat said, voice shaky, but amused.

He reached out and touched the little girl's arm, his heart skipping when she didn't pull away. "Frankie, I love this pretty lady." He glanced at Kat, his heart, he hoped, in his eyes, then looked back to her mirror image.

The girl smiled. "Me, too. I want us to live together like a family."

"So do I," whispered Kat.

Rome caressed his wife's cheek. "So do I." He blew out a nervous breath. "Frankie, sweetie, I asked Kat to be my wife. I'd like you to be my daughter. How do you feel about that?"

She worried her lower lip, thinking it over, and Rome was pretty sure he'd stopped breathing.

"Do I get to call you Papa?"

Oh, Christ. He blinked back tears. "Sure do. And that makes your auntie your mama."

She smiled and slammed her tiny fist in her palm. "Oh, boy! Wait'll I tell Zach and Zoe." She raced off, then raced back. "I forgot to give you a hug, Papa. Uncle London said you need lots of hugs."

Tears in his eyes, Rome swooped up his little girl, his mind racing on all he was going to do for her to make up for lost time. He hugged her something fierce, and she hugged him back. When he finally set her on her feet, she skipped off to find her cousins.

Fame and glory couldn't compare to what he felt for Kat and the spunky kid who'd just called him *Papa*. His wife grasped his hand, and something inside of him cracked. "Did you hear that?" he asked, thumbing her wedding ring. "That was the sound of me falling."

"For Frankie?"

Grateful for second chances and heavenly pacts, Rome kissed the woman who'd roped his heart twice and forever. They'd gambled on love and won. "For the three of us."

A special excerpt of *A Lost Touch of Bliss* by
Amy Tolnitch

CHAPTER 1

Wareham Castle, Cumberland, 1196

"Please come to Falcon's Craig," the note read. "I am in need of your unique services. I own Villa Delphino on the Italian coast. It is yours if you will aid me." Amice de Monceaux read the Earl of Hawksdown's boldly scrawled letter for the second time and crushed the vellum in her fist.

Then she started shaking. How could Cain ask this of her? Tempt her with the one thing he knew she had always dreamt of ever since her brother told her stories of the sun-drenched land. And why did he own the villa? That was her dream.

Her stomach churned with memories, too many, too

clear even now. After five years, she could still feel Cain's arms around her. And could still hear his calm voice saying, "I am betrothed," before he walked away.

The door to her chamber opened slowly. "Amice, dear? Are you in here?"

"Aye, Mother." Amice stuffed the vellum under her mattress and crossed the rush-covered floor to take her mother's arm.

Lady Eleanora pulled free and paced across the chamber, her pale fingers fluttering like butterflies in a meadow. "I cannot find Beornwynne's Kiss. Your father, the whoreson, must have hidden it again."

Amice took a deep breath, no longer startled by her mother's language. And, truth be told, she accurately described her late father. "Mother, the necklace is right here." She opened a trunk and lifted out a carved box, placing it in her mother's hands. " 'Tis safe, as always."

Her mother sat on the stone ledge in front of the window slit and opened the box. She gathered up the heavy gold and amethyst necklace in her gnarled fingers.

Amice laid a hand on her mother's shoulder and felt bones, as if she held a tiny bird beneath her palm. "Would you like to go sit in the garden, Mother?"

Her mother's brow furrowed, and she tilted her head to stare at Amice. "Where is Isolda? I told her to get my blue gown ready for the feast tonight."

"Mother, Isolda died last year." Amice kept her voice even, though she wanted to scream at the loss of the vibrant person who had been her mother and friend.

Blinking quickly, her mother looked around the

chamber, as if she expected Isolda to pop out from behind the bed at any moment. "Aye, of course." She gave a small laugh. "I was confused for a moment. Poor Isolda. How I miss her."

Amice squeezed her mother's shoulder and took a deep breath. "Come with me outside. 'Tis a beautiful day."

"What were we talking about?"

"Beornwynne's Kiss."

"Of course. I . . . forgot." Her mother dropped the necklace, grabbed Amice's hands and squeezed tight. Too tight. Amice felt her mother's frail body tremble.

"Mother," she began.

Her mother's gaze clouded. "Beornwynne's Kiss will protect me, see me safe across the river when I die."

"And you have it."

When her mother looked up at her, her gaze was far away. "Is this it?" she asked, her lips trembling.

Amice stared down at the top of her mother's head, the strands of silver hair mixed with white, and her heart splintered. "Mother, all is well."

Her mother patted Amice on the hand and rose. She wobbled and caught herself for a moment with her hand on the seat, waving Amice away with the other. "I believe I shall go down to the kitchen and see if Cook has prepared any meat pies."

" 'Tis a good idea." Amice watched her mother's departure with a heavy heart, the knowledge that she was dying an aching lump in her belly.

The only reason Amice remained at Wareham was to care for her mother. And by Michaelmas, her brother, the Earl of Wareham, would be wed to a woman who made it clear Wareham would have only one mistress.

Soon, she would have no place.

She closed her eyes and envisioned soft sand, a sparkling blue sea, and golden sunlight. Yes, there she could find peace. Take what Cain offers, her inner voice urged. Take it and flee to warmth and beauty.

How simple it sounded, but in her heart she knew it would take every scrap of strength and pride she possessed. Five years ago Cain Veuxfort had nearly destroyed her. Had taken her heart into the palm of his hand and then crushed it in his uncaring fist.

Her mouth curved in a wry smile. Now, it appeared he had a troublesome ghost who would not leave him alone. He needed her, the Spirit Goddess. She would be a fool not to take everything she could gain from Cain Veuxfort. Aye, he would give her what he offered and more.

And she would be free.

ISBN# 1932815260
ISBN# 9781932815269
US $6.99 / CDN $9.99
Paranormal Romance
Available Now
www.amytolnitch.com

A special excerpt of *Call of the Trumpet* by
Helen A. Rosburg

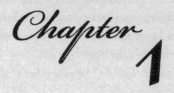

Chapter 1

Paris, 1859

THERE WAS NO LONELIER SOUND IN THE WORLD
than that of dirt thudding dully on the lid of a coffin.
Cecile sensed the priest at her side, felt his light touch on
her elbow, but she was unable to move. The thudding
continued and a misty rain began to fall. It did not move
her. She stared into the slowly filling grave.

"Mademoiselle . . . Mademoiselle Villier, please. It
is time to go, come along. You will catch a chill standing
in the rain like this."

Cecile ignored the priest, though not intentionally.
Her only awareness was of the terrible numbness that lay
like lead upon her breast and weighted her arms, her legs,
her very soul. If only she could cry. Something within
her might move then, and end the awful paralysis. But
she could only stare, watching until the coffin's lid was
completely covered with the dark, sodden earth.

"Come along now, mademoiselle. Really, you must,"
the priest urged.

"Excuse me. Excuse me, please. I will take the mademoiselle."

The priest moved gratefully aside, making way for the small brown man dressed entirely in white. The little man held a black umbrella over his mistress's head and gently touched her shoulder.

"Come now, *halaila*," he said quietly. "He is here no longer. We must go."

Cecile nodded slowly. She raised her eyes from the steadily filling grave to the jumble of headstones around her, elaborate statuary, crypts, and monuments of the Cemeteries Pere Lachaise. It was a city of the dead, and their cold, silent homes lined the brick-paved streets. Next to her father's grave stood a large crypt carved of white marble, on top of which stood the statue of a weeping woman. Cecile returned her gaze to her father's simple headstone.

It was exactly as he would have wished. There were only three things he had cared about in his life: his daughter, his horses, and the memory of the only woman he had ever loved. Cecile read the simple words on the stone.

Francois Louis Villier
1806–1859
Father of Cecile Marie Elizabeth
Husband of Sada bint Mustafa

Unresisting at last, Cecile allowed Jali to lead her

away. The narrow, uneven street sloped gently downward, and she leaned lightly on her escort's arm until they reached the waiting coach. Its black sides gleamed under a coating of rain. Four matched bays, all Arabs, stood quietly. A footman opened the door and lowered the steps.

Cecile turned, prepared to thank the priest, but saw only his black-clad back hurrying away into the mist. With a small shrug she climbed into the coach, Jali at her heels. The coachman cracked his whip, and the matched bays darted forward.

"I regret much that man hurt you," Jali said, sensitive as always to his mistress's every mood. "He is very rude. It was not necessary."

"It's all right, Jali." Cecile stared out at the passing tree-lined avenue. New-leaf branches glittered under their burden of rain. Distant thunder promised more. "He was merely impatient to conclude his business with me. He is no different from anyone else."

"*Halaila* . . ." Jali began, but Cecile silenced him with a wave of her delicate hand.

"Please don't waste your breath, Jali. You and I both know the truth. It's very simple. I am a half-caste, therefore I am shunned."

As she was right, Jali held his tongue. She knew the truth pained him, however, as it had pained her father. She was an alien, a stranger, in her father's land. She always had been.

The journey continued in silence as Cecile watched the passing landscape. Soon the city was left behind, and the coach entered the impossibly green, gently rolling country-side. An occasional château slipped by, sitting grandly at the end of its broad, shady avenue. Cecile's dark eyes narrowed as they passed one imposing structure in particular. Normally she blocked the unpleasant memories the sight of it evoked. But today was a day for remembering.

MEDALLION PRESS

www.helenrosburg.com

ISBN# 1933836148

ISBN# 9781933836140

US $6.99 / CDN $9.99

Historical Romance

Available Now

First, there is a River

Kathy Steffen

A family conceals a cruel secret.

Emma Perkins' life appears idyllic. Her husband, Jared, is a hard-working farmer and a dependable neighbor. But Emma knows intimately the brutality prowling beneath her husband's façade. When he sends their children away, Emma's life unravels.

A woman seeks her spirit.

Deep in despair, Emma seeks refuge aboard her uncle's riverboat, the Spirit of the River. She travels through a new world filled with colorful characters: captains, mates, the rich, the working class, moonshiners, prostitutes, and Gage-the Spirit's reclusive engineer. Scarred for life from a riverboat explosion, Gage's insight into heartache draws him to Emma, and as they heal together, they form a deep and unbreakable bond. Emma learns to trust that anything is possible, including reclaiming her children and facing her husband.

A man seeks revenge.

Jared Perkins makes a journey of his own. Determined to bring his wife home and teach her the lesson of her life, Jared secretly follows the Spirit. His rage burns cold as he plans his revenge for everyone on board.

Against the immense power of the river, the journey of the Spirit will change the course of their lives forever.

ISBN#9781932815931 • Silver Imprint
US $14.99 / CDN $18.99 • Available now
www.kathysteffen.com

"A refreshingly original twist on the vampire story.
Fast-paced and fun."
—Kelley Armstrong, New York Times bestselling author

The Vampire Shrink

LYNDA HILBURN

Denver psychologist Kismet Knight, Ph.D., doesn't believe in the paranormal. She especially doesn't believe in
vampires. That is, until a new client introduces Kismet to the
vampire underworld and a drop dead gorgeous, 800-year-old
vampire named Devereux. Kismet isn't buying the vampire
story, but can't explain why she has such odd reactions and
feelings whenever Devereux is near. Kismet is soon forced to
open her mind to other possibilities, however, when she is visited by two angry bloodsuckers who would like nothing better
than to challenge Devereux by hurting Kismet.

To make life just a bit more complicated, one of Kismet's
clients shows up in her office almost completely drained of
blood, and Kismet finds herself immersed in an ongoing murder investigation. Enter handsome FBI profiler Alan Stevens
who warns her that vampires are very real. And one is a murderer. A murderer who is after her.

In the midst of it all, Kismet realizes she has feelings
for both the vampire and the profiler. But though she cares
for each of the men, facing the reality that vampires exist is
enough of a challenge…for now.

ISBN# 9781933836232
Trade Paperback / Paranormal
US $15.95 / CDN $19.95
Available Now

"In her edge-of-the-seat page-turner *RUNNING SCARED*, Cheryl Norman brilliantly juxtaposes the triumphant power of love to heal against the damage people inflict in the name of love."
~ Jennifer Skully, author of *SEX AND THE SERIAL KILLER*, 2006 Daphne Du Maurier Award Winner

Cheryl Norman

RUNNING SCARED

Although newly divorced Ashley Adams thinks her ex-husband is trying to kill her, she's not Running Scared. Months of therapy and determination have strengthened her resolve to stop being a victim, while months of dedicated training have prepared her to run her first marathon.

Homicide detective Rick Edwards is coping with the deaths of his wife and daughter the only way he knows how—by focusing on his work. He is hoping to solve the murder Ashley witnessed during a training run, but first he must win her trust. And keep her alive.

But it doesn't take Rick long to realize Ashley Adams is hardly a damsel in distress. In fact, she may be the one woman who can save HIM. He has found danger?—has he also found love?—in the most unexpected of places.

ISBN# 9781933836416
US $7.95 / CDN $8.95
Mass Market Paperback / Romantic Suspense
SEPTEMBER 2008